SMOKE AND ASHES

Emily Slate Mystery Thriller Book 3

ALEX SIGMORE

Dark Woods Press

SMOKE AND ASHES: EMILY SLATE MYSTERY THRILLER BOOK 3

1st Edition

ebook ISBN 978-1-957536-10-1

Print ISBN 978-1-957536-11-8

Prologue

"GIVEN THESE FACTORS, YOU CAN CLEARLY SEE HOW THE supply along this axis defines the demand here, along this one."

Leon Spencer was doing everything in his power to stay awake, but he was fighting a losing battle. These evening classes after work had been a good idea at first, but four concentrated hours of nothing but economic theory two nights a week had begun to wear thin. These, combined with the course work from his other evening classes were pushing him to the limit.

He hoped taking night classes would be a new start, something to help him put the past few years...especially the past few months behind him. Plus, if he ever wanted a new career and out of his current job, he *needed* these classes so he could finally get that GED.

It wasn't that Leon was stupid, or lazy. He just hadn't finished school along with most other people his age. He'd been forced to drop out to take care of his ailing mother. Not only had he become her caregiver, but they'd needed money which meant he'd needed a job. He'd bounced around a while until he'd found most of what was open to him were jobs that required a lot of physical labor. Eventually, he figured if he was going to be out working his hands to the bone, he might as well help people while he was at it.

Leon had always been a strong kid. So when he'd applied to be a volunteer firefighter in his twenties, he'd been able to impress his instructors with how fast he could be, even carrying forty pounds on his back. It hadn't taken him long to go full-time, and it was a job he loved every day. It was a hell of a lot better than loading trucks or carrying steel around.

But after a while the job had begun to take its toll. His knees were beginning to give out and his back ached most of the day. Nearly fifteen years of lugging hoses and climbing stairs would do that to a person. He wanted one of those cushy jobs where you could sit on your ass and get paid for it. But for that, he needed to meet certain basic requirements. The captain had said he knew someone who could get Leon a nice, quiet office job, he just needed his high school diploma first. It was the least he could do for so many years of great service. Which meant the first step to Leon's new life was only a few short weeks away.

If he could stay awake, that is.

"That's about all for tonight," the teacher said, checking his watch. "Make sure you review chapters fourteen through sixteen and prepare your reports for Wednesday night. Remember, the report will count for twenty percent of your overall grade."

Twenty percent? How had he missed that? It meant Leon would be pulling a few more late nights in order to make sure his was up to snuff. He couldn't afford to mess something like that up; he needed a C or better in this class.

Leon gathered his book and laptop together, tucking them into his side bag.

"Spencer?"

Leon looked up to find the teacher staring pointedly in his direction. "Yeah, teach?"

"Can I see you a second?"

Some of the other students shot him furtive looks as they exited. Most were his age or older, all of them at different stages in life, working for the same goal. He wondered how many of them were also hoping to improve their career prospects.

Leon shuffled up to the front. "What's up?"

"I've noticed you've been having a hard time staying awake," the teacher said, shuffling his own papers on his desk.

Here we go. Another dressing down.

"Sorry, it's my job. We pull these long shifts and—"

The teacher held up his hand. Leon noticed his fingernails were expertly manicured. Not someone who worked with his hands. He reached into his bag and pulled out a small capsule. "Next time, give this a try."

Leon took the small bottle from him, quirking his nose at the label. "Four-hour energy?"

"Concentrated caffeine," the teacher replied. "I used to have the same problem. Take one about fifteen minutes before class begins. They'll get you through."

Leon gave him a small smile. At least the teacher was trying. "Thanks. 'preciate it."

"See you on Wednesday."

Leon nodded and headed out. The teacher was nice enough, but he could tell the man was just here to go through the motions. Maybe he was trying to build up his teaching hours so he could get a better job too. Leon couldn't imagine anyone would want to stay around and teach community college economics if they didn't have to.

After a quick stop to the bathroom—damn prostate issues, he thought this stuff wasn't supposed to happen until he was in his fifties—Leon headed out of the multi-story brick building to the adjoining parking lot. It was already past ten and it looked like he had a long night ahead of him reviewing his economics report.

When he reached the parking area, Leon noticed there was only one other car still in the lot other than his 2002 Toyota Tacoma. The car had its hood up and the owner was bent over in the engine, working on something.

Leon smiled. If there was one thing he knew, it was cars. He stopped a moment to toss his bag into his truck before heading across the lot to the vehicle.

It was a newer car, probably within the past five years, and it had a dark gray paintjob. He hoped he could help figure out the problem; these new cars were so fancy nowadays you needed a computer just to figure out what was wrong. Still, it was his job as a public servant to offer help if he could.

"Ho there," he called out. "Trouble?"

The figure turned, looking over his shoulder. Leon could tell he had dark hair that fell in his eyes and was probably a good five or ten years younger than Leon. Definitely another student though, but he must have been in a different class as Leon didn't recognize his face.

"Oh, hey," the guy extricated himself from under the hood. "Yeah, I don't know what happened. Wouldn't start. I was trying to figure out the problem before calling the towing company. Don't really have the money for that, you know?"

"I hear that," Leon said, peering into the engine as he got close. He didn't see any immediate signs of trouble. Though there was something familiar about the guy that he just couldn't put his finger on. "Do I know you?"

The other man shook his head. "I don't think so. You taking night classes?" He made a motion to the building behind them.

"Economics. You?"

"Public speaking," the man said, pushing the dark hair out of his eyes. It stayed back for only a second before falling back into place. "It's brutal."

"I'm sure you'll make it through. Has to be more interesting than learning about the law of demand."

The guy gave him an easygoing chuckle. "Maybe. You have any experience with this sort of thing?" he indicated the car.

Leon peered into the engine again. "Got a light?" the shadows from his and the other man's body were blocking a lot of the light coming from the parking lot overheads.

"Sure." He pulled out a cell phone and shone the flashlight from there into the engine itself.

"Perfect, hold it right there," Leon said as he inspected the components. All the belts were tight, caps were in place, nothing seemed to be rattling around. The entire engine was still cold, which meant he hadn't even been able to start it at all. Leon reached in, feeling for anything that might have come apart while driving, but nothing indicated a problem.

"Hey, can you turn it over for me? I don't——"

The next thing Leon knew, he was laying on the ground, his head pounding. He had just enough time to look up to see the man standing over him, a tire iron in his hand before he brought it down on Leon's head.

Everything went black.

Leon's eyes fluttered at the familiar smell, though he was so out of it, the significance of the aroma didn't immediately register. All he knew was he had the worst headache of his life and his arms and legs were sore as hell. What had happened?

"Oh good, you're awake," a voice said. It was a voice he thought he recognized, though he couldn't be sure. "Thought I might have been a little too rough with ya."

He knew that voice. The man. From the parking lot. He'd been helping him with his car. "Wha——" Leon muttered. As soon as he opened his mouth he tasted the sharp tang of blood, only to realize it was running down his face. The man had first struck him from behind, surprised him. Leon tried to wipe the blood from his face, maybe it wasn't too bad. Only he couldn't move his arm. Either of them. Or his legs.

Leon looked down in terror as he realized he'd been strung up like some kind of sacrifice. He was against a wooden wall made up of old slats, while his arms were spread wide, each of them tied to opposite sides of the wall. His legs were similarly bound in such a way that he felt like the living version of the Vitruvian man.

"Lemme...lemme..." he found he was having trouble forming words, much less get them out.

The man came closer, out of the darkness so Leon could see him plainly. He pushed his dark, greasy hair out of his face again, though there was a smile across his lips. Leon still couldn't place where he'd seen the man before...but he was *so* familiar. "Let you go? I assume?"

Leon nodded.

"Afraid it's not going to be that easy for you," the man replied. "See, Leo, ol' buddy, you did a bad, bad thing."

How does he know my name? He might not be able to enunciate clearly, but his brain still worked, at least for the moment. "Wha..."

The man's features darkened, and his hair fell back in his eyes again. His entire body seemed to radiate with rage. "Don't pretend like you don't know what you did. Don't play innocent with me!"

All of a sudden Leon recognized that voice. And it wasn't because the man was a student. "I...I'm sorry..." he squeaked out. He pulled at his restraints. There had to be some way out of this. Some way he could explain what happened.

"It's a little too late for sorry, don't you think, Leo?" the man said, approaching him. He had a small cannister in his hand. "But don't worry, you'll get what's coming to you."

"N—no," Leon said. This couldn't be happening. He was supposed to be turning everything around. He was supposed to be starting over. He couldn't let things end this way.

"Y—yes," the man said, doing a poor job of imitating him. "Now open up."

In one swift move, the man shoved something metal in between Leon's lips, forcing them open. Too late he realized it was a funnel, like the kind you use to change the oil in your car. He forced Leon's head back, so it was pressed hard against the wooden slats, then lifted the container in his other hand, tipping it into the funnel.

What felt like white-hot fire poured down Leon's throat. At first he was choking due to the fumes of whatever toxic substance was being forced into his stomach. He tried to retch, but the man held firm, continuing to pour. Finally, he ripped the funnel and container away, only to splash the remainder of the container's contents on Leon's body. Despite the fact he was choking on the substance, he had enough wherewithal to realize what the man had poured down his throat and covered him in: turpentine.

"Time to burn, Leo," the man said, lighting a match. "Tell the devil I said hi." The last thing Leon Spencer felt as he choked on the turpentine was his entire body igniting in a ball of flames.

Chapter One

"KAMILÉ MICHAEL, SIOBHAN DURAN, CAELAN BOYLE, OR Antionette Penn," I say, reciting the names from memory.

The older woman standing in the doorway tugs on her ear, her face pinched in confusion. "You're looking for all of those women?" she asks. Her glasses are probably two full inches thick, making her eyes look like literal saucers as she stares at me.

I blow an errant strand of brunette hair out of my face. It's about the only piece that isn't stuck to my head from the humidity. "No, ma'am. I'm trying to find if you have a record of any of them staying here, in the past year or so."

"Oh dear," the woman says. "The past year? I'd have to go look at my logbooks. And they're buried under a pile of boxes. I'm having my kitchen redone. By the time it's finished it's going to look brand new! And I'll be able to reach the upper cabinets. It gets hard for someone of my age to reach all the way up there. My husband used to do it, but he passed this last year and ever since it's just been more and more difficult—"

I glance at the woman standing beside me, Zara Foley. She's a good three inches shorter than me and keeps her platinum blonde hair cut short and smart. But even she has an incredulous look on her face as the older woman before us drones on about her woes. It's not that I'm completely unsympathetic, but we've been here ten minutes already, trying to get some basic information out of this woman and she's put up nothing but roadblocks. If I didn't know better, I would say she was intentionally stalling us.

"Mrs. Reese," I say, interrupting her. "I'm sorry about your husband. But you don't recognize any of those names? They're not exactly common."

She gives me a placating smile. "Trust me, dear. When you reach my age, you'll be lucky if you remember to put your teeth in every day. I have dozens of people stay here each month; I can't remember half of them."

"Is there any chance you can get to those logbooks?" Zara asks. "We could help move some things."

"I'm sorry," she says again. "But we just got everything moved and the workers are scheduled to be here any minute to get started. I don't want to interrupt them. You don't know how hard it is to find workers who have some available time these days. Back when I was your age, I could get anything done to my house I wanted, within a week. There were people ready and willing at the drop of a hat. But these days it seems like everybody's shorthanded. Just to get them—oh, look, right there." She points behind us and I see a pair of service vans pulling up, *Restoration Kitchen* written on the side of both.

"Good morning, Mr. Gulyak!" she calls out, waving.

I put my hands on my hips and take a deep breath, anything to keep me from verbally assaulting this woman. Instead, I reach into my pocket and pull out a business card. "Mrs. Reese, if you happen to uncover those logbooks, I'd really like to get a look," I say, handing her the card.

She takes a long look at it, adjusting her glasses so she can see it better. "Oh, I didn't realize you were with the FBI. Is this concerning one of your cases?"

I exchange a quick glance with Zara. "This is a...personal

matter. To me. Still, I'd like to take a look if you happen to unearth them."

"Sounds like you have an important job." She turns to Zara. "Are you in the FBI too?"

Zara shrugs. "Only when they ask nicely." Either Mrs. Reese doesn't get it, or she doesn't care for dry humor as she stares at us blankly.

"I'll try to remember," she says, holding up the card before slipping it into her apron. "Good luck on whatever it is you're doing." She makes a movement indicating we should step back and I realize it's to make room for the line of men coming up her walkway. "Good morning, good morning. I've got a fresh pot of coffee on for you."

The men beam at her like she's the best thing since sliced bread and I'm forced to accept Mrs. Reese is done with us for today. I shoot Zara another look, and we take our leave without any further conversation with the old woman.

When we reach the end of the block, still moving out of the way of men taking tools back and forth into the house, I have to stop and wipe the sweat off my brow. My hair is soaked and it's not even eight thirty. "God, it's humid down here."

"You're in the jungle now, baby. You gonna die," Zara cackles.

"I just might," I reply. I'm not used to weather like this. I didn't exactly grow up in the north, but I was used to mild springs with warm and sunny summers. I'd always heard about the Georgia heat, they weren't kidding. It's barely May and already the sticky heat is unbearable.

"So do we call this a bust or what?" Zara asks.

"I don't know," I say, shaking my head. The whole reason we're down here is because we're trying to track down the woman who took out one of my suspects before he could go to trial. Coincidentally this is also the woman I believe murdered my husband in January of this year. Thanks to a case Zara and I cracked eight weeks ago, I managed to find a list of this woman's registered names and addresses. The fact that she's known by at least four different names with addresses in three different parts of the country tells me that Zara's hunch is right: this is no ordinary killer we're dealing with here. This is a trained assassin, maybe even a hired gun. The problem is, I have no idea why she would want my husband dead. What's even more bothersome, is the other man she killed, Gerald Wright, seemed to know something about it. I was on my way to interview him, but she got to him first.

But despite the fact I have a list of names and addresses, Zara and I have been on her trail for a week and a half now and have come up with nothing so far. The first address in Florida turned out to be little more than a storage shed belonging to a local storage yard. When we forced them to open it, there was nothing inside other than dust. It looked like it hadn't been used in years.

The second address led us here, to Savannah, and right to the doorstep of Mrs. Abigail Reese, an elderly landlord who rents out rooms in her building for a month at a time. I have no idea if the woman we're chasing stayed here under one of her assumed names or all of them, but it's the first semi-lead we've had so far. If her name is in Mrs. Reese's logbooks, I need to see it.

"I guess it was too much to hope that Mrs. Reese kept her records on a computer like the rest of the civilized world," Zara says. I kick a rock as we make our way back across the street to the car. "Plus, it's not like she would have left a forwarding address anyway."

"I know, I just feel like I'm never going to catch up to this woman. She can obviously find me anytime she wants, I just want to level the playing field." I can't help but think back to the hospital in Stillwater, seeing the woman's dark brown eyes and bouncy blonde hair as she smiled at me. If I'd only known then she had just moments before done something to Gerald

Wright that caused him to have a heart attack, I could have stopped her. Arrested her. The ME ruled it completely natural, but I know better. I know because it's the same thing that happened to Matt.

"Are we thinking breaking in during the middle of the night? You saw she wears hearing aids, right? I bet she wouldn't even notice," Zara teases.

I pull open the driver's side door and slip in, turning the car on to try and feel the blissful blow of cold air. But it's gone up thirty degrees in here since we left it ten minutes ago.

"As tempting as that is, I'll have to pass. I don't think breaking and entering would look good on my record. Plus, she doesn't mean any harm, I'm just frustrated."

"Just a suggestion," she says. I tried to leave Zara out of this; I didn't want her in the middle of my mess. But being the type of friend she is and not willing to let me do this alone, she's sort of forced her way in regardless. She even took some time off work to come down and help me sort some of this out after we found all this information on Douglas Krauss's app. Right when she had begun working on her own cases as well.

"Is it bad I just want to go back to the hotel so my shirt will stop sticking to my back already?" Even Florida wasn't this bad. I learned quick that layers don't work down here. You pretty much have to wear something that breathes otherwise you're going to be suffocating all day.

We sit in silence a minute, watching the men pour in and out of Mrs. Reese's house while the air blasts in our faces. "What?"

I turn to Zara. "Hmm?"

"What are you thinking? You've got that look."

"Oh don't start with that again," I say, putting the car in gear.

"Tell me I'm wrong."

I wish I could. But Zara knows me better than anyone; she knows when I've got something on my mind.

"Your silence is deafening."

"Okay, smartass," I say as we drive past Mrs. Reese's house, back out to the main thoroughfare. "Let's see how those skills are developing. What do *you* think is going on?" I've been giving her a hard time ever since she got her promotion to field agent, considering she used to spend most of her time behind a screen working in Intelligence Analysis. I like to think I was instrumental in pushing her to move beyond her comfort zone and get out on the streets. And it turns out, she's got a natural knack for it.

"I'll go for a challenge," she replies. "Okay, so you're obviously disappointed that we can't find out if she stayed at this particular property and given that we've been at this two weeks with very little to go on tells me you're feeling disappointed and starting to wonder if this is still worth it."

I shoot her a look.

"So? How'd I do?"

"Completely off base," I say, though there's a smile on my face.

Zara puts her hands behind her head, kicking her short legs up on the dash. "Whatever. I nailed it in one. The student has become the master."

"Don't do that, this is a rental," I say, trying to shoo her feet down, but she just leaves them up, basking in the glory. I let out a sigh. "I'm just worried I'm doing all this for nothing. I don't have definitive proof she killed Matt *or* Wright. It's not a stretch to say I'm biased."

"Isn't that part of this, though? To find out if she did, and why?" Zara asks. "At least then you might have a sense of closure."

I've learned that nothing will give me closure about this. Nothing is ever going to make me feel better about losing my husband. I just have to live with that. But if there's even a small chance that someone murdered him, I need to bring them to justice. I can't fail him a second time. "I just don't know if we're ever going to find her. People like this usually end up disappearing and are never seen again if they don't want to be."

"We'll find a way, you'll see," she replies, flashing me one of her signature grins.

My phone trills in my pocket and I have to wiggle my hand to retrieve it from my pocket as it's sticking to everything. Finally I pull the phone out. "Emily Slate."

"Slate, are you still in Georgia?" I glance over to Zara and mouth *Janice*.

"Unfortunately," I reply.

"Good. I've got something for you. Listen up."

Chapter Two

MY BOSS ISN'T SOMEONE WHO APPRECIATES PRACTICAL JOKES. I know this because an unsuspecting agent attempted to show her his good humor by gluing everything down on her desk for her birthday a few years back. Needless to say, that agent found himself in Nome, Alaska, working at one of the most remote FBI satellite offices we have.

Which is why I have to get Janice to repeat what she just told me to make sure I heard her right. "I'm sorry, you want me to *what*?"

"I want you, and Foley, I'm assuming that's Foley I'm hearing in the background, considering you two seem attached at the hip, to head up to Charleston. We've got something up there I want your eyes on."

For Zara's benefit I switch the phone over to speaker as I pull off the road. "What's in Charleston that the office there can't handle?"

"Yesterday I got a call from an old friend at the ATF. He's concerned by what might very well be a string of serial arsons plaguing the city."

"So? Isn't that within their purview?" I ask.

"He's concerned because of the bodies that are piling up.

There've been two so far, and while the first one was initially ruled an accident, the second definitely was not. I want you to coordinate with the ATF on site, see what your instincts tell you about it. This could very well be nothing."

I shoot a glance at Zara. She just gives me a shrug and a "don't look at me" face.

"I'm flattered you want me up there, boss, but I'm kinda in the middle of something here. You approved my time off yourself."

There's what sounds like a laugh on the other side, but I can't be sure as I've never heard my boss laugh in my life. "Slate, you know better than anyone this job doesn't cater to your vacation schedule. When something comes up, it comes up. It just so happens you're close. Now get on it."

"Um, not to be a thorn here," Zara says. "But I *also* have approved time off and I—"

"Zip it, Foley," Janice replies. "It's not a great look for a new field agent to take two weeks off after just beginning her job. I approved it because I believed you deserved a little reprieve for your work on the Krauss case. But that approval begins and ends at my leisure."

"Right," Zara says, sinking back into her seat.

"Or I could order you back to D.C. right now and you could be doing the job the government actually pays you for."

"Nope, I'm good," she replies. "I like it down here, all this…warmth."

Janice waits a beat. I know from experience that means she's doing a mental reset. "The ATF agent on site is a man named Stan Farmer. He's expecting you. How long will it take you to get up there?"

"Charleston isn't far," I reply. "We can probably be there in two to three hours. We'll need to pack."

"Good. Keep me updated on your progress. And feel free to coordinate with the local FBI office if you need additional

resources." She hangs up abruptly. I pull up maps on my
phone and plot a course to Charleston. Yep, two hours.

"Well," I say, staring out the windshield as a small swarm
of small, red bugs lands right in the middle. "Maybe it's not as
hot up there."

We're not on the interstate long before the GPS puts us back
on surface roads heading into Charleston. Though we come in
through the suburbs, so we don't get a good look at anything
until we're almost on top of the city.

"Where are we headed again?" Zara asks. She's been
uncharacteristically quiet most of the trip. I'm not sure if
something is going on or not, but I trust her to talk about it
when she's ready. Personally, I was partially relieved when
Janice called. This whole hunting down an assassin thing is
starting to feel like a little too much. Like I've stumbled onto
something I should never have seen. And to be honest, I'm not
sure I'll ever be able to make any progress. Though I do still
have two more addresses on my list from Krauss's app. Unfortunately both of them are on the west coast, and will take
significantly more resources to reach.

"A place called Paintball City," I say, checking the GPS
again. It's located in the West Ashley part of the city, which is
fortunate considering that's the area we have to drive through
to get into Charleston proper. From what I understand,
Charleston is a very historical city, with a lot of culture and
heritage. Did I happen to book us in a hotel that's close to the
center of the downtown area so we could partake? Maybe.
It'll be a lot better than that motel on the edge of Savannah I
had to spring for since I was using my own money.

That's one nice thing about this job, the perks.

"Who in the hell would kill someone in a paintball yard?"
Zara asks.

"Have you ever played?"

"Me? Oh no. I don't care to be shot by what's basically a water-filled BB. I had a friend who took two to the chest, point-blank range. They left welts for weeks afterward. You?"

"A little bit. During college. But it got old quick since most of the players were guys and a lot of them got *way* too into it, if you know what I mean."

"Boys love to play soldier," she replies.

"I think it helped with my application though," I reply. "My marksmanship scores were higher than average. Probably because of all my practice."

"That's B.S." She laughs. "There's no way those clunky things handle like a real weapon."

I give her a wink. "Maybe I'm just deadly with whatever weapon I pick up."

"Now *there's* the Emily I haven't seen in a while." She gives me a little shove. "Nothing like a little murder to bring you right back, huh?"

I really think these past two weeks have been restorative for me. Even though we haven't made much progress on finding our mystery woman, just leaving the pressure of the job for a bit and hanging out with a good friend have done more for me than anything else so far. I still haven't fully processed what happened to me…to my life five months ago. And I think it's going to take a lot of time to come to terms with it.

Following the GPS, I turn off the aptly named Savannah Highway into the parking lot of what looks like a military bunker set off from the side of the road. Beyond it are large open fields, all with high fences. Some are completely unobstructed, while others have obstacles and woods inside the perimeter and others have nothing but wooden structures. It seems Paintball City offers something for everyone.

The parking lot is empty except for two cars, three black and whites, and two large fire trucks.

"Didn't Janice say this happened yesterday?" Zara asks.

I nod. So why are all these vehicles still here? I could understand keeping a local cop car or two around to keep watch, but the fire engines?

I pull up to an officer standing close to the entrance who stops us with his hand up. "Sorry, field is closed. There was a fire here last night."

I show him my badge. I probably should have changed into something more formal before we left Savannah, but it's just so damn hot I wasn't prepared to sweat through my suit. I'm sure I look like a college kid out for a fun afternoon of paintballing in my tank and torn jeans. "Slate and Foley, FBI. We're looking for Agent Farmer."

The cop points us in the direction of the "bunker". We thank him and pull around so as not to block any of the other vehicles in the lot. Once we're out of the car, I head back to the trunk and open my suitcase, pulling out a button-up shirt. It's not much, but it's better than going over there sleeveless.

"Trying to impress somebody?" Zara asks, sidling up beside me.

"Just trying to make sure we're taken seriously," I reply. "You'll figure it out soon enough. They're looking for any reason to dismiss you. Don't give them the chance."

Zara grumbles and opens her suitcase, slipping on her blouse and coat to match. I hang my badge on my belt so it's clearly visible and pull my arms through my holster, wearing it over my shirt. It's not the best, but it will have to do.

The bunker is actually the main office of the yard, and the door is wide open for us to walk right in. A couple of fire-fighters are outside, their coveralls on, but their jackets off. I catch Zara give one of them a wink as we walk by and hurry her forward before things can escalate.

The inside of the main building is a flurry of activity. More firefighters in here moving past us in both directions, a cop stationed at the door who is about to stop us until he sees our badges, and medical personnel speaking to one man in particular. I'm pretty sure I've just found our contact with the ATF.

"Agent Farmer?" I ask, walking up behind him.

The man turns, revealing a grizzled face and a beard that hasn't been trimmed in a while. His gray hair tells me he's probably in his fifties, but his eyes are sharp, even if his clothes seem almost threadbare. He's wearing a tweed jacket, even in this heat, with a white button-up and slacks and he has something of a belly hanging over his belt. To me, it looks like a man who has seen too much of this job and the job has turned him inside out.

"And you are?" he asks.

"Agent Emily Slate. FBI." I indicate to Zara. "This is Agent Foley. We spoke on the phone."

He regards us for a moment. "I thought you'd be older."

"I used to do a lot of undercover work for the Bureau. Been with them about four years now."

"Huh," Farmer says, apparently not impressed or entertained by either fact. "Well. Welcome to the shitshow. Just to make something clear here. I'm in charge of investigating the fires. What you do with the bodies once I'm done, is your business."

I hold up my hands. "We're here purely on an advisory role only."

Farmer grumbles something under his breath. But it's loud enough for me to catch "*half my age*". I can see how someone like Farmer wouldn't be too happy about us giving him pointers about a case. If there even is a case here.

"My boss said there's no definitive proof this is a serial yet, is that still true?" I ask.

Farmer looks over to the medical personnel he was just conversing with. Looks like a local medical examiner, but definitely not a coroner. "That's TBD. We're still working on the details."

"Okay," I reply. "So what's with all the extra equipment out there? Wasn't the fire yesterday?"

"Last night," he replies. "And they're there because it took them nearly seven hours to put this thing out. We were lucky it didn't spread to the surrounding marshland. Could have been bad."

That's something I hadn't even considered. When Janice said Arson, my mind immediately went to someone's house or a building of some kind. I hadn't thought about an open-air fire that could have easily spread to the surrounding trees and bushes.

"They're sticking around to make sure there aren't any more flareups," he adds.

I glance out through the shop's main window on a row of picnic tables that separate this building from the paintball yards. "Can we go see it?"

Farmer sighs. "I guess that's what you came for, isn't it? C'mon."

Chapter Three

EVEN THOUGH THE FBI ROUTINELY INVESTIGATES ARSON cases, I haven't been on many. Most of my previous work history centered around drug rings or missing persons. So I'm more than happy to hand off the more technical aspects of the job to Farmer. He's the expert, after all.

He leads us past the picnic tables over to a charred metal fence. I notice on one of the tables sits an evidence marker with the number "4" written on it.

"What was that over there?" I ask.

"The man's wallet was left on the table for us to find," Farmer says. "It's how we knew who the victim was. It wasn't like we could make a positive ID from what was left."

"So then whoever did this wasn't trying to cover their tracks," Zara says. "They wanted us to know who they'd killed."

"Mm-hm," Farmer grunts.

"Or it could be a decoy; they might be trying to throw us off the trail and cover up the identity of the person they really killed," I say.

"It'll be Leon," Farmer says.

"I'm sorry?"

He turns to me as we reach the charred gate. "There's no conspiracy here. The body will match the wallet once we get the dental information back."

I appraise him. "You seem awfully sure about that."

He doesn't elaborate on why he's so sure, only takes a nitrite glove out of his pocket before he opens the gate for us. Though I notice he doesn't put the glove on, he just uses it so he doesn't touch the metal with his bare hand. "This way."

It looks to me like the flames licked the metal gate, but didn't make it much farther than the yard itself. And they don't seem to have spilled into the adjacent yards, which is probably due to there not being a lot in this course that could burn. It's not heavily wooded, instead it's filled with a lot of obstacles and wood plank construction clustered near the center.

Thankfully we're outside, otherwise the smell would be overpowering. Even though the fire is gone, I can still taste the smoke on the air and the acrid sting causes my eyes to water. The whole area has been drenched by the firefighters, only adding a swampy, wet aroma to the place. Underneath our feet, the ground still crunches, even though the charred black grass has been soaked down. I only now realize just how large of a job it would have been to get this fire under control, given the size of the obstacle course.

"What time did the fire start?" I ask as we make our way around some of the burned wood supports of what used to be a blind.

"First call came in around midnight. Someone a couple of blocks away saw the glow and could smell the fire on the air. They had to dispatch four trucks by the time they realized what they were dealing with."

We pass a couple of firefighters who are trudging away from the direction we're heading. They don't look up or even acknowledge us. I don't deal with fire departments often, but from what few interactions I've had with them, they're usually an open and friendly bunch. At least more so than the local cops I encounter.

As we get closer to the center of the yard, the destruction becomes worse. Here most everything is coated in a thick layer of char, if it hasn't burnt away entirely. There are a few posts driven into the ground which used to hold something up, and there are a couple of vertical logs that are completely black. It looks like they used to be obstacles paintballers could use to hide behind. The smell here is even worse, and I have to cover my nose and mouth not to inhale. I look back at Zara who is doing the same thing, her eyes wide.

Farmer, however, seems completely undisturbed. He must have lungs of steel. He leads us to what used to be a wall of some kind, though most of it has burnt away. I can tell by the amount of damage that this was probably the flashpoint of the fire. "This is where you found him?"

Farmer nods. "What was left of him, anyway. Not much more than bones by the time we got here." He points to the edges of the wall, where some charred metal chains still hang. "Though he was still strung up, both arms spread wide, and his legs bound together and to the wall. Almost like he was crucified."

"Are you thinking there's a religious component at work?" Zara asks through her shirt. I had the same thought.

"That's for you to figure out," he replies. "I'm here for the fire."

"Fair enough." I take a long look at the site, though it doesn't look like there are remnants of any kind of pyre. The chains are blackened, but have cuffs where they clamped around the victim's appendages. So someone was prepared for this; it wasn't a rush job. I take my time walking around the site, looking for any other evidence, though the fire and subsequent extinguishing of it have left little remaining. What would motivate someone to do something like this?

"Thoughts?" I ask Zara.

"Looks ritualistic," she replies. "But that could be a misdirection."

I turn to Farmer. "What can you tell us about the body?"

"I'm not a forensics expert," he replies. "I investigate fires. You'll have to talk to the coroner if you want detailed information."

"Okay," I reply, trying to hide my frustration. He's being willfully obtuse, though I can't figure out why. Is it really because we're that much younger than him? "What can you tell us about the fire itself?"

Something flips in Farmer, and he goes into analytical mode. "This is the flashpoint, obviously," he says. "We're looking at an accelerant, more than likely kerosene or another liquid, though we won't know for sure until we get the data back from the labs. You can smell it in the air." I had noted a strange smell mixed in with all the burn and char, though I can't quite place it. It's only a remnant. "Fire spread out from here, moving in all directions. My guess is the perp doused the entire area before lighting it up. The fire burned hot and long because it had plenty of fuel in the form of these boards and obstacles. The wall here," He points to the wall with the chains, "was also doused in the accelerant. My guess is he poured it all over the victim as well."

"He didn't want to take the chance he would survive," Zara says.

Farmer shakes his head. "Doesn't look like it."

"And you're sure it's this Leon person," I say. "What can you tell us about him?"

Farmer lets out a long sigh. "That's part of the reason you're here. Leon is a local firefighter. Had it been anyone else and we probably wouldn't have called you in."

I screw up my features. "Doesn't the ATF routinely handle cases of arson when a firefighter...or any public servant is involved?"

He nods. "We do. But Leon is the second firefighter in as

many weeks to die in a fire. The first one was a man named Sam Phelps, who perished in the line of duty. His death was originally ruled an accident, but after this…"

"You're not sure anymore," I say. "You think someone might be targeting local firefighters and taking them out one by one."

He makes a gesture in our direction. "You said it, not me. Enter our FBI profilers. They tell me you're familiar with this kind of thing."

I exchange a quick glance with Zara. "Not this exactly. But we've recently just solved a serial kidnapper case."

"Well," Farmer says. "Looks like you have your work cut out for you."

Chapter Four

"WHAT MAKES YOU SO SURE IT WAS LEON SPENCER YOU FOUND here?" I ask as we make our way back through the burnt maze to the front of the yard again.

Farmer doesn't look back as he answers. "We've already tried to contact Leon Spencer, and no one has seen him since yesterday. His truck was found in the local community college parking lot this morning, with all his stuff still inside. I called in the locals to process it."

"Any family?" I ask.

"No, but he's divorced. His wife and son live in Atlanta. They'll be notified as soon as we get the positive ID from the medical examiner."

"Any enemies?"

He opens the gate, allowing both of us to step through before closing it. I notice he uses the glove again. At least he's not incompetent. Farmer strikes me as someone who is probably exceptionally good at his job, as he's probably been at it a long time.

"Considering I haven't had time to do a full psychological workup on him, I can't speak to that point, Agent Slate," he snaps. I should have expected as much, but I figured it was worth asking so we could get a jumpstart on this case.

"What about the other firefighter? Anything connecting the two?"

He shakes his head. "Not that I've found so far. They were from two different stations. The only thing connecting them right now is the proximity of their deaths and the fact they both died in a fire."

"But you said the other one, Sam, he was killed in the line of duty. Which meant he was responding to a fire that was already ongoing?" I ask.

Farmer nods, leading us around the bunker building, back to the parking lot. "Like I said, I don't know if they're connected, or if this is just a massive coincidence. But that's not my area of expertise."

"I'd like to take a look at those case files as soon as possible," I say.

Farmer nods. "You coordinating with the FBI satellite office here?"

Until we know what this is, I don't see any reason to pull more people off their current cases. And given we'll need to stay in close contact with Farmer, I'd rather stay as close as possible. "For now, we'll just coordinate with you," I reply. "Since we're all working on this together."

While the look he gives me isn't friendly, it's not outright loathing either, which is a nice change of pace. "You know our building? Off Highway Seven?"

"I'm sure we can find it."

"I'll be there if you need me." He hands me his card with his cell phone number on it. "And remember, we called *you* in on this. So I expect to be kept in the loop."

I take the card. "Of course."

His phone rings and he takes it off his belt before flipping it open. "Farmer." He pauses then turns away from us. "Yeah.

Okay, thanks for putting the rush on this. Right, your tab is always open with me." He hangs up and turns back to us. "That was the coroner. They just confirmed it was Spencer's body. Matched his records with his dentist." He blows out a long breath like he was hoping it wouldn't be true.

"You said locals are on site where his truck was found? I'd like to go take a look," I say, trying to pull him back to the conversation. In all honesty, he looks somewhat rattled by the news.

"Yeah, it's Carolina Palmetto. Not far off 526." He glances back at the bunker. "Now I get to go in there and tell them another one of their own just died."

I can relate. Giving news to families is hard enough. But firefighters are like cops, they're all an extended family on the job. When something happens to one of them, it happens to all. I don't envy Farmer's position.

"We'll let you know if we find anything at the college," I say. He nods, then heads back to the bunker to meet with the rest of his staff.

"Poor guy," Zara says when he's out of earshot. We both head back to the rental vehicle. "Still, he's something of a curmudgeon."

"It doesn't matter," I reply. "He could be the grinch for all I care, as long as he doesn't actively obstruct the case."

"That's right," she teases. "I forgot you have a sordid history with grumpy old cops."

"It was one time," I insist. "Plus, he's not like Chief Burke. He's actually competent." I turn to look back at the fire trucks. The teams of firemen are replacing all their equipment, preparing to leave after a hard night's work. "What do you think?"

"I think I wouldn't want to be Farmer right now." All her earlier bravado is gone. "Word is going to spread fast, if it hasn't already."

"Given his ID was just on display like that? Yeah, I'd say

so." But there's something about it I don't like. It's too easy. Why go to all this trouble to kill someone, just to announce it to the world? "I think we need to start digging into Leon Spencer's life before we do anything else. Find out who hated the man enough to burn him to a crisp."

"Did you see any other evidence anywhere else in the yard?" I ask.

"The place was raw. There wasn't much left."

"We'll have to catch up with Farmer's forensic team when they're done. At least they'll be able to tell us if the killer left anything else behind other than the wallet. But if they were this brazen about it, I doubt the team will find anything. Someone obviously spent a lot of time planning for this."

"You're thinking about the chains."

I nod. "Let's get out to the college. I want to see if there are any security cameras that picked up anything. Or maybe somebody saw something last night." We head back to the car, and I catch Zara smiling as we do. "What?"

"Nothing," she says, slipping into the passenger seat. Somehow, despite the fact we've only been out of the car less than thirty minutes, it's sweltering inside again. Sweat seeps through my shirt.

"Oh no," I say, doing my best to get myself comfortable despite the fact I feel like I'm almost swimming through the air in here, as thick as it is. "Spill it."

"You," she says. "Three hours ago, you were moaning about not getting anywhere with your mystery woman and now you're already wrapped up in another case, the whole thing forgotten. It's enough to give someone whiplash."

"I—" I want to protest, but it's not far from the truth. This is a welcome distraction, one which I need now. Plus, I've never been able to resist a good puzzle. "It's like Janice said. If you don't like it, you can head on back to D.C."

"And miss all this? No way."

It only takes us about twenty minutes to reach the community college. It's a complex made up of at least a dozen brick buildings, some interconnected and others off to the side on their own. But it isn't difficult to figure out where we're going, flashing police lights draw our attention to one of the parking areas where local cops are directing people away from the scene. They've also coordained off the area around a pickup that sits near one of the tall light poles. After showing our credentials, the locals let us through, and we park a few spaces away. A small crowd of students has gathered on the far side of the lot, looking in our direction.

"Who is in charge here?" I ask as Zara and I approach, our badges on display again.

An older gentlemen, smoking something menthol—I can smell it from here—turns to us and I see him roll his eyes before we're even ten feet from him. "What do feds want with a missing person?" he asks. Clearly the word hasn't gone out to everyone yet.

"We're coordinating with the ATF," I reply. "Farmer called for us. Agents Slate and Foley."

"Christ," the man says under his breath. "I'm Sergeant Henlion. How many agencies do we need working one case?"

"We're here in an advisory capacity," I reply. "I assume this is Leon Spencer's truck?"

"Yeah," he says, putting the cigarette out under his foot. "Been here all night. Campus security called it in this morning."

"Anything inside?" I ask.

"Books, laptop, school supplies. Looks like Spencer is finishing his degree."

"Anything else?" I ask. "Signs of a struggle?"

Henlion shakes his head. "Nothing like that. Truck was locked. No tracks, but we're still pulling prints." He nods to his team which are giving the truck a once-over. "Should know pretty soon if anyone else touched it. They find out if it's Spencer yet?"

Zara and I exchange looks. "Unfortunately it looks like it," I reply.

"Damn," he says, pulling out another cigarette. "Somebody's out there hunting them down. I tell you one thing; it's making my guys nervous."

"Your guys, why?" I ask.

"Why else? All of our departments work closely together. I knew Leon. Not well, but I knew him. We all did. And what's to say this guy doesn't start coming for cops next?"

"We haven't confirmed the same person is responsible for both deaths," I say. "The first one was ruled an accident."

"Uh-huh," Henlion says, sucking on his cigarette. "And I'm the prince of France."

"Sergeant?" The three of us turn to see a beat cop trotting up with a young woman in a long, plaid skirt and sweatshirt. She's probably not older than twenty. "This is Ms. Laghari. She said she can show us the camera footage from last night."

I instinctively look up and around, but don't spot any cameras around the vehicle. "Where's the closest one?" I ask.

The young woman with black hair points to the building. "There, right above the door."

It's so far away I know any footage from the camera will probably be worthless, unless they have a telescopic lens attached. Still, it's worth a look.

Five minutes later the three of us, along with Ms. Laghari and the beat cop are all squeezed into what amounts to an A/V room close to the college offices. Laghari is running the cameras back, though only one of them for this building looks out onto the parking lot; the same one she pointed out before. The entire time, Spencer's truck is visible at the top left portion of the screen, though it's pixelated.

"There," I say as she keeps winding back. "Looks like that

was when class got out." As it keeps going back more and more cars pull "into" the lot and students get out of them, walking backward to underneath the camera. "Play it from here."

We watch at normal speed as everyone goes to their cars, though I notice no one has approached Spencer's truck yet. After all the other cars are already gone, a man appears just off to the right of the screen, heading for the truck. He's hard to see because he's not in the middle of the frame. By the time he reaches the truck, he's little more than a bunch of pixels.

"Isn't there any way to clean this up?" Henlion asks.

"No, sir," the girl replies. "This is all we have."

It looks like Spencer, or at least, who I assume is Spencer, stands by his truck a moment, then walks around and off screen. "Where is he going?" Zara asks.

"Can you keep rewinding, back before everyone gets out of class?" I ask. I note the time stamp when Spencer disappears off screen: ten twenty-two p.m.

"Sure," she says, and it speeds backward again.

"What are you looking for?" Henlion asks.

"Something pulled him away from his truck last night. I want to see if the camera caught anything out of the ordinary earlier in the evening. I'm not sure what."

She keeps rewinding all the way until six p.m. when cars start disappearing from the lot again, indicating that was when people first started getting there for class last night. I didn't see anything else out of the ordinary. "Can you make us a copy of that entire video, from twelve p.m. yesterday until this morning?"

"Sure," she replies.

"But there was nothing else there," Henlion says as Zara and I squeeze our way out of the room.

"Still, I want to get a closer look," I tell him.

"Whatever happened, the perp was smart enough to stay

off the camera," Henlion says. "You're not going to find anything."

I shrug as the young woman gives me a thumb drive she just ejected from the computer. "Thanks." I toss it to Zara who snatches it out of the air. "You never know what you might find when you take the time, sergeant."

I can tell I've probably pissed him off, but it doesn't matter. Zara and I make our way back to the parking lot, but before we can get there, we're stopped by one of Henlion's men, who is being followed by a timid-looking man with glasses and a sweater vest. "Agents?" he asks. "You were looking for Mr. Hoffman?"

"You're the economics teacher?" I ask. Before we looked at the footage, I had the office pull Leon Spencer's schedule. Turns out he had econ class for four hours last night.

"What is this all about?" the man asks. "I saw at least three police vehicles outside."

I thank the officer who leaves Hoffman with us. "Is Leon Spencer in your class?" I ask.

He nods. "Leon, yeah. He's not the best student, but he tries hard."

"Was he in your class last night?" Zara asks.

Hoffman nods again. "What's going on?"

I take a deep breath. Spencer's death isn't public yet, and Hoffman doesn't need to know what happened. Still, part of me wants to tell him just so it won't come as such a shock later. "Did anything happen last night? Anything strange?"

"Strange how?"

"Was Leon acting any different? Did he seem nervous at all?" I ask.

Hoffman purses his lips. "No, in fact I caught him nodding off more than once last night."

"We noticed Leon left a little later than everyone else. Was everything okay with him?" I ask.

"Oh," Hoffman says. "Yeah, that was me. Gave him some

concentrated caffeine to help him on tomorrow night's class. They all have big papers due, and they have to present their findings in class. Leon tries hard, he does, and I know his job can be taxing. But if he can't stay awake during class, I don't know how he's supposed to retain these concepts."

I shoot Zara a look. "Has Leon ever had problems with any of the other students?"

"Not that I know of. He mostly keeps to himself. Doesn't bother anyone."

This is looking more and more like a dead end. I'm not sure what to think, but it looks like we can rule out any of his classmates doing this to him. Though we should probably check his other classes, just to make sure. I can see from the look on Zara's face she's thinking the same thing.

"Can you please tell me what's this about? Has Leon done something illegal?"

"Mr. Hoffman, I'm sorry to tell you, but Leon was found dead this morning. The police are here because his truck is still in the parking lot."

"Dead? Are you sure?" he asks.

"We're sure," Zara replies. "They just confirmed it was him about an hour ago."

"I can't…" Hoffman says, putting a hand to his head. "I was just talking to him last night. *Dead?*"

"Did you happen to see anything out of the ordinary when you left last night?" I ask. Hoffman seems lost in thought. "Mr. Hoffman?"

"Oh, no, sorry. The teachers have a different lot on the other side of the building. I left through there. But I didn't see or hear anything."

"What time did you leave last night?"

He rubs his forehead again. "After I spoke to Leon, I stayed maybe another ten minutes to catch up on work. Then headed home. They've got me teaching two different shifts and it's murder on my sleep schedule." He seems to realize what he's said too late, as his eyes go wide.

I pull out a card and hand it to him. "If you think of anything else. Call."

We leave Hoffman standing in the hallway, a dazed look on his face.

Chapter Five

ONCE WE'RE BACK OUTSIDE, ZARA AND I CHECK THE PARKING lot to see if we can find anything that might have drawn Leon Spencer's attention away from getting into his own vehicle and driving home. But other than a few oil stains at random intervals all over the lot, we don't come up with much.

Finally, we head back to the car and crank the A/C as the sun has hit its peak. Despite how hot it is now, it's only going to get worse. Not wanting to draw the ire of Sergeant Henlion any longer, I drive us down to the street and park so we can start doing background work.

"Found anything yet?" I ask Zara. At least I was able to get us into a shady spot out of the killer sun.

"Not a lot. Like many forty-something men he doesn't have much of a social media profile. Though, going back far enough I see pictures of his wife and kid. He never deleted them."

"I wonder if they were still on good terms," I say, scrolling through what little I've found on him as well.

"I can't do a full background check on him until I can access our servers. We'll need to swing by the satellite office at some point."

"I figured as much." Our first priority, as strange as it seems, is not to find Leon's killer, but to determine if the two deaths are related. Because if they are, that indicates someone has a much higher chance of striking again. However, if they were just after Leon and have made their point now, they might not go after any other victims. "Anything on Phelps?"

"Haven't even started yet," she replies. "It's very difficult to do this kind of work, cramped in a little car parked on the side of the road somewhere."

An idea strikes me. "Did you find out where Leon was stationed?" I ask.

"Um..." She scrolls back through her phone. "Firehouse six. It's in downtown."

"Let's see what his co-workers have to say. They might know something no one else does, especially if they heard about the first death."

"Should we inform Farmer?" she asks.

I weigh the pros and cons. He did say to keep him in the loop. But at the same time, we're not doing anything out of the ordinary here. We're just making some inquiries. "If it turns up something, yeah, we'll let him know. Until then, we're just two unassuming agents, asking some questions."

Zara shakes her head. "You're terrible. You can justify pretty much anything, can't you?"

"Look who's talking, Ms. I-take-off-after-six-weeks-on-the-job." We both share a laugh. I think the only reason Janice hasn't canned me yet is because despite not always following procedure to the letter, I do follow the spirit...and I get results. Farmer has enough to deal with at the moment, no need to waste his time if we don't come up with anything.

It takes us another twenty minutes to get into Charleston proper. The streets here aren't very wide, and none of the buildings are very tall. It all *feels* very historic, just like I'd suspected. As if the entire city was built in the 1800's and just refused to grow up. As we were coming in, some of the tallest spires I saw were from churches.

"Take a right here," Zara says, watching her GPS. The further into the city we've driven, the smaller the roads have become. We're now on a two-lane that's tight with even this small car. How an SUV or pickup would drive down here with traffic in both directions I don't know.

"There it is."

I look over and see a historic-looking building, clad all in brick with two archways in the front and the CFD logo emblazoned over each one. There are two thin doors situated between the arches and two more on the outside of the arches. A second floor sits atop the first, each window with a different type of ornamentation. And, of course, there's a large American flag waving in the breeze out front.

"Now that's a fire station," Zara says.

"Pretty much exactly how I'd picture one in my mind if someone told me to imagine the perfect firehouse," I say. I can just imagine horses pulling a water wagon out of there, trotting down cobblestone streets. The building sits in between a small storefront on one side and what looks like a house on the other, despite the fact we're in the middle of downtown.

It only takes me a minute to find a parking spot across the street and when we step out, thankfully there is a breeze blowing through that has cooled the air from earlier in the day.

"How do you want to play this?" Zara asks. "Do we tell them?"

"I'd be surprised if they didn't already know by now," I reply. "I didn't catch the station numbers of the engines that responded to the fire, did you?"

"I think one was station twelve," she replies.

We head up to one of the main archways which is already open, one of the station's trucks sitting right inside. I catch sight of a man sitting inside on a wooden bench, reading a book. He looks up as we enter. "Can I help you?"

"Special Agents Slate and Foley," I say, showing him my badge. "Is this where Leon Spencer was stationed?" The man stands, putting his book away. As is the case with most firefighters, I can tell he's ripped. His arms have to be as big as my thigh, easily. His hair is cut close to the scalp, but he's got an easy demeanor about him.

"Leon? Yeah, he runs trucks out of here, why?"

"And you are?" I ask.

He sticks his hand out. "Conrad. Jace."

"Jace," I say, giving it a quick shake. "Do you know when Leon's last shift was?"

He shrugs. "Not sure. Captain changed up the schedule last week. I haven't seen him since Friday."

"Do you know Leon well?" Zara asks, picking up that Jace is still talking about him in the present tense. They haven't heard yet.

"I've only run with the guy once, and that was on a training drill. Our schedules don't overlap much."

I catch a few of the other firefighters milling around near the back of the station. Some of them watching us. "Is your captain in? We'd like to speak with him."

"Sure, he's upstairs." Jace points to the far-right corner where a staircase begins before turning ninety degrees following the wall upstairs. "His is the only office with a door."

"Thanks." We head up the stairs, but I notice Zara has a silly smile on her face as we do. "You better wipe that off if you don't want him thinking you're nothing but a lovesick schoolgirl."

She smacks me on the arm. "Let me have my fantasies, please, and thank you. I don't go around knocking the wind out of your sails."

"Yeah?" I ask. "Then go back there and ask him out."

"It's called a fantasy for a reason," she says. "As in, I'd never do it in real life."

"Coward," I say as we reach the top of the stairs. There are a couple of other guys up here, one in what looks like a nice, updated kitchen while a few others are in a rec room down the hall whooping at each other.

The room with the door is right in front of us. I give it a light knock. "Come in."

The man behind the desk is probably in his late fifties, though most of his hair is white. Like Jace, it's cut short, and he's got a trim mustache to match. He looks up, surprise on his face when we enter. "Pardon the interruption, Captain," I say. "I'm Special Agent Emily Slate, FBI. This is Special Agent Foley. We were hoping to ask you a few questions."

The captain shoots the phone on his desk a brief look, then stands, extending his hand. "Kirk Henry," he says. "What can I do for the FBI?"

"We're here about one of your firefighters," I say, taking a seat across from him. Zara does the same. "Leon Spencer."

Henry nods at the phone. "I just received the call from ATF notifying me. I was about to go inform the rest of the crew."

"We're sorry for your loss," I say. I should have expected Farmer would give Spencer's captain a heads up, but that also means he's probably already informed the family as well. "Had you known Leon long?"

Henry shakes his head. "Thank you. It's always tough losing a good jake. But I didn't really know him that well. He transferred over here from Station twelve a few weeks ago."

I shoot a look at Zara. Station Twelve was on-site at the paintball yard. Which means that some of Leon's old co-workers probably had to put him out. No wonder they looked so dour out there. But his transfer hadn't come up in what little background we'd done on him. "Transferred, why?"

Henry makes a gesture. "Who knows. You'd have to ask

the Assistant Chief. He's in charge of all that. I just take what I'm given and do the best I can with it."

"Was he good at his job?" Zara asks.

"Spencer had been on the job for fifteen years, I think," Henry says. "He was slowin' a little, but still pretty good for an older guy. A lot of the young ones looked up to him."

"Did you know he was going to community college?" I ask.

Henry nods. "Yeah. He told me he couldn't do this forever, and joked he wasn't smart enough to take my job, so he had to find something else to do. I helped fix his schedule so he wouldn't miss too many classes." There's a certain fondness in how he talks about Spencer.

"Any trouble with anyone in the station. Or anyone else that you might have noticed?" I add.

Henry holds both hands out. "What can I say? Everybody liked Leon. Despite his claims, he was a smart guy. We're really going to miss him around here. I heard it was pretty gruesome down there."

I swallow. "We haven't seen him for ourselves yet, but from what I understand, yeah."

He points at us. "You two may not want to get involved with that. Burn victims are a lot more traumatic than victims of gunshot or knife wounds. I'd hate for young women like yourselves to be burdened with something like that. Trust me, I've seen my fair share of crispies. It's not something that ever goes away."

I stand. "Thanks, but I'm sure we can handle it."

"Suit yourselves," he says. I motion to Zara that we should go. She's giving Henry a hard look but finally gets up to follow me out. "Nice meeting you ladies," he calls as we're crossing the threshold.

Once we get back outside, I can practically feel the anger radiating off her. "Nothing like a little baked-in misogyny to get you fired up, am I right?"

"I just love it when men tell me that something might be too gruesome for my sensitive female eyes," she replies in mock sarcasm.

"That makes two of us. But at least he did give us one good nugget of information."

She looks over at me. "The transfer?"

I nod. "Yep. What are you willing to bet Leon was originally stationed in the same unit with Phelps? Two victims, one station."

"We'll have to check the records to verify," she replies.

I turn the engine over. "Sure will. *Now* we give Farmer a call."

Chapter Six

AFTER INFORMING FARMER THAT LEON HAD BEEN transferred from another station, he told us to meet him and his team over at the Charleston County Coroner's office, which is where they were examining Leon's body. I couldn't tell if he was encouraged by the news or not; he's a difficult man to read. But he was able to confirm for us that Phelps had been part of Station Twelve before he died.

As we're on our way over there, I give Janice a call.

"Simmons," she says in her characteristic flat tone.

"Giving you a heads up," I say. "Looks like it's something after all."

"Serial?" she asks.

"Looking that way. Turns out both victims were from the same firehouse here in the city. But we're looking at completely different M.O.'s, so it's not conclusive yet."

"Okay," she replies. "Get yourselves comfortable down there. And I want regular updates on your progress. Foley?"

"Yes, ma'am," Zara says.

"I'm pulling you back here."

"But—"

"Slate is more than capable of handling this on her own and you have your own cases still sitting on your desk. In case you've forgotten."

Zara grumbles something under her breath. I hate to lose her, but I can't really blame Janice. Our leaves of absence were due to be up soon anyway. Though it's going to be a lot harder for me without her here. I work better when I have someone to bounce ideas off of, or in Zara's case, someone who can distract me so I'm not overthinking a case.

"I'll be on the next flight out," she says, begrudgingly.

"Good. Slate, don't let those ATF guys walk all over you. You've got operational authority here, use it."

"Thanks, Janice. I will." The woman hangs up without another word. She never has been one for small talk.

"Well, this is a load of bullshit," Zara says. "Joke's on you though, because now you have to keep *both* of us in the loop. I want to know what's happening every step of the way."

I chuckle. "I doubt you'll have time to remember, in between all your other casework."

She opens her phone, tapping away furiously. I'm sure she's probably booking the next flight back to D.C. "Guess you better make a detour."

It takes me another forty-five minutes to get out to the airport and back to the coroner's office. While I understand the need for Zara to get back to her own caseload, I feel a deep sense of loneliness after I watch her head off into the terminal. I hadn't realized just how much I'd been leaning on her these past few weeks while we were searching for the woman who killed my husband.

We've grown a lot closer ever since Matt's death, though I never would have expected it. Zara is one of those people who is a natural at getting others to open up around her, where I'm more likely to keep things close to the chest. I know I come off as rude or standoffish sometimes, but I just don't feel like intruding on someone else's wellbeing. She doesn't see it as an intrusion though; she sees it as a way to get to know someone better. We complement each other well; I just wish I could work more cases with her. I never would have found Krauss without her help.

"Where's your partner?" Farmer asks as I get out of the vehicle in front of the unassuming one-story brick building that is the County Coroner's.

"Have you been waiting for me this entire time?" I ask. I catch the whiff of cigarette smoke on the air, but don't spot any on the ground or discarded anywhere. Must be from employees around the corner.

The shadow of a smile crosses his unshaven face before it's gone again. "Waiting for you? No, I needed some fresh air after looking at *that*. The building has good ventilation, but I can still taste it in the back of my throat."

I hesitate for just a second. "That bad, huh?"

"Trust me, you have no idea how bad it can get. You ever see a full body burn victim before?"

I shake my head.

"Then I hope you have a strong stomach." He leads me into the building, waving off the woman posted at the small window just inside the door. She gives me a questioning look, like she can't figure out why someone who looks like she's in high school is in a place like this.

"You never answered my question," Farmer says, pushing through a set of double doors.

"Agent Foley had to return to D.C.," I say. "I just dropped her off at the airport. She was the one who figured out Spencer and Phelps both used to be in the same station."

"I should have picked up on that earlier," he says. "Didn't

have time to do a full workup on Leon. Not with everything else going on."

"Did your forensic teams find anything else at the paint yard?"

Farmer pushes through another double door, leading us to a third door secured by an electronic lock. "Still waiting to hear back. But it's not looking promising. You have the security footage from the school?"

I hold up the thumb drive Laghari gave me.

"Good. I want my guys to review that as soon as we're done here." He holds out his hand. Part of me feels like giving this up is like submitting to his authority. Should I push to keep some kind of control here? Janice said I had the authority, but at the same time I'm just one agent, while Farmer has teams of people working for him. In the interest of the case, it's better I don't let my ego win. I hand over the drive just as Farmer knocks on the locked door. If he noticed my hesitation, he doesn't say anything.

The door beeps and the light on the pad beside it turns green. Farmer opens the door, allowing me to go first into a long hallway which branches off into examination rooms. Looks like they have at least three or more, meaning they must have a robust staff if they're equipped to do that many inspections at once.

He points to the first room where two people in white medical coats stand over what looks like a large piece of charred meat half covered by a blue sheet. Both have gloves and masks on. "Slate, this is Dr. Olivia Lewis and her assistant, Levi Allison. They're some of the best this city has to offer. This is Agent Emily Slate with the FBI."

The first person turns to me, though all I can see are emerald green eyes since she has a mask and a surgical scarf keeping her hair out of the way. "Pleasure," she says. "Due to the nature of the crime we've been anxious to finish the autopsy of Mr. Spencer here." She backs away from the table and pulls her gloves off. I notice the tips of the fingers are covered in what looks like soot. She unties her mask and tosses all three of them in a nearby trash can before holding out a hand. I give it a good shake. "I was just going over some of the specifics with Agent Farmer here when he suddenly needed to take a break."

Farmer just grunts and moves to the far side of the room, his eyes on the table.

"You made a positive ID using his dental records?" I ask, doing my best not to stare at what Dr. Lewis's assistant is doing to the body.

"That's right. Now it's just a matter of finding the details. And so far, it's looking pretty grim."

"What do you mean?" I ask.

She steps to the side, allowing me to take in the full image of Leon Spencer's remains. His entire body looks like one long piece of charred meat. Most of the skin has burned away, though the assistant, Allison, is pulling pieces of the upper crust back, revealing dark pink layers underneath. I can clearly see Spencer's skeleton in multiple places, especially around the face. As I step closer, it's like I have passed some invisible wall as the smell immediately hits me. I can only describe it as a combination of burnt hair and overcooked bar-b-que. I cover my face with my arm, though it does little to stop the stench. I see what Farmer meant; I can taste it all the way in the back of my throat.

"The body was cooked, inside and out," Dr. Lewis says. "Which tells us this was a long, sustained fire. But if you'll notice, more of the skin and muscle has burned away around the neck and face."

"What does that mean?" I ask, my voice muffled.

"There was concentrated accelerant in those areas. It also appears Mr. Spencer was still alive when he was ignited."

"You can tell that?"

She nods. "There is soot in what's left of the airways,

telling us that he was still trying to breathe in while he was burning. Though, this case is somewhat more unusual." She turns to Farmer. "Did your forensics team determine the accelerant used on the site?"

He shakes his head. "Not yet. It will take them a while to process what little was left. But it looked to me like a common liquid. Kerosene maybe."

"It's a good guess," Lewis says. "But I think you'll find it was turpentine. Levi?" She walks over beside me, as her assistant pulls back a large section of charred skin, which reveals Leon Spencer's cooked insides. The smell is immediately worse. I'm not sure I'll ever be able to eat pork again, the smell is so similar and yet it has a hearty tang that must be unique to humans. My stomach lurches, but I force it to hold. I'm not going to lose my lunch all over the inside of Mr. Spencer.

"Look here," Lewis says, using a laser pen to point to one of the charred organs inside the body. "This is what used to be the stomach, and yet we're finding the crust of the burns is as thick here as anywhere else on the body. Which means more than likely he burned from the inside out at the same time."

"Jesus," Farmer says.

I squint, pushing through the discomfort to actually look. "How is that possible?"

"We also found trace gasses still in the lining here, where it's burned through. They were trapped in pockets. We first noticed them when we opened him up. The fumes are consistent with what you find when you burn turpentine and are quite toxic. Fortunately, we were able to take a sample before the ventilation system took care of the rest."

"You're saying he had turpentine in his stomach?" Farmer asks.

Lewis nods. "If there was anything left of the throat we would probably see massive irritation and inflammation. But given he was still alive at the time of the burning; the turpentine must have been added to his body just before ignition. More than likely, they doused his body as well, which is why we're seeing so much charring. Then the flame naturally followed the easiest fuel source, as in it probably traveled right down his still-coated throat and ignited the reservoir in his stomach. Whoever killed him wanted to make sure he burned inside and out."

I find I can't look anymore and turn away. It's just too gruesome. Add that to the fact someone was sick enough to force Spencer to drink turpentine before killing him…I'm not sure what to think. What I do know is we need to find this guy, fast. I walk over to the nearest table and place my hands on it to steady myself.

"Anything else?" Farmer asks. He sounds perfectly cool and collected. And yet all I can see in my mind is Mr. Spencer's "crust" being pulled off him like he's a Sunday roast.

"We're still working on him, I'm sure we'll find more as we go along. Let me know if they find any other accelerants out there. This is difficult enough, given the state of him," Lewis says.

"Thanks, Doc," Farmer says, then heads out.

I turn back to the two of them, doing my best to remain stoic. "I appreciate your help."

Lewis nods. "Good luck finding this guy. I don't have to tell you; I'd rather not do another one of these if I can help it."

That reminds me. "Did you work on the other firefighter case as well? Phelps?"

She nods. "I did. But he wasn't in nearly the condition this man is. He died of smoke inhalation before anything. Only about twenty percent of him was actually burned when they pulled him out. Still not a way I'd like to go, but better than…" she gestures to the table.

I nod. "Thanks. I may be in touch for a follow up."

"Anytime," she replies. "Unfortunately, my door is always open."

It takes me a few minutes to gather myself before heading back outside. I expect Farmer will be there waiting for me, but I find he's already left in his vehicle.

So much for professional courtesy.

Chapter Seven

"MISS ME YET?" ZARA ASKS.

I'm sitting at a small table in a hole-in-the-wall restaurant I found near the hotel I booked in downtown Charleston. I picked the one place I didn't see on any advertisements and that wasn't screaming "tourist". The host ushered me into the back, sat me at a table with a water and I've been waiting ever since for a menu. But to be honest I'm not that hungry after seeing Leon Spencer this afternoon. I'm definitely not getting anything grass-fed.

"You mean have I been able to survive the seven hours since you left without going mad?" I ask. I was feeling sorry for myself, so I put Zara on a video call. "Barely. Got a look at Spencer. I'm starting to think the fire captain was right, that wasn't something I needed to see. Or smell."

"Let me guess, you're not coming to my cookout next month."

I give her a face and she busts out laughing. "It's seriously messed up, Z. The guy poured turpentine down his throat and lit him on fire."

Her eyes grow wide. "No shit."

"Yeah. I've got to give Janice a full report tomorrow. And Farmer isn't being very cooperative."

"There's a surprise."

"He's *not* being not cooperative either, he's just…abrasive." I sigh. "Sorry. I didn't mean to call just to complain. How was the flight?"

"Sat in the terminal for two hours waiting," she says. "Only to get back here to a mountain of work. It's going to take me a month to get through all this. I think Janice has been adding to my workload while I've been gone. Kind of like a passive-aggressive punishment for leaving so abruptly."

I shake my head. "She wouldn't do that passive-aggressively. She'd do it full aggressively."

Movement in my field of vision pulls my eyes away. A waiter approaches with a menu. "Ma'am. Want anything else to drink?"

I didn't see a bar when I came in, there's no telling what they've got. "Do you have bourbon?"

"Yes, ma'am. You'd be hard pressed to find a restaurant around here that didn't."

"I'll take whatever your house is, straight. And make it a double."

He leaves the menu for me and makes his way to another table.

"Double huh?" Zara asks.

I glare at her. "Trust me. I need to get this taste out of my mouth. I feel like I've still got Leon Spencer in my throat."

"Don't say that too loud, someone might get the wrong idea." She grins.

It takes me a second to catch up to her. "You're terrible."

"I'm also pissed! I should be there with you, trying to find this bastard."

"Look at it this way," I say. "If this thing gets much worse, I'll have to requisition some help. I'll bring you right back down."

"What do you mean gets worse? If someone else gets killed?"

I nod. "Given that we now know both victims are from the same station, I think it's fair to assume they're being targeted, at least provisionally. But we still have to figure out why. And given the drastically different ways in which they died, I'm not sure Farmer is ready to buy in to the whole theory yet."

"You think he's going to be a problem?"

I shake my head. "I hope not, but I do feel bad for the guy. He's clearly been to too many fires in his career."

"Yeah, well, don't feel *too* bad for him," she replies. "When I got back the first thing I did was some digging on Stan Farmer. He's got a long history of being pals with some of Charleston's more powerful public servants. I haven't found anything *illegal*, but it doesn't speak well to his character."

"You're fishing," I say. "It doesn't mean he's dirty."

The waiter returns with my drink, setting it on a small coaster on the table. "Do you know what you'd like to eat?"

I haven't even looked at the menu. I scan it a second. "I'll take whatever your signature seafood dish is. But no red meat, understand?"

"We have plenty of pescatarian options, don't worry," he says. "I've got just what you need." He saunters off.

"That wasn't smart," Zara says.

"What?"

"Putting your meal in his hands. He's going to bring you back something in a fish skull, I guarantee it." She gives me a wicked grin.

"I'm not sure I'm going to eat anyway. I'm really just here for this." I hold up the drink and mock toast her, then knock back half of it in one gulp. It burns all the way down which would normally be a bad thing, but in this case, it's like cleaning out my system with bleach. For the first time in three hours, I don't taste ash on my tongue.

I smile at her, but she doesn't return it all the way. I can tell she's hesitant about something. "What?"

"I wasn't going to bring it up, but now that I'm back, do you want me to go pick up Timber?"

I let out a long breath. When I knew we would be leaving D.C. for a few weeks, I arranged with my brother-in-law and his wife to watch my pit bull. Matt and I rescued him after he'd been rehabilitated from a dog-fighting ring. And ever since Matt died, he's been the one thing still in the house that always reminds me of my husband. But with the longer hours I've been working and the fact I've been out of town so much lately, I finally decided to take my sister-in-law up on her offer to let Timber stay there on a semi-permanent basis. Right now it's fine because I'm here. But as soon as I come home to an empty house, I know it's going to be almost unbearable. But I have to do the right thing for him, not for myself. And in this situation, it's giving him a home where he's not alone all the time. It wouldn't be so bad if I wasn't so estranged from Matt's brother. He partially blames me for what happened, and I can't really blame him for that, knowing what I know. Had I been there, I might have been able to stop this woman from finding her way into our house and taking the life of the only man I ever loved.

"Ah, shit. I knew I shouldn't have mentioned it," Zara says. "I can tell by your face, I just opened the floodgates, didn't I?"

"There are no floodgates to open," I say and drain the rest of my glass. "It is what it is."

"We'll find her, Em, I promise you that." She's wearing the stern look she gets sometimes when things get serious. I know she believes we can find this woman, but I'm still not so sure. And given I need to focus on the task at hand rather than chase down someone who doesn't want to be found, I feel like it's a finish line I'll never reach. It's just too far.

I motion to the waiter to bring me another round. "If you say so."

"Oh yeah, I forgot to tell you. Guess who was back in the office this afternoon when I walked in?" I shrug, my mind too scattered from thinking about Timber, Matt, Leon Spencer and everything in between. "Nick Hogan."

"He's back?" I ask.

"Seems so." A couple of weeks ago, Nick had tried to coerce me into giving up one of my suspects so he could take the credit. Fortunately for me, that plan backfired, and he was gone the day Zara and I made the report to Janice. I wasn't sure if he would be back or not.

"Did he say anything to you?" I ask.

"Didn't even acknowledge me. Though I noticed his case-load is gone from his desk. In fact, I think *I* have some of his old cases."

"Then what's he doing there?" I ask.

"Maybe it's like you after what happened. Maybe Janice put him on probation, and this is her attempt to see if he's worthy of coming back or not."

"I just don't see how she could bring him back, after everything he did. I thought for sure he would be gone for good. That maybe they'd let him come in and pack up his desk, but that would be it."

"Pssh," Zara says. "If they were going to do that, they'd just mail his stuff to him in a cardboard box. They wouldn't risk the security of the building for one man."

"I just hope he stays out of my way when I get back. I don't plan on going easy on him."

"Nor should you."

I catch sight of the waiter approaching again, this time with something in a bowl along with another bourbon. "Okay, food's here. I'll talk to you tomorrow once we have a plan in place."

"Good luck," she replies. "And hey, don't let Farmer get to you. He has no idea what you can do."

"Thanks." I end the call and put my phone back in my pocket just as the waiter sets down the bowl. Shrimp, oysters, okra, and a variety of other items sit on top of a bed of rice pilaf. I look up at the waiter.

"It's a low country seafood gumbo, though I told them to hold the sausage."

The smell is heavenly, and it erases all thoughts of this afternoon. I don't think I've ever smelled anything like this before. Though there's no way I can eat all of it. "Thank you," I say.

"Enjoy."

I take a moment to appreciate the meal before taking a fork full and tasting it. The explosion of flavors is enough to make the stresses of the day melt away.

Though in the back of my mind, the sight of Leon Spencer still lingers, his skeletal face staring back at me. Now it's up to me to make sure it doesn't happen to anyone else.

Chapter Eight

Through the fog of inebriation, Greg eyed the ball on top of the little tee in front of him. He wrenched his arms back, club in hand, and swung as hard as he could, connecting with the little white object. The ball took off in a beautiful arc, though his follow-through was almost enough to take him off balance. He recovered without losing control, though.

"Four!" he yelled, despite the fact there was no one on the field. But given the circumstances, that was one of the cleanest tee-offs he'd ever made. He always golfed better when he'd had a few, even if it was just at the driving range.

"Whoa," Dan said, shielding his eyes from the spotlights that illuminated the range. "I think that's two-hundred."

"Check again, Danny-boy," Greg said, peering out into the over lit area. "Two-twenty-five at least."

"I dunno. Looks more like two hundred," his companion replied.

Greg spun on him. "Are you blind? C'mon!" He walked over and grabbed what had been a frosted mug of beer when they'd first started. Greg drained the last of the now-warm liquid. "You're up."

"Yeah," Dan said, walking up to the tee and placing the ball. He moved like he had molasses in his pants.

"What the hell is wrong with you? You've been mopey all night."

Dan squared his legs and leveled his club. "Maybe I just don't feel like golfing."

"This isn't golfing," Greg replied, trying to retrieve anything from the bottom of his mug, but it was already empty. "This is driving. If you weren't such a pussy, you'd go out on the actual course with me one day."

Dan swings, barely connecting with the ball, sending it on a pitiful trajectory for the fifty-foot line. "Golfing just isn't my thing," he replied.

"Never seemed to bother you before when the rest of us would get together."

"Yeah?" Dan asked, walking past him. "That was before."

Greg made a face. He was so sick of this. He'd heard of nothing else for weeks, and now Dan was starting in on him too? They'd made a mistake. And he'd seen to it to fix the mistake. It was over. "Look, all of that's in the past. We can't do anything about it now."

"We could go to the police," Dan replied.

Greg stepped up to the green again, placing a ball on the tee. It toppled off and he had to replace it. "And you can go to hell." He swung with all his might, sending the ball out past his last drive. "Ha! Look at that shit!"

"Yep," Dan said, dropping his club back in his bag. "Can't beat that."

Greg turned to him. "Wait, where are you going? It's only —" He looked at his watch. Ten p.m.? When had it gotten so late? "They're open until eleven. We could do one more drink."

"I think you've had enough," Dan said, hoisting his bag on his shoulder. "You need me to call you a ride?"

"I'm not paying to get back over here in the morning to get my car. I'll be fine." Dan eyed him a minute, which only made the heat on Greg's neck rise. "What are you, my wife?"

"If only we could all be so lucky," Dan muttered, but it was loud enough Greg didn't miss it.

He stormed up to Dan. "What did you say to me?" His face couldn't be more than two inches from Dan's. He could smell the other man's musk.

"Back off, Greg."

"You wanna start something?" Greg almost wished he would. Dan had been getting on his nerves for weeks now. They all had, even after the transfers went through. They were brothers after all, you weren't supposed to disrespect your brothers.

"I just want to go home," Dan replied. Greg played out the scenario in his mind. Dan had about twenty pounds on him, but Greg was faster. He could do it; he could take him down if he wanted.

"You gonna hit me or can I leave now?" Dan asked. Greg hated the blasé way he said it, like Greg hitting him would be nothing but an inconvenience. He should do it to show him just how *inconvenient* he could be. Dan waited a moment more, before pushing past him, heading back out through the gate to his car.

"Yeah, next time I'll just save you the trouble and call Ricky or Leon instead."

Dan threw him a middle finger as he walked away, not bothering to look back. That did it. Greg went back to the driving green, setting up another ball on the tee. Except this time he stood on the other side of the green, facing out toward the parking lot. He'd have to clear the gate, but there was a good chance he could do it. He wrenched his arms back and brought the club around with all the force he could, except he missed the ball entirely and his swing through was so wild it threw him completely off-balance, spinning him into the next stall over, which was thankfully empty.

"Hey!" Greg looked over at the elderly driving range manager a few stalls down, looking out of an elevated pen. "We got a problem here?"

"Cool it, gramps. I'm a public servant," Greg said after he'd regained his footing.

"I don't care if you're the fucking mayor. You hit a ball anywhere other than out at that yard, I'll have you arrested."

Greg rolled his eyes and returned to his game. But without someone here to watch him, he'd lost all desire for it. He sighed and replaced his club into his own bag, going over and picking up the bucket of balls to return to the front.

Just as he was about to take them back, he decided to leave them. Let the old man come get them. He probably needed the exercise anyway.

Greg hoisted his bag over his shoulder and headed back for his car. On the way his cell vibrated in his pocket. "Fuck," he said, fumbling for it. He was sure it was Melanie, calling to ask where he was and when he was getting home already. She probably wanted to complain that she'd had to deal with the kids all night and remind him that he wasn't pulling his weight around the house.

Except when he looked at his phone, he recognized the number, even though he had it listed under the name *Evan: Racquetball*. "Hey you," he said, answering.

"Heyyy," her soft voice said over the speaker. "I was thinking about the other night. I'm not sure I can wait until Friday night to see you again."

He smiled, feeling the familiar bulge in his pants. "Yeah? You liked that, huh?"

"Mm-hm," she purred. "Can you stop by tonight?"

Greg checked his watch again. Ten-oh-five. "I could swing by for a quickie. But I've got a long day tomorrow and need to be back home by eleven."

"You could always stay over here," she said. Even though they'd only met a few weeks ago, she'd already started pestering him about staying the night. But if he did that, Melanie really *would* get suspicious.

"One night soon," he replied. "When I don't have to work early the next morning."

"Okay," she replied, though he could hear the disappointment in her voice. But honestly, he didn't care. Life was full of disappointments, and she was too young to know better. He was just teaching her a valuable life lesson.

"I'll be over in ten," he said. "You know what to do."

"I'll be waiting," she said, her breath heavy on the line before she hung up. God*damn* that girl was hot. She knew it too. Knew just how to use it in every way that counted. And Greg was going to take full advantage of that. And here he thought this night was going to turn out shitty. Instead, an unexpected bonus.

He reached his SUV and the back tailgate unlocked automatically, opening at his proximity. He heaved his bag of clubs inside, then adjusted himself in his jeans. Just thinking about her was enough to—

The next thing Greg knew, he was on the edge of consciousness, his face planted in the bed of his car. His whole body had gone slack, and he could feel himself slipping back. In a second he'd be on the ground if he didn't get his feet back up under him. He tried to press up, but only then did he realize there was someone else behind him. He turned only to see one of his own clubs coming down right on his face.

Greg awoke to the smell of something acrid. At first it was just the smell, but the more he came back to consciousness, he realized the smell was fueling a massive headache that caused his entire brain to throb. "Wha…" he said, opening his eyes, only to find it was dark in here. He was in a large room of sorts, though he couldn't tell where. And he was laying on something hard, something that dug into his left shoulder.

"What's going on?" he managed to say, though he realized his words were slurred. It must be from the beer earlier. "Where am I?

"Greg Perry," a voice said from the darkness. "Never the brightest of the bunch, were you?"

Greg tried to sit up to see who was speaking, only to realize he'd been bound to whatever he was lying on. A thick rope wrapped around his midsection, binding his arms down. Another bound him at the neck and yet another at his legs. And they were tight. He tried to struggle, only to find he choked himself if he pulled too hard.

"What is this?" Greg yelled, even though it made the headache worse. And what was that smell?

"Gregory, you did a very bad thing," the voice said. He thought it was a man's, but he couldn't see anyone in his limited field of vision.

"Yeah, and what was that? Fuck your mother?" He could tell the voice was young. How had someone gotten the drop on him? They must have been waiting for him in the parking lot.

"It's funny you should put it that way," the voice said, amused. "Because if anyone is fucked, it's you."

"Let me out of here, you psychopath," Greg said, struggling against the ropes.

"I'm really disappointed in you, though I guess I shouldn't have expected any better. Your colleague was much more penitent than you seem to be."

"Yeah? And what do I have to *penitent* for?" he spat.

"I think you know," the voice said. It was closer now. "Two months ago."

"I don't know what you're talking about," Greg said. How

could anyone else know about that? Unless one of the guys talked. He bet it was Dan. Bastard had been in a weird mood for weeks now. He must have finally cracked. You couldn't trust anyone anymore! Well fine, if he wanted retribution, he'd get it. They all would. If Greg was going down, then he wasn't going down alone. Dan had just dug his own grave.

"Let's not play games here, Greg," the voice said. "You know *exactly* what I'm talking about."

"What do you want?" he yelled, even though his head continued to pound.

The voice was silent a moment. "I only want retribution. I want it to be fair."

"Yeah, well life's not fair," Greg said. Strange, he'd just thought that about Kyla earlier. Wait, where was his phone? If this little bastard had it—

Finally, the form came into view, though Greg couldn't see his face because he had on a hoodie, which covered his hair as well. Greg was about to rip him a new one when he produced what looked like a metal funnel out of nowhere and stuck it in Greg's mouth. The action was so sudden he barely had time to register what was happening, though he felt one of his teeth chip. This fucker was going to have a lot to pay for when—

Fire poured down his throat, burning the insides of his mouth all the way down to his stomach. He was pouring something in the funnel! And from the smell Greg could only assume it was kerosene or something similar. But that was toxic; it would eat away at his insides in a matter of minutes. He tried to cough it up, but the liquid kept pouring. His gag reflex finally kicked in, causing him to sputter some of it back up, though he could still feel it burning him from the inside.

"I hope it was worth it, Greg. I really do," the voice said, before lighting a match. The flame lit up his face and Greg recognized him at once. How could he have not put it together before? He tried to speak, to protest, but it wouldn't stop burning. And before he knew it, the match was flying in his direction.

Greg Perry watched in horror as his entire body ignited at once. Only then did he manage to scream.

Chapter Nine

MY BUZZING PHONE WAKES ME FROM A DREAMLESS SLEEP. I reach over and smack it a few times, trying to get the alarm to turn off, only to realize it's not my alarm, someone is actually calling me.

I grumble and grab for the too-bright device that's the only source of light in the room. Clearly Zara is back to her old habits again, and it's only been what, a day? But as I look at the number I don't recognize it.

"Slate," I say, groggy and still on the edge of unconsciousness.

"It's Farmer. Professional courtesy. We've got another fire."

My eyes snap open and I sit up. "Where?"

He gives me the address. "It's a local bar, looks like the fire started around two-thirty a.m. I'm on the scene now; they're still trying to get it under control."

I pull the covers off and head for the bathroom, flicking on the light. "Anyone inside?"

"Impossible to tell at the moment. But I thought you should know."

"Thanks," I say, running the tap. "I'll be there in a few." I hang up and splash some water on my face which shocks me into a full waking state. *Another* fire? Whoever is doing this, they like setting these things at night, which could be indicative of needing to maintain a level of secrecy, or perhaps that's when they know a response will take the longest, because people are less likely to see it immediately in the middle of the night. Either way, it could just be a coincidence. I'm sure a city of this size fights fires all the time. But something about it screams pattern to me, and given how close in proximity it was to the fire that killed Leon Spencer, I'm not willing to take any chances.

I dress quickly, forgoing any skincare. I pull my hair back into a ponytail to keep it out of the way and grab my gun, wallet, and keys on the way out the door.

Fifteen minutes later I pull up to the scene, which I could see from two blocks away. All the flashing lights and haze of smoke gave it away. A sign out by the road identifies this place as *Billy's Backwash*, what looks to be a local dive bar. From what I can tell of the building, it wasn't very big, maybe large enough for a bar and a couple of booths, though I can't see the entire building with all the trucks blocking it.

A fire crew has a hose attached to the nearest hydrant and is dousing the area with water while another crew is cutting through what remains of the front door, trying to create an access point. I stay off the property and park in the next lot over for a small strip mall. A local patrol car sits at the entrance to the property and as I'm making my way over, one of the officers runs up to me.

"Slate," I say, showing him my badge. "I'm looking for Farmer."

"The ATF guy? He was over with one of the trucks last I saw."

"Thanks." I head over, careful to avoid the working crews

and staying far back from the building. I see Farmer yelling at one of the firefighters, but I can't hear what he's saying over the noise of the water blasting and everyone else yelling out orders. The entire place is organized chaos.

"My guys are doing their best to get inside, what more do you want?" the fireman Farmer is yelling at says.

"To get inside quicker! There could be someone still inside," he says.

"Look, this is a concrete building, with only two windows and a door. It's not the most easily accessible place. If there was someone in there, let's hope they died quick because otherwise they would have been cooked. Buildings like this are essentially ovens."

I come trotting up. "Still no word on any victims?" I ask.

The fireman stares at me. "What are you doing on my job? Get out of here."

"She's FBI," Farmer says before I have a chance to respond. "Slate, this is Captain Padilla, he's with firehouse twelve."

"Where Leon Spencer was originally stationed," I say.

"That's right," he says, disdain in his voice. He's not a tall man, but I can tell he's got a muscular build, along with dark hair and auburn skin. Padilla wears a neat goatee that's trimmed perfectly which makes him look a little younger than he probably is. "Which means I don't need a lecture about doing my own goddamn job!" He faces Farmer as he says it. "We get in there when we get in there. We'll let you know what we find." He pulls a helmet on and trots over to the crew working the hose, showing them where to focus it.

"Thanks for the call," I tell Farmer once he's out of earshot. "You didn't have to do that."

He puts his hands in his pockets as he stares at the crews working. "No point in requesting you be here if I'm not going to keep you in the loop. I hope you'd do the same."

We watch in silence for a few moments as the crews

continue to douse the building. The crew at the entrance finally gets past the door and makes their way inside, all of them in full gear. "Odds they find another body inside?"

He clears his throat. "Hundred percent."

I turn to him, trying to mask my surprise. "Do I want to know why you're so sure?"

He motions to the sign near the road. "This place is well-known to cops and firemen alike. A lot of them come here after hours to cool off. No way it's a coincidence."

I look around the vehicles. "Have you done a perimeter check yet?"

He shakes his head. "I've been trying to get a handle on things out here first. Haven't had time."

"We should probably notify the owner too," I say.

"I'll handle that," he says. "If you want to walk the area. My guys will be down here in a few minutes as well."

I nod and head back to the patrol car that is keeping any traffic off the scene. "Officer, could you come with me, please?"

He nods and follows me. "Begin a perimeter sweep, I want to start cataloging evidence."

"What am I looking for?" he asks.

"Are you familiar with this place?" He nods. "Then anything out of the ordinary. Anything you wouldn't normally find here. Start over on this side and work your way back. I'll take the opposite side of the building. But stay far enough back until they've cleared the building, got it?" Fortunately the lot surrounding this building is wide and expansive, enough so that there's plenty of space on both sides without us needing to get near to the building, which is still smoldering.

"Yes ma'am," he says, heading off to the other side of the building, holding his belt while he trots. I'm already missing Zara's keen eye for observation. I just have to hope this cop is good at his job.

As I make my way around the right side of the building,

the pavement turns into gravel and weeds sprout up from every crevice. "One contained!" I hear one of the firemen call out from inside the building. From where I'm standing it looks like the hose crew is decreasing the pressure, which must mean they're fairly certain there won't be any more flareups. If the fire started around two-thirty, that means it burned for at least half an hour before it was fully under control. If Farmer's hunch proves to be right, I'd be willing to bet an accelerant was used again, but I try to keep my mind open. It's possible this fire isn't related. Being a bar, this could have been a grease fire, or faulty electrical, or a dozen other things. But even as I'm walking around the building, I can feel the heat coming off the cinder block. It has to be unbearably hot in there.

Using my phone's flashlight, I search the ground for anything that looks odd. Other than a couple dozen cigarette butts, I don't see much. The gravel has some ruts where people have driven through here to get to the back of the building. Along the side, I pass one small window which has been blown out, though I can't see into the dark structure inside without any lights on. Instead, I keep walking, realizing the building is larger than I'd first assumed. If this was a local hangout, it's possible they had pool tables or other entertainment set up farther back in the building, on the other side of the kitchen.

As I reach the back of the building, I scan for any vehicles. The gravel lot back here is large enough to hold at least ten or twelve of them, and other than an open back exit, the only other thing here is a dumpster off in the far corner. It's far enough away from the building that I don't think it was in danger of igniting. Back here there are also two other firemen, both visually inspecting the back of the structure. They briefly look up to acknowledge me before returning to their duties. It looks like they might have come through the building via the exit door.

I sweep my light over the area, though I don't see much of

anything. It will be hard to tell if any of these spots are fresher than the others until I have some daylight.

"Agent?" I hear a voice call out. I look over to see the officer has appeared on the other side of the building and is motioning to me. I trot over to him.

"Find something?"

"It's something all right," he says and leads me away from the building off to the far-left corner of the property. His torch is more powerful than the little light I have on my phone and as we approach the area, I can see it's been disturbed somehow. The gravel has been raked back to make a small clearing in the dirt.

"What the…?" I say, staring at the clearing. Someone has taken red spray paint and drawn a circle with a horizontal line through it, then drawn two smaller circles on the outside of the big one, both on either side of where the line bisects it. "Some kind of graffiti?" Though usually graffiti like this is tagged on walls or other surfaces where it won't get destroyed easily. I could kick some dirt around and this would be gone in an instant.

I bend down for a closer look, and that's when I see it. A small, brown billfold lying on its side in the upper half of the bisected circle. I retrieve a pair of gloves from my pocket and pull them on before carefully removing the billfold and opening it. Inside I'm greeted by the face of Greg Perry, staring back at me from his driver's license. And underneath that, I extract a second form of identification that makes my stomach drop: his firefighter's ID card.

Chapter Ten

"I ASSUME YOU'VE SEEN THESE KINDS OF PATTERNS BEFORE?" Farmer asks, his hands on his hips as he stares at the image spray painted into the dirt. I showed him Perry's wallet, but put it back in place for the forensics team, which has just arrived.

"Something like it," I reply. "Though this is much more ritualistic. The man I chased didn't want anyone to know what he was doing. This one obviously does."

"Then you think it's a man," he says.

"The statistics bear that out," I reply, looking over my shoulder. A couple of the local cops huddle a few feet away, whispering to themselves. A couple more of the firefighters are still inspecting all around the building. "We need to clear this area. I don't want to contaminate this scene any more than we already have."

Farmer turns, "Officers, will you set up a barrier around the entire property? Once they have that building clear, I don't want anyone in except for the forensics team."

Two of the officers exchange glances then head off to build a perimeter. "Do you get that a lot?" he asks me.

"What?"

"The *attitude* from local law enforcement."

"Depends on the place," I say. "But yeah. It's not uncommon. Then again, they don't work for either of us."

Farmer mumbles something unintelligible. I'm sure he's frustrated at this situation; so am I. This makes three men now, all firefighters. And I'm willing to bet once we start looking into Greg Perry, we're going to find he's from the same station Leon Spencer and Sam Phelps were from.

"Hey, Stan."

The voice causes us both to turn at the same time. Captain Padilla stands at the back door to the building, his jacket and helmet covered in soot. Despite the amount of smoke from the fire, the winds of the evening have mostly carried it off, though it's impossible not to notice.

"We got one vic inside," Padilla says. "Looks like he was alone."

"When can we get in there?" Farmer asks.

"Now. Just be careful. Part of the roof caved in. My guys were able to shore up the parts that are still up. You should be safe as long as you stick to the main path from the back door to the front."

Farmer shoots me a look just as the forensics team comes around the building. I point to the area on the ground. "Start here, then move outwards until you're about two hundred yards in all directions."

The team is dressed all in white scrub suits, and they begin pulling on their masks as they approach. Farmer is already headed to the back door and I trot to catch up.

"You find something out there?" Padilla asks as he leads us into the back entrance of Billy's Backwash.

"Maybe. Not sure yet," Farmer says. I'm about to correct him when I remember Padilla was Leon Spencer's old captain. If Greg Perry was from the same station, it means Padilla has just lost another "brother". I like that Farmer is keeping his cards close to the chest; it's something I'd do in the same situation. We have no idea who could be perpetrating these crimes and until we do, it's best to keep as much information from getting out as possible.

"Watch this here," Padilla says, ducking under a two-by-four to bring us into the kitchen. Everything is soaking wet, though there doesn't look to be too much damage back here. Though a heavy detritus of tile, wood and metal cover the floor. Everything else is mostly stainless steel, tables, appliances, and the like; things that wouldn't burn as easily as carpet and wood. Still, scorch marks are easily visible around the door that leads out, and in a few other places. I look up, seeing the hole created from the roof partially caving in, which is probably what I'm walking on. My nose is full of acrid smells, ranging from burned wood to something that's probably toxic. Too late I wonder if any part of this building had asbestos in it. Then again, if it had, it probably wouldn't have burned so quickly.

Padilla leads us through what's left of the door frame out into the main dining area, though that's a generous term. There are a few tables and chairs, most black and charred, or collapsed all together, along with a couple of what used to be pool tables, all lined up down and around a corner. In the middle of the room, stretching from the front door all the way down to the kitchen entrance is a bar, though all the bottles that once sat on shelves behind it have melted and the entire area is nothing but black soot. On top of the bar is another burnt human form, who I can only assume used to be Greg Perry.

"Here," Padilla says, handing both of us N95 masks. "You're gonna need them." I slip mine over my mouth and nose, and approach the body. Smoke is still coming off it and within seconds I can already smell the exact same thing I smelled when we examined Leon Spencer's body. Except here it's a lot stronger. I hate how it reminds me of the smell of bar-b-que ribs, or roast beef, neither of which I'm ever going to be able to touch again.

The body is partially curled up on its side, its legs drawn close to the chest and its arms pulled in. Again, the skin and muscle around the neck and head are almost completely gone, leaving little more than a charred skeleton behind. Given the similarities between this body and the body of Leon Spencer, I have to assume we are definitely working with the same killer.

"No bonds this time," Farmer says, his voice slightly muffled. As soon as I open my mouth, I can feel that awful taste back there again, despite having the mask on.

"No, look," I say, pointing at the ground. A couple remnants of what looks like rope remain attached to the metal footrest that runs the length of the bar. "Just a different kind."

"Hell of a thing," Padilla says, coming up beside us, his own gas mask on. "I've seen a lot of burnt bodies, but none like this one."

"What makes this one different?" I ask.

"Around the head up there," he says. "Usually people cook through pretty evenly, as gruesome as that sounds. But looks to me like this guy burned extra hot around the head area for some reason." He turns to Farmer. "Is this what happened to Leon?"

Farmer doesn't acknowledge him. "I'm not at liberty to talk about ongoing cases."

"Uh-huh," Padilla says. "I'll take that as a yes. You better stop this, Stan." He then turns to me. "Or you. Somebody is out there hunting us, and I'll be damned if I'm gonna let this happen to me."

"Why would it happen to you?" I ask.

"It could happen to any of us," he says, clearly agitated. "No fireman in the entire city is safe."

"Calm down, Joseph," Farmer says. "We don't know *who* we're dealing with yet."

"Exactly my point. You don't know who or what could be

doing this. And from my count, this could be number two. What if it's another one of us? What if he's from my house?"

"Don't you mean three?" I ask. Padilla stops his little grievance speech to give me a confused glare. "Sam Phelps?"

Recognition dawns on his face. "Right. Phelps. Possibly three then. What's it going to take? Ten? Twenty?"

Farmer turns to him. "What do you want me to do? Shut down the city? Tell people to stop lighting things on fire? This is the whole reason I requested the FBI be involved, in case it turned out to be something like this."

"Then you," Padilla says, pointing at me, "better figure this out. Otherwise we start taking the law into our own hands." He storms off, weaving around the debris until he reaches the front door and disappears.

"How do you think he's going to react when he finds out it *is* another firefighter?" I ask.

"Mmm," Farmer says, and I can tell he's not paying attention. I glance over at what has him so interested, and he seems to be investigating the area of the bar around the victim's head.

"What is it?" I ask.

"Since this man seems to have been laying flat on his back, I was looking for any telltale signs that might give us a clue as to how he got here. Any blood would have burned away in the fire, but I was hoping to see if he had any contusions or damage along his skull."

"You're trying to figure out how the killer is capturing these men. Men, who by all accounts, are stronger than your average male."

"Exactly," he says. "Each one has to have been taken by surprise in some way. Phelps by responding to a call, Spencer being distracted by something in the parking lot and now Perry, assuming this is him."

"I think that's a safe bet," I say.

"So do I," he replies, standing up straight again.

"We need to figure out where he was last night. And who saw him last."

"I'll have one of my guys pull his phone records," Farmer says, which surprises me. I figured he'd just tell me he'd take care of it then try to ditch me again.

"Do you think the same accelerant was used?" I ask.

He doesn't respond right away, instead continues inspecting the corpse. I'm not sure how he can get so close to it; the smell has to be permeating every inch of that mask. "I can't say for certain. Looks possible."

I take a few steps back and look around at the ruined building. Whoever lit him on fire had to get out of here before it became too large—before it raged out of control. And this isn't like at the paintball yard where the unsub could have just run in any direction to safety. He would have had to either go out the front or the back door. And while I'm sure he wore gloves, there might be something left behind we can use.

"Knock, knock." I look up to see Dr. Lewis and her assistant Levi—the latter who looks absolutely exhausted to be up at this ungodly hour—appear in the doorway. She spots the body, and her face darkens before she turns to Levi. "Check with the medics. We're going to need a sturdy, but light stretcher to get up under him without disturbing him too much."

Levi nods and heads back out before he can enter all the way. It's funny, I don't think I've heard him say one word.

Dr. Lewis puts on a pair of gloves and her own mask before approaching us. Her hair is tied back like mine. If I were taller, we'd probably look like mother and daughter. "Got an ID for me?" she asks.

"Indications are it's Gregory Perry," I reply. "Another member of the city's bravest."

Lewis *tsks*. "Doesn't make your job any easier, does it?"

I shake my head. "I was hoping that due to the amount of time between the first death and the second, we'd have more time before he struck again. But it seems like he's moving up his timetable."

Farmer gives a curt nod to Lewis before turning back to me. "Why would he do that?"

"Could be a number of reasons," I say. "This might have always been the original plan, or he could be using opportunities as they present themselves, which obviously won't follow a schedule. The other possibility is he knows we're on the case now and he's afraid he won't have enough time to finish what he started. He could be in a rush."

"And people in a rush make mistakes," Farmer says.

"Exactly." I turn back to Dr. Lewis. "How long until we have a formal ID?"

She checks her watch. "I can confirm with Mr. Perry's dentist as soon as I know where he went. Is that something you can get for me?"

I nod. "I'll check with the CFD, they should cover his dental insurance and will have a record of who he's been seeing most recently."

"I'd appreciate that, agent," Lewis says. "Now if you'll excuse me, I have to try and move a body without destroying it." She pushes her way past us to get a better look at the body on the bar.

Levi comes back in with a pair of medtechs on his heels, wheeling a gurney. Farmer seems content to stand around and watch, but I've seen enough for one night.

I head back out into the night air.

Chapter Eleven

IT TAKES A FEW HOURS TO FULLY PROCESS THE SCENE. I consider heading back to the hotel, but once I'm awake it's almost impossible for me to get back to sleep again, especially now that I am certain we are dealing with a serial arsonist who also just happens to be targeting firefighters.

After Dr. Lewis confirmed the body was Perry after all, Padilla immediately left the scene. His behavior seems somewhat off to me, though I can't put my finger on why. Maybe I expected him to show more remorse for someone he used to work so closely with. Or maybe I'm overthinking how close firefighters really are. You hear about it all the time, how guys like this are always in each other's weddings, or they're the godparents of the other's children. But it's also got me curious about what's so special about the firemen in this city. The killer obviously has some kind of score to settle, and so far he's showing no sign of slowing down.

While Padilla and his truck might be gone, there's still a contingent of men on site from firehouse nine, keeping an eye on the place while the forensics teams comb over every inch of the place, searching for any more clues or anything the killer might have accidentally left behind. It's a stretch, considering how clean he's been so far, and I don't have my own people on site. I'm sure the ATF's teams are perfectly capable, but they're not the FBI.

From the hood of my car I sit, watching the scene and trying to think. The sun has already broken the horizon, which is giving some much-needed light to the area. The teams will be able to finish up a lot quicker as soon as it's a little brighter out. Farmer stands over the scene, his arms crossed, watching from a distance. He's a very solitary person; something I can relate to. And so far he's been straight with me. So I owe him the same courtesy.

"Agent," I say, walking up behind him. He barely looks over his shoulder but gives me a quick nod. "I've been thinking. I need to deliver the news to Greg Perry's family."

"I've already assigned a couple of my guys to do that," he says.

"I figured as much, but I think it would be better coming from me."

He finally turns. "What's the strategy?"

"Whatever is going on, someone is out for blood, and someone else knows why. I want to see if Greg Perry ever brought any of his problems home with him. If maybe his wife can shed some information on this whole operation."

"It's risky," he says. "She could just shut down."

"True, but so far, we haven't been able to talk to anyone's family. Leon Spencer was divorced with his family living in another state. Sam Phelps wasn't in a relationship as far as I can tell. Perry was still married with kids. It's worth a shot before I take a run at Padilla."

He shrugs. "If you want to go tear the woman down and break the news that she's a widow that's your business. I hate doing that."

"Fair enough," I say. "I'll let you know what I find out." I head back to my car, somewhat annoyed that he's not willing to come and help. But I guess I shouldn't be surprised. It seems all he wants to do is get to the bottom of these fires, which means analyzing them from the ground up.

"Oh, and Slate," he calls over his shoulder as I reach my car door. "Don't be surprised if she slams the door in your face."

"Thanks." I suppress a grimace. What does he think, I've never done this before? "I'll keep it in mind." Once I'm in the car I shoot him a glare, but he's already turned his attention back to the building.

I connect with Zara once I'm in the car and fill her in on the details while she gets me the rest of the background information on Greg Perry. It turns out he had a couple of run-ins with the law when he was younger, but nothing serious enough to keep him off the city payroll. Once he turned hero firefighter, it was like he left that life behind him, at least on paper. She manages to give me his current address while at the same time squeezing in complaints that she's not here with me giving these guys the business.

Once I finally get her off the phone, I give Janice a quick call but only catch her voicemail. I leave her a detailed message about the developments over the past twelve hours, then head over to Greg Perry's house.

The address is in a modest neighborhood. Nothing too flashy, but not deteriorating either. It's a nice, one-story ranch house with a pitched roof and two-car garage. The front is clad in mostly stone and the abundant array of flowers out front indicates someone takes a lot of pride in their gardening. I have a suspicion it isn't Perry himself, but I've been wrong in the past.

It's only seven-thirty in the morning, so I'm reasonably sure I haven't missed Mrs. Perry yet. But I also have to weigh the moral obligations of what I'm about to do. The deceased was this woman's husband, and no matter what the circumstances, learning of a death like this is difficult. I should know. So I'll have to be delicate in asking about his work, or if he had any problems. But I'm hoping she'll be willing to help me try and find the person who did this. I know I'd be more than happy to assist in any way I could if someone wanted to find the woman who killed Matt.

I walk up to the door and ring the bell, then step back far enough so that she can see me through the long windows that frame each side of the door.

Sure enough, a moment later a woman with blonde hair peeks out one of the windows. At first her face is twisted in fury, but as soon as she sees me, her eyebrows raise and the anger disappears. I hear the click of a deadbolt and she opens the door. She's still in her fluffy nightgown, but I see she's at least had enough time to do her makeup. "Can I help you?" she asks.

I hold up my badge. "I'm Special Agent Emily Slate with the FBI. May I come inside?"

She glances behind me, like she's expecting someone else. "What is this about?" the woman asks.

"Are you Melanie Perry?" I ask. She nods. "This concerns your husband."

She tenses, the grimace returning. "Why am I not surprised. Here, come in," she says, opening the door wider for me.

I step inside and am immediately assaulted by the smell of pancakes and syrup. In the background I can hear children attempting to talk over each other. A tingle runs down my spine.

"Do you want something to drink?" Mrs. Perry asks, closing the door behind me.

"No thank you, do you have somewhere we can sit?"

"Trust me," she says, leading me further into the house. "Whatever he's done, I can handle it. It's not like this is the first time." The kitchen is at the back, right off the main hall-way. In the room across from the kitchen I see the children. Both look to be less than five years old, and a pang of regret hits me. For them both to lose their father so young, neither of them will be the same again. I only had my mother until I was twelve. Losing her hurt more than anything I had ever felt. And I didn't see that pain again until Matt died.

"All right, let's get it over with," she says. It takes me a moment longer than it should to respond. "Agent Slate?"

"Yes, sorry, I've been up since three a.m." This happens every time. And now Zara isn't here to cover for me.

Mrs. Perry grabs a coffee cup from the counter. "I know how those nights go. We're no strangers to inconsistent sched-ules around here." She shoots a glance at the kids over my shoulder, but they seem completely involved in whatever they're doing.

"You said you're not surprised to see me, what did you mean by that?" I ask. I know I should just get right down to it, but her attitude intrigues me. Maybe things between them weren't as close as I had assumed.

"Just that Greg does some stupid shit sometimes. And the only reason he gets away with it is because he knows some of the cops through his job. No matter how much of an asshole he can be, it seems some people can't help but to just gravitate toward him."

I take a deep breath, unsure how this is going to go. "Mrs. Perry, I'm sorry to be the one to inform you of this, but Greg died early this morning, in a restaurant fire."

She stares at me, blinking once, twice, then cocks her head. "I'm sorry. What?"

"We don't know the exact circumstances yet, but we're fairly sure he was placed in the fire intentionally."

Her face is totally blank. I see this sometimes. People either can't process what I tell them, or they go into a kind of shock upon hearing the news. Everyone deals with grief in different ways. Finally, she sets her mug down, then walks over to the kitchen table which is still littered with the remnants from the children's breakfast, and takes a seat in one of the chairs, just staring off into the distance.

I gently take the seat across from her, giving her the time and space to digest what I've told her.

"He's…dead?" she finally says.

"I'm very sorry," I reply.

I catch her shoot a glance over at her phone, which is sitting beside her purse on the same counter where her mug remains. When she looks back, her eyes have begun to tear up and she wipes them away expertly, without smudging her makeup. "I'm sorry…I just didn't…when you rang the doorbell, I thought you were him."

"What time was he supposed to be home?"

"He was out at the driving range with one of his work buddies, which means he's usually not home until around midnight." She lets out a long breath; she's looking at her kids again.

"Were they close with their father?"

She shrugs, shaking her head. "They're kids. They think the world of him. I don't know how I'm going to tell them."

I notice after the first few tears have passed; she's managed to hold herself together well. Some people can do that because they think it's bad manners to cry in front of strangers, but I feel like it's something more in this situation. "I don't mean to be rude, but you are handling this very well. I've done this a lot and most of the time it ends up with a lot of screaming and yelling."

She draws in another long breath before releasing it. "The result of a strict mother, I suppose. Then again, if you knew Greg like I know—knew—him, you'd understand," she said. She looks over at her phone again. "I actually didn't expect him to come home at all last night."

"Why is that?"

She gets up, retrieving the phone and hands it over to me after opening it. "I received a text from him last night, a series of them, actually. All screenshots of recent conversations he's had with another woman."

I take a look at the screenshots of texts between two people. "The name at the top of the texts says Evan: Racquetball."

"Read them," she says. "It's obvious. Greg never was the sharpest knife." She retrieves a bottle from one of the top cabinets as I'm going through the messages. She's right, and from what I can tell, *Evan* sounds pretty young. I can't help but wonder if this has something to do with his death.

Mrs. Perry tips the bottle into her mug and brings it back over, taking her seat across from me. I can smell the sweet tang of Kahlua coming from her mug. "I figured that was his way of telling me he was leaving me and the kids to fend for ourselves while he made off with a younger model, as they say." She takes a long sip of her drink. "Either that or he just wanted to hurt me. Neither would have really surprised me."

"Has he done this sort of thing before?" I ask.

"Not directly. But he could be manipulative. Using the kids to…well, no sense in talking about it now."

I disagree. But pulling on that thread while she's in a delicate state could cause her to shut down. And right now I need answers more than I need to worry about Mrs. Perry's wellbeing.

"What time did these come through?" I ask.

"About one a.m. I'd fallen asleep on the couch and my phone woke me up. Honestly, I wasn't even that shocked. Things haven't been very good between us for a long time now. I figured this was just the final nail in the coffin." She scoffs. "But I at least thought he'd still help support the kids. Now…I don't know what I'm supposed to do." She takes another long drink. I need to get as much out of her as I can before she gets sloshed, even if it is absolutely understandable.

"Do you have any idea who this 'Evan' might be in real life?"

She shakes her head. "No clue."

I square my shoulders. She hasn't asked a word about how or where we found him. Part of me finds that suspicious, but another part of me thinks perhaps she's too wrapped up in what this is going to mean for her and her kids. It's obvious there was no love lost between them, yet I feel like I need to press the issue to try and get what I need. "Mrs. Perry, I know this is a difficult time, but right now we believe Greg was murdered."

She takes another drink like it doesn't even faze her. "Greg had a big mouth. I guess someone finally wasn't willing to take anymore." I catch something of longing in her eyes, almost like she wishes she was the one who had shut him up. I can't ignore the possibility.

"Do you know Leon Spencer?" I ask.

Her eyes light up. "Sure. Leon and Greg worked at the firehouse together before he was transferred. He was always so nice to me and the kids whenever I'd bring them over to sit in the big trucks."

Transferred? Greg's ID showed him as a member of firehouse fifteen. I can't help but wonder if Greg also came from firehouse twelve. I would have asked Padilla on site after the identification, but he left too quickly.

"Why, you don't think Leon killed Greg?"

I shake my head. "No. Unfortunately Leon was killed as well."

Her eyes go wide and this time tears fall almost immediately. "Oh my God." Mrs. Perry covers her mouth as silent sobs radiate from her. She has to put her mug down.

Her reaction seems genuine, which means I can effectively cross her off the suspect list. Despite how she might have felt about her husband, she's clearly more broken up about Leon. Which means she didn't know he was dead and thus she couldn't have staged Greg's death to match. "What is happening?" she asks when she regains control of herself. "Who is doing this?"

"That's what we're trying to find out," I tell her. "Do you know of anyone who would want your husband dead? Anyone who he might have wronged?"

She shakes her head, wiping her eyes again. This time her makeup does smudge. "Like I said, Greg had the unique talent to be able to piss anybody off. But I don't know anyone who would want to hurt Leon. He was nice, gentle."

"You never heard Greg complaining about anything the past few weeks?"

She finally manages to pick her mug up again, taking another sip. "I wish I knew. But we didn't talk anymore. If he was having problems with someone, he hid it from me. Just like he hid everything else, apparently." She glares at her phone.

I spend another ten minutes with her, but by then she's getting good and tipsy, and I start to worry if she's going to be able to take care of her kids the rest of the day. She assures me she'll call her mother who can come over and help start to deal with all of this. But before I leave, I make sure to get Greg's phone number, along with copies of the texts he sent to his wife.

Once I'm sure I can leave Mrs. Perry, I head back to my car, texting Zara along the way.

Hey, u busy?

Yes. But who cares? Is this about the case?

Yep. I need ur help.

Chapter Twelve

"So. Greg Perry was cheating on his wife, huh?" Farmer
says like it doesn't surprise him. He's leaning back in his chair
inside his division of the ATF building. "We need to look at
the wife."

"I already cleared her," I say, standing on the other side of
his desk. Why do I feel like he's trying to be my boss here?
"She didn't know about Leon, and she had no motive to kill
him. Plus, when I checked her cell records, they matched up
with what she told me. You can go question her if you like, but
I doubt you'll get much out of her."

He shrugs. "What about this other woman? Did she know
he was married?"

"I've got Zara trying to find her now so I can ask her that
myself. But even if she did, what cause did she have to kill
either Leon Spencer or Sam Phelps? I'm more interested in if
Perry ever told her anything about what was going on in his
personal life. Men will spill their guts to their mistresses and
not think twice about how it can be used against them."

Farmer chuckles. "That's certainly true."

"Did you find out anything else about the fire?"

He taps a file folder sitting in the middle of his desk with a thick pointer finger. "Same accelerant as at the paintball yard, though the restraints were different, obviously. The first time was using chains, this time ropes, which strikes me as odd. Though ropes would have been easier to wrap around that bar to hold him down. Coroner thinks it's the same as with Spencer, turpentine poured down the victim's throat just before ignition, causing him to burn inside and out at the same time. The bar itself was soaked in it, but the surrounding area was left alone."

"To give the killer time to get out unharmed," I say.

He nods. "That, and possibly to contain the fire."

"What do you mean?" I ask.

"It doesn't look like our firebug is going for maximum damage. It seems to me he's just trying to burn his victims, and not leave a wide trail of destruction. With Phelps most of the house burned, yes. But Spencer and Perry, their sites were more concentrated. Did you notice at the paintball yard how the flames hadn't jumped over into any of the adjoining arenas?"

I had, but I thought that had been more from luck than an intentional choice.

"You're saying the killer is trying to limit the amount of fire damage?"

He holds up both hands. "Why not douse the entire bar in the stuff to make sure it's completely destroyed? It would have burned a lot faster. And a skilled arsonist could get out without a problem before the flames became too hot."

"Maybe he's not skilled," I say. "Maybe he's cautious."

"Possibly," Farmer says. "But most arson cases I investigate are designed to do the most damage possible. Whether that's to a building, a complex, a forest, whatever. Firebugs love the flames, and they want to see them get as large and spread as far as they can. They don't limit how much burns."

It's an interesting angle that I need to incorporate into my profile. "Do you think the old woman that died in Phelps' fire was an accident?"

"What do you mean?" he asks.

"If someone is targeting firefighters, but *only* firefighters, then it's possible she could have been unintentional collateral damage. What if the fire that killed Phelps was meant to kill *only* him and that's why the killer changed tactics? Maybe he realized he needed to exert more control over the fires, direct them, so that they only killed the person he intended."

Farmer's eyebrows raise as he considers the prospect. "That's not a bad theory."

"Unfortunately, that's all it is at the moment," I say. My phone buzzes in my pocket and I pull it out to see Zara is calling. "Hey."

"Kyla Griffin, four-twenty-five Baker street, apartment six-oh-one," she says.

"That was fast," I reply.

"Don't forget I used to work down there, I still know all the tricks," she replies. I can hear the smile in her voice. "Looks like she's either unemployed or works from home. I can't find an employment record with anyone. She drives a black Tesla model three and lives alone as far as I can tell."

"Wow, you really did your homework."

She scoffs. "It's what happens when you get the interesting cases and I have to deal with tax evasion up here. You owe me a dessert when you get back."

"I do, thanks," I say before hanging up.

"News?" Farmer asks.

For a brief moment I consider not telling him. He's a good investigator, I know that much, but at the same time I can tell he resents me. Whether that's because I'm a woman, I'm young, or because I'm in the FBI, I don't know. Part of me wants to figure this out on my own. But at the same time, I can't put my personal feelings ahead of the case. "Just got the

information on Perry's mistress. I'm going to head over there
to see if I can catch her."

With a grunt he pushes himself up. "I'll come with you.
There might be something to this whole thing and I wouldn't
mind being there."

Great, just what I need, someone who thinks they're my
babysitter. "It's really not necessary, I do this kind of thing all
the time."

"C'mon," he says, heading past me. "Time is wasting. I'll
drive."

The whole way over to Kyla Griffin's apartment I'm flexing
my hands, trying not to let my frustration get the better of me.
It isn't often I'm in a situation where I'm continuously forced
into the proverbial backseat, but right now my desire to figure
out who is killing these firefighters and why overrides my
pride. There will be time enough for that later.

Farmer pulls up in front of the apartment complex, which
is actually a series of buildings all set at different angles to
each other. Signs on the sides of the buildings indicate which
ones hold which apartments, and it takes us a minute of
driving around to find the building that houses six-oh-one. In
one of the parking spots out front is a Tesla model 3, telling
me we definitely have the right place.

"Looks like she's still home," I say. "Good."

"It's been a while since I've done a home call," he says,
pulling into a spot across from Kyla's vehicle.

I get out and head up the walk, not waiting on Farmer to
catch up. We'll have a much better chance of getting something out of her if I'm the first one she sees and not him.
Apartment six-oh-one is on the first floor of the complex, the
door facing an interior open hallway with three other doors. I
rap on hers before Farmer has made it the full way up the

walk but by the time I hear rustling on the other side, he's already at my side.

The door cracks open, though the chain is still on so it can only open so far. I see a mop of auburn hair framing a porcelain face on the other side "Yeah?"

"Kyla Griffin?"

"Yeah," she says. She sounds even younger than she looks.

"May we have a word? It's about Greg Perry."

She looks us up and down. "Sure, just a sec," she says, closing the door. We wait a beat but I don't hear her removing the chain. A moment later I give the door another knock. "Ms. Griffin? We just want to talk."

"Showed your hand too early," Farmer says.

Gritting my teeth, I knock again, this time harder. "Ms. Griffin." I put my ear up to the door and can't hear anything on the other side, though I do detect the slightest hint of an odor I hadn't realized was there before. "Shit," I say.

I take off running back the way I came, around the side of the building to where the walk-out patio on Kyla's unit leads out onto the grass. The sliding glass door is wide open, the curtain on the other side fluttering. I turn and see her running toward her car, her keys in hand. I'm off like a shot after her, not even bothering to tell Farmer what's going on. If we lose her, we could lose any insight into Perry's death. But I can't very well arrest her; she hasn't done anything wrong, at least as far as I'm concerned.

I reach her just as she reaches her vehicle, opening the door. I manage to slide my entire arm between the door frame and the door itself, and she attempts to pull it closed, trapping my arm in between. I cry out in pain, but manage to keep upright.

"What are you doing?" she yells at me.

"Look, we just want to talk, I don't care about the hash," I say, keeping my arm in the way of her closing the door. She could slam it in there a second time, but I really hope she doesn't.

"Get out of the car!" Farmer yells. I look up to see he's got his weapon out and pointed at Kyla through the windshield.

"No!" I say, holding my other hand up. "Put that away! It's fine, I've got this." The poor girl looks terrified. Her hands are up and she's practically shaking in her seat.

"Get out of the car, now!" he yells.

She does as she's told, still holding her keys in one hand. I back out of the way. I don't have the authority to tell Farmer what to do, but at the same time, he's completely botching any chance we have to get the truth out of this girl.

Once she steps away from the car, I get in between him and her and he immediately lowers the gun. "What are you doing?"

"I put my arm in there on purpose to stop her," I say. "She didn't assault me if that's what you're thinking." I turn back to Kyla who now has tears streaming down her face. "Look, it's okay," I say. "You didn't do anything wrong."

"I don't know anything about Greg, okay?" she says, her voice even higher-pitched than before. "I just met him a few weeks ago."

"Let's go back into your apartment," I say, holding out my sore arm. There's going to be a bruise there for sure.

She shakes her head. "Can't."

"Because of what you're growing?" I ask.

Her eyes flick to me, then to Farmer, then back to me again, which answers my question. "Like I said, I don't care about that. Neither does he. Neither of us are with DEA. I'm with the FBI and he's ATF. We're investigating a series of fires."

She looks over at him and thankfully Farmer seems to have picked up on my call. His weapon is away, and he's taken a few steps back. Kyla visibly relaxes and I put my arm around her, leading her back toward her apartment. "Look, I know I'm not supposed to have it, okay, but I only sell it to people who need it medicinally," she says. Unfortunately, medicinal marijuana is still illegal in South Carolina, but I'm not about to bust her for something as innocuous as that. I don't plan on adding it to my report either, and I plan on making sure Farmer does the same.

"As far as anyone is concerned, we're just here to chat," I say.

"What do you want to know about Greg?" she asks as we reach her sliding glass door. She pushes through the curtains inside and I follow, finding myself in a moderate apartment. It's mostly clean, though there is a huge dresser cabinet on the far side of the wall next to the small bar that attaches to the kitchen. I don't have to open it to know what's in there.

"Let's take a seat," I say. Kyla hangs her keys back on a keyring and sits down on her couch. It didn't really register before in all the chaos, but all she's wearing is a black tank top and boy shorts. It looks like she's just woken up, despite it being nearly noon.

I take a seat across from her. "How long have you known Greg Perry?"

"Just a few weeks. We met at a dive bar."

"Billy's Backwash?" Farmer asks.

She looks up. "No, it's a Mexican place. El Taqueria, out by Comstock."

"How would you describe your relationship?" I ask.

"Mostly physical. I'm not stupid; I know what he was looking for. He knew what I was looking for. It was mutually beneficial."

I take a breath. Now that she's calmed down some, she seems more confident. "When was the last time you heard from Greg?"

"Last night. He was supposed to come over, but he never showed. I tried texting a few times, but I know better than to call after eleven."

"Because of his wife," Farmer says, and there's an accusatory undercurrent in the words.

"Yes, because of his wife," she replies, a little heat rising in her words. "Greg hadn't been happy in that relationship a long time. And I'm not naïve enough to think I was the first woman he'd fucked outside of his marriage."

"What time did you hear from him last night?" I ask.

"Around ten, ten-thirty. I did a little preening after we talked but I guess I shouldn't be surprised he didn't show."

"You spoke to him on the phone?" I ask.

She nods. "Yeah. Half the time it's the only way I can lure him over here. I know what my voice does to that man."

I shoot a glance at Farmer, no doubt he's thinking the same thing I am. "When you spoke to him, did he seem… agitated at all? Upset?"

She shrugs one bare shoulder. "Maybe a little. But he was always like that. I'm not sure I've ever seen him completely calm. Why, what's going on? Did he get arrested or something?" Interesting that this is the second woman to assume that about Greg Perry. I'm going to have to get Zara to do a deeper dive into this man, he obviously had a reputation.

"Kyla, I'm sorry to inform you, but Greg was killed last night."

Her eyes go wide. "What?"

"We believe he was intentionally burned to death in a fire," I say. I catch the bottom of her lip quiver as she tries to process what I've told her. "Do you know anyone who would wish him any harm?"

"No," she says, breathlessly, like she can't even comprehend the question. "Why would someone kill him? What did he do?"

"That's what we're trying to find out," Farmer says.

"He never said anything to you about any shady deals, or people who might have been after him?" I ask.

She shakes her head slowly, but I can see her mind is

somewhere else; I'm not even sure she's hearing me. She's probably trying to figure out if this can come back on her in any way.

"Were you here all last night?" Farmer asks. She nods, looking up at him. "Didn't leave your apartment?" She shakes her head, again, wordless. "I don't suppose anyone can corroborate that?"

Her eyes shift to the side, like she's looking down her hallway. "Actually, now that you mention it, I think there was something going on," she says.

I lean forward. "What do you mean?"

"Sometimes he'd come over and he'd be more frustrated than usual," she says. "I figured it was just problems with his wife. But whenever I'd ask him about it, he'd get angry and shut down." She pauses. "Though, sometimes I'd do it on purpose. Angry sex can be the best sex, after all."

"But he never told you what happened?"

She shakes her head. "All I know is it happened a few months ago, before we met. He said it was all in the past and wasn't something I needed to worry about."

It hasn't escaped my attention she obviously is attempting to distract us from something about last night, though I can't imagine she had any more to do with Perry's death than his wife did. However, I need to be able to do my due diligence. I may be able to overlook what's growing in her closet, but I can't overlook a potential alibi.

"Kyla, we need to know if you had someone else here last night who could corroborate your story."

She bites her lower lip. "It's not that I had someone here, per se, it's more like I was...I was just here, okay?" I glare at her. "Fine," she says, getting up from the couch. She leads us down the hall to her bedroom, and when the door opens, I'm not sure what I'm expecting, but it isn't that.

She's got a three-monitor station set up with a professional gaming chair and a huge computer with a transparent casing and LED lights running along the inside of it. It kinda reminds me of a spaceship the way she's got everything integrated together. "I was online last night, okay? For like, six hours."

"Doing what?" Farmer asks, looking over my shoulder.

"Fortnite? Ever hear of it?" she asks, her tone sarcastic. "I was playing with at least thirty other people at any given time."

Zara is going to be sorry she missed this. She's a big gamer too, and I bet she would love to take a look at this setup. We return to the living room and go through a few follow-up questions, but it's clear she doesn't know anything more than what she's told us. Though I find it curious she was embarrassed about her hobby. I wonder how much Greg knew about it, or even cared. Regardless, we're done ten minutes later, though I do leave her my card in case she remembers anything else.

"How's your arm?" Farmer asks as we head back to the car.

"Fine," I say, even though it's throbbing. "How is your trigger finger?"

"I was just assessing the situation," he says. "From where I was standing it looked like she was attacking you." He shakes his head. "And you let her off on those 'plants'."

"First off," I say, "I don't give a shit about a couple of plants growing in someone's home. Regardless of what the state says, it's not worth upending her entire life for. You wanna throw her in jail for growing and distributing, then go right ahead. But it isn't going to help anyone, and her customers will just find it somewhere else. And second, when I need your help, I will *ask* for it. That could have turned bad quick. I'm trying to make connections with these people, not scare them into submission. Regardless of what your generation thinks, that's not the way to get a witness to cooperate."

He doesn't reply for a few minutes, so I assume the matter

is closed. My arm really does ache though, she slammed it in there good. I'll have to make sure there isn't any internal damage.

"I'm not like that," Farmer finally says as we turn back on the main highway. "I don't shoot first and ask questions later."

"Looked like you were pretty close to shooting first back there," I say.

"It was the wrong call. You were right," he finally says. I glance over at him. "Guess I'm rustier than I thought."

Chapter Thirteen

Since Kyla Griffin couldn't give us much more to go on, I figure our next best bet is to head to where we know Greg Perry was last seen: the Four Links Driving Range. There are tons of golf courses around Charleston, but only one dedicated driving range, so it isn't hard to find. And given that was where his wife said he was last night, it's the first place we need to look.

Farmer pulls into the small parking lot which bumps up to a wooded area off to the east. The range is right off the parking lot, separated only by a metal gate that isn't even chest-high. We head around the main gated area to the service counter which sits just behind the fifteen stalls that make up the range. It looks like this place has been here for decades and doesn't offer any of the amenities of the more modern places that have full food and drink service. This is a mom-and-pop operation all the way.

Speaking of which, I think I see pop himself sitting behind the counter, reading an honest-to-God newspaper. "Excuse me," I say. There are only two other people here practicing their swings, so I'm surprised he didn't hear us approach. But then again, when I get a good look at him, I realize he's probably close to eighty.

"Afternoon," he says without putting his paper down. "Interested in some balls?"

I look over to the buckets of golf balls sitting just on the other side of the counter. He also has a wide array of clubs available for rent. I show him my badge and Farmer does the same. "I'm Agent Slate with the FBI. You wouldn't happen to have security cameras on your establishment here, would you?"

He shakes his head. "Nope. Don't wanna pay the companies for upkeep. You know they charge extra just to monitor the damn things? They ain't gettin' my money." He *thwicks* his paper and goes back to reading.

"How late are you open?" I ask.

"Eleven a.m. to eleven p.m., six days a week. Closed Mondays."

"Can you tell us who was working last night? We're looking for information about someone who might have been here."

He folds the paper together, setting it down. "I was here last night. Was slow. Ended up closing early after the last car left."

I pull up a picture of Greg Perry from his firefighter ID on my phone. "Was this man here last night?"

"A'yuh," he says, his face morphing into a sneer. "Tried to hit a ball out into the parkin' lot. Drunk-ass bastard."

"He was drunk?" I ask.

The man points a little further down to a small stall where it seems they do serve alcohol and snacks after all. I underestimated this place. "I never should have served him that second pitcher," he says. "But business is slow. That's the only thing keepin' us afloat anymore."

"I assume you have a valid liquor license," Farmer says, inspecting the stall. The man points to a small bulletin board behind him, covered in flyers for all sorts of local events. With effort he stands, moving some of them aside to reveal the license. "You need to have that out in the open where everyone can see it."

"Alright, alright," he says. "Keep yer britches on." He pulls the laminated license down, along with a couple of thumbtacks and probably half the flyers before slapping it on the counter between us. "I'll tape it up in a minute."

"Back to the man," I say. "You said he *tried* to hit a ball into the parking lot? Why?"

"Hell if I know," he replies. "Cause he was a bastard, that's why. He left right after. Didn't even bring his balls back. I had to go out and get 'em. Everyone's supposed to bring any unused balls back to the counter. It says so right there on the —" He looks back to the sign that had been up, but has now fluttered to the ground after he removed the license. "Goddammit."

"Did you happen to notice anything else?" I ask. "Was anyone with him?"

With effort, he bends down to pick up the errant sign. "Yeah, for a while, another man was here. But he left first."

"What did this other man look like?" Farmer asks.

"Preppy boy. One of them collared shirts. He drove off about five minutes before the bastard left."

"And you didn't see anyone else last night? No other cars?" He shakes his head. "Alright, thank you," I say, stepping back from the counter.

We head back out to the parking lot. There are three cars here now. I assume two belong to the people who are out driving, and the other to the old man. "You notice anything?" I ask.

"Perry's car is missing," Farmer says.

"Exactly. So either he drove somewhere else that wasn't his house or Kyla's place and was taken from there, or the unsub took him and his car from here." I shoot a quick text to Zara asking her if she can send me the latest GPS data from Perry's phone before it turned off. I have no doubt it's been destroyed by now.

"You think he'd be bold enough to take him right here?" Farmer asks.

"He was bold enough to take Leon Spencer from the community college parking lot," I reply. There are only two lights in the entire lot. And the woods that it bumps up to would provide good cover for someone half-drunk walking back to their car. I make my way over to the wooded area, searching around. There's some of the standard debris and trash. But I also happen to spot something in the soft dirt. "Hey Farmer," I call him over.

He joins me to find me staring at a couple of footprints. They look recent. "You better call your forensic teams out here," I say.

"Damn." He pulls out his phone and makes the call. While he's doing that I head to the entrance-slash-exit of Four Links, looking for anything nearby that might have a camera. Unfortunately, it's a two-lane road with not much else around. There's a collapsing barn on the far side of the road in the middle of a wide stretch of property, but nothing else in either direction for a few blocks at least. No chance of getting any camera footage unfortunately.

"They're on their way," he says when I return. "We'll have to let the proprietor know we'll be sealing off this area until further notice."

I get a text back from Zara. While I think it's going to be Perry's GPS info, she's sent something else.

Just confirmed, Perry transferred away from firehouse twelve two weeks ago.

Firehouse twelve. Just like Leon Spencer and Sam Phelps.

"You seriously think Padilla has something to do with this?" Farmer asks. I took over the driving duties as we make our way over to Greg Perry's old firehouse to have a chat with Captain Padilla, the commanding officer in charge.

"How could he not?" I ask. "Three of his former crew have now been killed, two of them violently. It's what connects them all together. We need to know what he knows. I want to push him a little, see if he's hiding something." I already suspect that he is, but I'm holding that part close. It seems to me Padilla and Farmer have some history together, and I'm not about to let Farmer's emotions get in the way of this investigation.

"Look, I've known Joseph a long time. He and I worked together a lot back when we were both younger. Kind of watched out for each other in our respective fields. There's no way he's a part of this."

"I'm not saying he is," I lie, already vindicated in my hunch. "I'm just saying he might know something and not realize it."

It only takes us a few more minutes to reach the firehouse; it wasn't that far from the driving range. Though it's later in the day than I want it to be, considering we had to wait on Farmer's guys to come on scene and begin processing. He's assured me the site is in good hands and that everything will be cataloged. They'll be taking casts of the footprints to see if we can't match them up with a particular brand of shoe.

When we arrive at firehouse twelve it's different than the one in downtown Charleston. It's a one-story for starters, and only has one garage for an engine. We head in through the front door and through the station until we reach the offices near the back.

"I'm going against my better judgement here, Slate," Farmer says.

"Yeah, well you owe me one for that stunt back at Kyla's,"

I reply. He grumbles something unintelligible as I knock on Captain Padilla's door.

"Yeah," he calls from the other side. His eyebrows raise when we enter. "Stan, what's going on?"

"Hey, Joe," he says. "We need to have a talk."

He smiles, but it doesn't reach his eyes. He's not happy about us being here, that much is clear. "Sure, what can I help you with?"

"We're trying to find out why someone is targeting the men who used to be on your crew," I say. "We're looking at three deaths total. Two of them in the past week."

"Yeah, I'm aware," he replies. "I've just launched an internal investigation. Someone obviously has a grudge against my guys."

"Any leads so far?" I ask, not sure if I believe the investigation line.

He shakes his head. "I've been running into dead ends."

"What makes the men on your crew so special? And not the men who are on your crew now. But the ones that were here before they were reassigned."

"I mean, they all worked together for a few years," he says. "I'm sure you know how it is, you get close to the people you work with." I actually *don't* know how that is, but I motion for him to continue. "These guys become like family. But they're all above reproach. Couldn't ask for a better crew to trust with your life."

"Why the transfers then?" I ask. "Both Leon and Greg were transferred to different stations two weeks ago. What spurred the change?"

He shrugs. "You'll have to talk to the Assistant Fire Chief on that one. I only handle my station here. He approves all transfers."

"Does that mean the men requested the transfers themselves?" I ask.

"They didn't come from me, if that's what you're asking,"

he says. "Sometimes, guys just want a change of scenery. Leon was looking to get out altogether. It's why he was going to school at night."

"You knew about that," I say.

"Of course. Like I said, we were all close, even after they left." I don't miss that he's now including himself instead of the crew being separate from him.

"Did anyone else transfer out with Leon and Greg?" I ask.

He shakes his head. "No, everyone else is still here. We've got twenty-six firefighters that run out of this station. Two moving to a different station isn't really that uncommon."

I shake my head. Twenty-six? At this rate we're going to end up with twenty-six more bodies in the ground if I can't figure out what's going on.

"Have any of the guys talked about problems they're having? Personal issues? Anyone following them?" I ask.

"I've been asking myself the same thing ever since I found out about Greg. I'm wondering if I've missed something obvious. But no one has come to me with anything."

"Sorry about this, Joe, we're just trying to figure out what connects these three men. There has to be something," Farmer says.

I want to rub my temples out of frustration, but I'm not about to let Padilla see it. The last thing I need is him dismissing me because he sees me as too emotional. Normally I wouldn't worry about it so much, but with Farmer not giving me much support, I feel like I'm on my own out here.

"I don't envy your job, that's for sure," he says, though he directs his attention more to Farmer than to me.

"Is there anyone else that's still part of his company who was close with Sam, Leon and Greg?"

"Sure, Daniel, Jay. Ricky if he were here, but he's got today off. Maybe a couple of others." I look for any tells that he might not be telling the truth, but from what I can see, he's being honest about that much, at least. But he's holding something else back, I just can't tell what or what it even relates to. What isn't he telling us?

"Do you mind if we take a look around?" I ask.

He shrugs. "I suppose not. What are you looking for?"

"I'm not sure. What did you do with their old lockers?"

"They should still be empty," he replies. "We haven't gotten anyone in to replace them yet."

I nod, standing. "Thanks for your help. We'll let you know if we find anything." I turn and head out, looking for the employee lockers. Though I hear Farmer utter, "Thanks, Joe," like he's apologizing for me.

Once we're back out of his office, Farmer heads over to the employee area, but I catch him by the arm before he can get very far. "I would have appreciated some support in there."

"It's like I said, I've known Joe a long time. He's not involved in this."

"Hallmark of a good detective," I say sarcastically, "Make sure you let your personal relationships interfere with your investigation." I release his arm and push past him, leading the way.

And here I was thinking we were starting to make some progress.

Chapter Fourteen

THE DOOR TO THE MEN'S LOCKER ROOM IS PROPPED OPEN, SO I
walk right in. Given that I haven't seen a woman since I've
arrived, I'm willing to bet there isn't much cause for decorum
around here.

The room is the same as any gym locker room I've ever
been in, and smells about the same. A mixture of soap, body
spray and body odor, all amalgamated into one noxious cock-
tail that I'm sure men like this think makes women's panties
drop. A line of lockers runs along the wall and another runs
the middle of the room while sinks sit along the opposite wall.
Beyond those is an opening which leads to the showers if the
sound of running water and steam is any indication.

There are a couple of men in here, most in various states
of dress, and some with nothing but towels on. They all turn
upon seeing me enter, those in conversation ceasing immediately.

"FBI," I say, holding up my badge. "I'm looking for the
lockers that belonged to Phelps, Spencer and Perry."

A few of the guys exchange looks; they've already heard
the news from Padilla, no doubt. Still, it takes them a minute
to respond to my request.

One guy wearing a towel that sits right below his chiseled chest and hugs his hips points at a locker close to where he stands. "This was Perry's." As I make my way over I catch sight of Farmer coming into the locker room behind me. He seems to be sulking. Good.

As I reach the locker, I notice that all of them have combination locks built in, just like the lockers back in middle and high school. The one I'm looking for sits open, empty. The man stands close by and as I approach he puts his foot up on the bench that runs the length of the lockers, which allows his towel to fall open up, exposing his leg and leaving little to the imagination.

"You know what they say about firefighters, right?" he asks. I ignore him. "We gotta keep our poles waxed."

"*Jesus Christ,*" I mutter under my breath.

"Give it a rest, Walker!" one of the other firemen yells. Walker gives a smile and backs off.

I perform a visual inspection of the inside of Perry's locker, finding nothing of note. There's a shelf at the top, a couple of hooks inside for his jacket and other equipment, and a small metal box built into the bottom, which looks like it might hold shoes or boots. I have to get on my tiptoes to reach on top of the shelf, making sure nothing was left behind, though I don't expect it. Though as soon as I finish searching the overpowering smell of body spray consumes me.

I turn to see Walker has returned and is smiling down at me. "Can I give you a hand there?"

"No," I reply, pushing him out of my way. "Spencer and Phelps?"

"Leon's locker is over here," another man says. I leave towel boy behind and reach the second locker, noting Leon's name is still on the outside, whereas it wasn't on Greg's. I wonder why they would leave Leon's name up when he's obviously transferred out? Another inspection leaves me with nothing.

I head around the island of lockers so I'm facing the shower room just as a naked man exits as he's drying his hair. "Whoa!" he yells, then scoots back, covering himself as fast as he can. The rest of the room breaks out in cackles as I inspect the other names on the lockers. I find what I'm looking for: Sam Phelps' name is still on his locker as well. It sits right in between Mackenzie, D. and Olsen, J. Olsen's locker is marked with a symbol I recognize that gives him rank above the others.

"Why didn't somebody tell me we had girls in here!" the startled man yells as he storms off to his locker. The room is rife with laughter now and I use the distraction to inspect Phelps' locker. Again, I find nothing of note inside. I hadn't really expected to, but I figured it couldn't hurt.

"Olsen?" I call out.

A man who had been shaving by one of the sinks walks over. His hairy chest is clearly visible, but at least he has pants on, though his face and chin are covered in shaving cream. He's barely begun. "Here," he says.

"Jay Olsen?" I ask. He nods. "Padilla says you were close with the three men that were lost."

He hangs his head. "We all were. We're brothers here. I assume you're investigating their deaths."

I nod. "Is there anything you can tell me about why these three men were targeted?" I ask. "Was there anything they shared in common? Other than being part of the same firehouse?"

I notice a couple of the other guys seem to be trying to busy themselves as not to look like they're eavesdropping. But they're not very good at it.

Olsen shakes his head. "Greg was a right jerk when he wanted to be. Hell of a firefighter but get a couple drinks in him and he'd always get nasty. On the other hand, Leon was about the best kind of brother you could want. He was a little older, so he saw a lot of us come up. And Sam...Sam was just a good guy. He was my best man at my wedding." He wipes his hands on his towel. "I just can't believe they're all gone. But they didn't have a lot in common."

"Did you notice any of them acting strange before they died? Like they were worried about something or had some reason to be concerned for their own safety?"

He turns his mouth down as he shakes his head. "Don't think so. I never noticed anything, at least."

"You say Phelps was your best man. What about the other two, did you spend a lot of time with them?"

"Sure. We'd spend weekends at each other's houses, go out for drinks, help with whatever needed doing. You know, family stuff."

"Were you aware Greg Perry was having an affair?" I ask.

He averts his eyes, showing no surprise. "It wasn't a secret he and Melanie were having problems," Olsen says. If Olsen knew, that means everyone in this room knows. Which means I could have more suspects than I can count on all my fingers and toes combined. The killer knew Greg's "secret" and was determined to out him to his wife. Otherwise, why send the texts at all? Whether he sent them or made Greg do it, I can't say. All I know for sure is he wanted to expose the man, which indicates either a deep loathing for him, or an attraction to his wife. But given the killer murdered Leon in the same way, I'm assuming it's the former for now.

I notice Farmer sulking in the corner of the room, not really paying attention to anyone. He's leaning up against the wall and I've seen the way his leg bounces before. On suspects who are antsy for a smoke. It *was* him I smelled at the coroner's office after all. But he's not about to light one up next to a firehouse.

"Who was closest with Leon?" I ask.

"That would probably be Ricky," Jay says. "He's not quite as old as Leon was, but he's one of the older guard here.

Though Ricky can be blunt. He's not one to beat around the bush."

"And he's off today, I understand."

Olsen nods. "He'll be back on duty on Sunday." I huff. I can't question every one of these men, not in time to prevent another killing. But at the same time, what choice do I have? One of them has to know something that they're not sharing with the others, because there's no way this many people could keep a secret this long. Not like this. Little white lies are easy enough to cover, but something big enough to get three people killed causes even the most hardened person to speak up. I know the answer is here somewhere, I just have to suss it out.

"Alright," I say. "Thanks for your help." I turn and head back out, though before I leave, I catch Walker throw me a wink. I ignore him for a second time and make my way back out to the main section of the firehouse where the truck sits. Farmer isn't far behind me.

"Find what you need?" he asks.

"No," I say, frustrated and not turning back. "We're going to need to set up an interview schedule for every person in there," I say. "There's no other way about it."

"Absolutely not," he says.

I do a one-eighty so fast he actually takes a step back. "Look. Someone in there knows something. And they're not going to talk until we squeeze. I want to get them out of their comfortable space and into an interview room. See how well they hold up then."

"That will take a week to execute," he says. "You really think we have that kind of time?"

"Agent?"

I glance over and see one of the men from the locker room approaching us. He's not as big as some of the other firefighters, but he's still obviously in good shape, though his dark brown hair is somewhat longer. And his face isn't as hardened as some of the others. If I'd had to guess, I'd say he hasn't been in the unit very long. Maybe a year or two. "Yes?" I ask.

"Dan McKenzie," he says, though he doesn't hold out his hand. "I thought you should know; I was out with Greg last night. We went to a driving range."

"Four points," I say, shooting Farmer a look. At least now we know who our mystery man last night was. That saves me some time.

"Yes, ma'am," he replies. "Greg was pretty drunk. I tried to call him a ride but he wouldn't have it, so I just left him there."

"Did you see anyone else around? Any other patrons or anyone hanging around the parking lot?" I ask.

He shakes his head. "Greg was pissed about having to go home but it was already ten o'clock and I needed to be here early this morning. He was yelling at me the whole way to my car."

"Did he say anything else?" Farmer asks. "Anything about his problems with his wife?"

McKenzie shakes his head. "No, he was just being Greg. Anyway, I just thought you should know." He makes a motion to head back.

"Did you know the other two?" I ask, not wanting to lose this opportunity. "Sam and Leon?"

McKenzie hesitates for a second, and it's the same hesitation I thought I saw with Captain Padilla. "Yeah. Both were really good guys. They didn't deserve what happened to them."

"I'm not sure anyone deserves to be burned alive," I say.

McKenzie turns back to us, though he glances over his shoulder. "I know Sam…he had something on his mind."

"Something like what?" I ask.

He gives me a pointed look. "Just…he was weighed down with something. Sam was a good person; you could always count on him to do the right thing." Speaking of being weighed down, McKenzie looks like he's about to break under the weight of whatever this is. I was right, the answer is here.

"And what was the right thing?" I ask.

"McKenzie!" We all turn to see Padilla standing at the far end of the hall. "Fall in. We've got drills and you're leading the group."

McKenzie gives me one last look and trots off back to the locker room. "Can't this wait?" I ask Padilla. "I'm trying to conduct an investigation."

"We've got a schedule to follow here, Agent," Padilla says. "If you want to talk to my guys, get me a list. I'll have them come to you when their schedules allow." He gives us a wave then heads into the locker room himself.

"I hope you saw that," I tell Farmer.

"Yeah," he replies. "I did."

Chapter Fifteen

WE'RE BACK IN THE CAR, SITTING IN SILENCE. IT'S BEEN THIS
way for the past ten minutes as we head back to Farmer's
office. I didn't bother fighting to drive back, I think I've proven
my point. At the very least I've made Farmer question his own
motives in this case. Padilla is clearly hiding something, and
McKenzie knows more than he's letting on. He was on the
verge of telling us too, I could see it in his eyes. But I'm sure
now if we get another shot at him, Padilla will have put the
fear of God in him, and he'll clam up.

I think maybe we can take another run at Olsen, but he
seems too cool and clear-headed for me to rattle. And then
there's the other twenty-four of them in there. But I find it
interesting McKenzie was out with Perry the night he died.
Given Perry's reputation, only a rookie would be stupid
enough to go out and get drunk with the guy. But it confirms
what the driving range proprietor said: Perry was drunk, and
it would have been easy for someone to sneak up on him.

"Give me your assessment of things," I finally say,
breaking my silence since it seems Farmer is content to remain
stoic.

"I'm not sure," he finally says. "What I think is telling me something different from what I feel."

"Which one tells you Padilla's involved in this?" I ask.

He shoots me a glare of epic proportions. "Does McKenzie seem to you like the kind of man who could burn a couple of bodies by pouring turpentine down their throats?" I ask.

He shakes his head. "Unlikely. He doesn't strike me as the type."

"Me either," I reply. "He's got no rage when he talks about the victims. Our killer is full of it, it's obvious all over the scenes. McKenzie seems almost…repentant."

"Strange for a man to feel regret for something he didn't do," Farmer says.

I have to agree. Maybe McKenzie didn't light the match, but he's involved in this somehow. I just can't see it yet. "He said Phelps had something on his mind. Something that was bothering him. And all of this started with his death." I check the clock on the dashboard. It's almost six p.m. and the sun is only going to be up for another thirty minutes or so. "How far to the site where Phelps died?"

"It's about ten minutes away," Farmer says.

"I want to check it out."

"Why?" he seems perplexed I'd even be interested.

"Because it's the one site I haven't seen yet. And in the face of not being able to make any progress, I want to go back to the beginning. See what started all of this."

Farmer sighs, then puts on his blinker and does a U-turn. "I already told you, it seemed like an accident," he says.

"But it obviously wasn't," I reply. "Which means someone missed something along the way." I do my best not to accuse him because I need his help out there, but it seeps through anyway. Farmer isn't a stupid man.

"You mean *I* missed something." The anger in his voice is palpable.

"I mean you weren't looking for foul play, so it might not have been obvious. Plus, he could have been the killer's first victim; he might not have known exactly what to do. But he learned from it, and he's only grown more brutal as he's gone on."

Farmer is silent the rest of the way. I find myself wishing Janice hadn't pulled Zara back to D.C. I could really use her help right now. She's good at field work, even if she doesn't have a lot of experience yet. Still, I'd at least have someone to bounce ideas off of. Farmer is more like a black void. I toss something out and get nothing back.

We pull into a nice-looking neighborhood in West Ashley. It's a little dated—the buildings all look like they hail from the sixties or seventies, though a few have been renovated. At the end of the block sits the burned-out husk of one of the buildings, with caution tape still around it.

"Who owns the house?" I ask, getting out of the car and pulling on a pair of gloves.

"It belonged to the woman who was found inside, a Mrs. Orla. She didn't have a will, so at the moment the property is contested by her two grown children and their families. It's up to the courts to decide what happens."

I duck under the tape and walk up the cracked sidewalk. As I get closer, the grass around the property become charred and burnt. "What can you tell me?"

"Standard wood-frame home, so it burnt quick. Looks like the fire originated in the kitchen as that's where the damage is the heaviest. I was thinking grease fire or something with the stove, since she had natural gas and an open cooktop. It wouldn't be hard for an older woman to slip and for something to catch fire."

I walk through the burned front entrance. The door is half off its hinges, splintered where it looks like an axe took it out. "I assume this is how Phelps got in?"

"We assumed so," Farmer says. "The back door was still locked."

The inside of the house is little more than burnt remains. The wooden floors groan under me as I step, trying to remain light on my toes. A living room sits off to the right inside the doorway, the remnants of a burnt loveseat and table all that remain. Off to the left is a dining room, turned-over chairs and the skeleton of a smashed chandelier draw a picture in my mind of happier times shared around the broken table. A staircase leads up to the second floor, but half the steps are missing or broken. I can't get up there without a ladder.

As I move around the staircase to the back of the house, I find the kitchen. Farmer is right, there's no doubt the fire started here as it's where the damage is the greatest. The appliances that remain have all been charred down to metal, the plastic in them having long melted away. However the tile on the floor and around the counters is in surprisingly good shape, just covered in a layer of soot, which I wipe away with my gloved hand.

"They found her in here," Farmer says, standing in the doorway. "She was face down, right over there." He points to the area beside the refrigerator.

"What about Phelps, where was he?"

"Upstairs," Farmer says. "The assumption was he was checking the other rooms for anyone else when he was caught and unable to make it back down the stairs in time."

I walk around the room, shaking my head. It really does seem like an accident. It isn't like the other sites at all. "Why was Phelps in here by himself? Don't fire teams come in three or four at a time?"

"Padilla told me he ran ahead of the others against his orders. That he breached the door before the rest of them were ready. By the time the others made it into the house, it took them time to find him upstairs. They had to bring in ladders to get up there to him."

I put my hands on my hips, making a circle in the room then heading back out to the staircase. "Does this really make sense to you? A trained firefighter, running into a blaze by himself? Then getting himself trapped? Why didn't he just break one of the windows upstairs and jump? It would have been better than dying by asphyxiation."

"I did an investigation and found his oxygen tank malfunctioned. More than likely he wasn't getting any clean air, but maybe thought he could push through or that it wasn't a big deal. But based on what I could tell, his tank was delivering carbon dioxide to him instead of oxygen."

"Slowly putting him to sleep," I say, nodding. "So Phelps breaks in here, off protocol, skips the old lady in the kitchen, runs upstairs, faints, then subsequently dies from asphyxiation. Meanwhile, the rest of his squad is making their way in, but the stairs are too damaged from the fire, and by the time they get the old woman out, she's already gone. Do I have that right?"

He narrows his eyes, though I can't be sure if it's because he is skeptical of me or his original assessment. "Why don't you tell me what you think happened?"

"I'm not a fire investigator," I say. "You know this better than I do. It just seems strange to me that Phelps would make so many careless mistakes when his life—and the life of his team—was on the line."

"It's a fair point," Farmer says, finally relenting. "I can't say that you're wrong. But what are you saying, that someone *made* him run into a burning building without all the proper precautions?"

I shake my head. "I'm saying maybe our killer wasn't as bold as he is now. Maybe he figured the best way to take out his first victim was to sabotage his breathing equipment. Though I can't explain how he would have convinced Phelps to run in there by himself."

"If the theory holds, he would have had to," Farmer says.

"Otherwise the other guys would have noticed and pulled him out before he stopped breathing."

"Exactly," I say. "And unless someone has invented mind control without my knowledge, I don't see how anyone could have convinced him to do it."

"There's always another option to consider," Farmer says. I look at him expectantly.

"Someone *placed* him there. Before the fire."

Chapter Sixteen

"Now that is a sweet piece of ass," Ricky said as he watched the group of women walk past his car. They all wore tight little dresses designed to accentuate every curve and barely cover their best assets. That was why he'd park here, right along the street where he could get the best look at them. Heels that pumped up their calves and pushed out their butts, all of them carrying tiny purses that could barely hold an ID, phone and maybe a little vial of coke, for the bathroom later. Just enough to get fucked up but not enough to blackout. And they say guys are the ones drugging women in the clubs? No way, they're out there doing it to themselves. Whatever they needed to get in the mood, right?

As one of them bent over to fix the strap on her six-inch stiletto, Ricky leaned over to the passenger side of his souped-up Camry to get a better look. He gave a little whistle just as the woman stood back up. She turned back, the purple eyeshadow and lipstick practically begging him to get out and follow her. But then she sneered and shot him the finger.

"Well, fuck you, too," he yelled, settling back into the driver's seat. He was just trying to be nice. What the hell did they dress like that for if they didn't want guys to look at them?

Ricky drummed his fingers on the steering wheel as REO Speedwagon blasted from his speakers. He always thought he should have been born a decade earlier. The music was definitely better; not that pop trash they played on the radio these days. A couple other groups of women passed by, but no one gave him much of a look. Seemed like everyone was more interested in getting out of the chilly air rather than mingling outside. If he was going to score tonight, he'd have to do it the hard way. Sometimes he could reel one in from just the car alone, though they were usually skanks. To get the quality meat you had to go straight to the butcher, not wait out on the street for the scraps.

Ricky cut the engine and stepped out, straightening his collar after he unbuttoned the top button. His job ensured he stayed fit, which seemed to be enough these days. Half the time he didn't even have to talk to the girl. As the night wore on, he'd pop a few more buttons, giving everyone out there a good look. Inevitably one of them would spy his glistening abs out on the dance floor and that would be all she wrote. The only bad part was he had to pretend to dance to that shitty music.

Still, it was hard to argue with the results.

Ricky headed over to the club entrance, flashing Ernesto a fifty which he took without pause, letting Ricky through. Good ol' Ernesto, Ricky was probably putting that guy's kids through college.

Inside the entire place seemed to vibrate to the rhythm of the bass, and it was both bright as shit and dark at the same time. Strobe and spotlights flashed all over the place and within five seconds Ricky could tell the place was past fire capacity. It always was, but he was off-duty, so he didn't give a flying fuck. The place was so crowded it would be difficult out there. Time to try a different tactic.

He headed over to the bar and snagged two shots of tequila from the bartender. He made his way across the dance floor, spying a particularly hot number dancing with her friends a few feet away. Ricky held the shot glasses precariously and as he made his way across the floor the girl backed into him right on cue, knocking one of the shots out of his hand and spilling it all over his pants.

"Ohmygod, I'm sorry!" she yelled over the thumping bass.

"Don't worry about it," Ricky said, holding up the other one. "I've still got one!"

"But your clothes!" she said, and he saw her take a look at his open shirt, her eyes travelling down there for just a millisecond. "Let me get you another one."

Ricky smiled. "If you insist."

"I'll be right back," she yelled to her friends who both shot Ricky a look but neither made a move. He'd made the right call. You could always tell the good Samaritans; they just had a look about them.

"What was it? Tequila?" the girl yelled. He nodded, with the other one still in his hand. "One shot of tequila!" the girl called out.

When the bartender came back with it, Ricky shot him a wink and he rolled his eyes, walking away. "Wait, I need to pay," the girl said.

"Don't worry about it," Ricky said. "They know me here, they'll just put it on my tab."

"But...I was the one who spilled it," she said.

"Like I said, it's not a problem." She held out the shot to him and he just clinked his glass to hers. "It's yours."

"Really?" she asked. She looked back over at her friends then gave a little shrug. "Thanks."

They both shot them at the same time, Ricky's mouth burning from the sensation.

"Needs salt!" the girl yelled. Ricky threw up a peace

symbol to the bartender who quickly poured two more and brought them over. "Salt and lemon!" the girl said.

"You heard the lady," he said which produced just the smile he'd hoped for. It was almost too easy.

A number of shots later—Ricky had lost count—the girl was hanging on his every word. She'd said her name at least twice, but he hadn't paid enough attention to care. In a couple of hours he'd never see her again. But right now, she was his.

"You're a firefighter?" the girl yelled; her words slightly slurred. She ran her hand down his chest, stopping right when she got to the ridges that made up his abs. "That's so cool." Then she began laughing like it was the funniest thing anyone had ever said.

"You wanna get out of here?" he asked, making a motion for the door.

She practically licked her lips. "Let me just tell my friends." Hook, line, and sinker.

A couple minutes later they were in his car and her hand was on his crotch, giving him a couple of squeezes. At this rate they wouldn't even make it to his apartment a few blocks away. That was okay, the backseat worked too.

Ricky pulled out of the spot, not bothering to check his mirrors and gunned it down the street, causing her to squeal in delight as she grabbed him even harder. He pulled down a side street a couple of blocks from the club, looking for a good place to pull over.

The girl reached for her seatbelt when the car jerked forward, and Ricky nearly hit his head on the steering wheel. The girl screamed again, this time out of fear.

"What the fuck?" Ricky said, checking his rear view. Headlights shone back at him. Some asshole had run into his car!

"What's going on?" the girl asked. The impact seemed to have sobered her some.

"Somebody just bought himself a huge repair bill," Ricky said, getting out. He'd sunk more than a few paychecks into this vehicle, tuning up the transmission, widening the wheelbase and of course going with the underglow kit. Not to mention all the other modifications he'd made. No one had ever hit him before, and now, just as he was about to score, some jackass comes along and ruins his night? He was going to beat this guy senseless first, then blame it on the accident.

The driver's door was open on the other vehicle as well, and when Ricky looked inside the still-running car, there was no one inside. "What the hell?" He looked around, thinking maybe the guy got out to throw up or something, but didn't see anyone around.

"What is it? What's going on?" the girl asked.

"Shut the hell up," Ricky yelled back. Where was the other driver?

"You know what? Fuck you, I'm outta here," the girl said, getting out and storming off in her heels in the direction back to the club. At the moment Ricky didn't care; he needed to find this asshole who decided to ruin his entire evening. If the guy ran, there was a good chance he didn't have insurance, which meant his own insurance would have to cover the damages. He knew how these things worked; his rates would be going up and he'd have to spend a fortune just to get the car back to how he had it.

The other guy's car was nothing special, just a Hyundai Accent, which could be decent with a couple of mods, but was nothing more than the standard model. Would he really leave it running?

Suddenly Ricky felt the ground rise up to meet him and before he knew it, his face was against the pavement. Blood filled his mouth, and he was sure he'd broken his nose. He struggled to comprehend what was going on and felt the back of his head. It was warm, wet, and sticky, and when he pulled his hand away, it was covered in blood. Ricky's adrenaline kicked into high gear, and he attempted to push himself up, only to feel something strong and hard drive into his stomach, forcing all the air from his lungs and causing him to pull himself into a ball.

Something strong and hard grabbed one of his wrists and began dragging him across the pavement. Ricky could barely get a breath out, much less fight back, but he managed to get to his knees and begin crawling before he felt another sickening crunch across his face.

More than one tooth came loose and somewhere in the back of his mind Ricky was sure he'd need dental reconstruction at the very least. Funny that he was concerned more about that than what was actually happening to him, but his alcohol had dulled his senses somewhat.

He felt himself being wrenched up by his wrists again, though this time he didn't fight back; he barely had the energy. Something hard and cold clamped itself around one wrist and then the other as Ricky was pushed back into the driver's seat of his car. His seatbelt was strapped across his lap and for the first time he had the sense of the other person doing this to him.

They were strong, that much was for sure. But he couldn't see their face, hidden under a hoodie. And they had gloves on. "Wha...wha..." His mouth felt like mush. It was already swelling from the dislodged teeth, and he found it difficult to speak.

"Shut up," the voice said and the familiar tang of turpentine filled Ricky's nostrils. All of a sudden he jolted back, but his hands had been secured around the 'oh shit' handle of his own vehicle, suspended up by his left side. His body was restrained to the seat by the seatbelt, and he couldn't wiggle his way free.

"You're the one who killed Leon and Greg. What th' fuck

do you want with us?" he managed to say through his broken mouth.

"What do I want?" the man replied, emptying an entire can of turpentine all over the outside of Ricky's car. He grabbed another can and began dumping it through the open back window. "You know what I want. And there's only one way to get it."

Ricky thought he recognized the voice, but he couldn't be sure. "Look man, it wasn't my idea, okay? It was Greg. He started the whole thing."

"You all had a hand in it," the man replied. "And you're all going to pay."

"The cops are on to you," Ricky said, only growing more desperate as the man finished emptying the container. "Jay called me. Said they were at the station not more than five hours ago."

"Doesn't matter," the man replied, pulling out a metal funnel. He jammed it into Ricky's mouth, causing Ricky's gag reflex to kick in. He wretched all over the inside of his car. The man pulled his head back and jammed the funnel in a second time, then poured what felt like fire down Ricky's throat. No longer was he worried about fixing his teeth or his mouth. All he was worried about was living through the next five minutes.

When the man removed the funnel, Ricky tried to make his gag reflex kick in again, and was only partially successful as he felt like he threw up some of the poison. Something was dribbling down his shirt.

The hooded man took a few steps back from the car and lit a match. "You deserve this Ricky. Reap what you sow." He flicked the match through the back window of the car.

Ricky screamed.

Chapter Seventeen

I FLOP BACK ON THE BED IN MY HOTEL ROOM, COMPLETELY exhausted from the day. I had planned to get a drink at the bar downstairs, but decided I just needed sleep instead. On the way back over after Farmer dropped me off, I picked up a burrito from a local shop. I know it's probably sacrilegious to eat Mexican food in a town like this, but right now I just need fuel and sleep.

I can't get Farmer's theory out of my mind, that the killer might have had enough access to Phelps that they were able to stage the entire scene. If that's true, then it's definitely someone the entire firehouse knows. Otherwise, how would they have access to his equipment? More than that, how would they have been able to get him into the house without the old woman knowing? Unless she was already dead before the fire started. But if that's the case, why the change in tactics?

What am I missing?

I pull my phone out and make a video call. Zara's face pops up a second later. "Please tell me you asked one of those firemen out on a date."

"What do you think?" I ask.

"I think you're sitting in your room alone, like usual," she replies.

"Yeah, and what kind of wild night are you having?" I ask.

"It involves killing orcs, I can tell you that much."

I smile. "That reminds me. I saw this setup this morning. You would have loved it. The girl had...well, I don't know what all of it was, but it glowed and looked expensive."

"Transparent case?" she asks. I can hear the excitement in her voice.

"Yeah, I think so. I thought if I got too close it might transport me fifty years into the future."

I can practically hear her swoon. "I'm gonna kill Janice for making me miss that," she says.

"How are your cases going?" I ask.

"Boring as hell. Not nearly as interesting as chasing down a serial arsonist, I can tell you that much. I'm looking at this one guy...I think he's embezzled like twenty grand from his employer, which just happens to be a federal contractor. So you know, riveting stuff."

I turn over, staring at the window which looks out onto the street. "Somebody's gotta do it."

"Yeah, Nick," she replies. "I mean, since he's the one who tried to blackmail you, shouldn't he be busted down to doing this stuff?"

I perk up. "What does Janice have him doing anyway? He can't be back on full duty."

"Nah, he's still chained to his desk. I don't know what he's working on, but he looks miserable most of the time. Hasn't said a word to me ever since I came back into the office."

"Good," I say. Nick doesn't deserve to be in the FBI, not after what he pulled. I'm surprised Janice even took him off leave. Part of me is anticipating returning to the office so I can confront him again.

"So how's Stanley?" Zara asks, mocking me.

"Grumpy as ever," I reply. "But he had a good insight today, something that's thrown a wrench in the investigation."

"Lay it on me," she says. "Let's figure it out."

"Okay," I say, and I proceed to give her all the information we've learned so far. I describe each of the scenes to her, along with the states of the victims, including Perry. I end with Farmer's theory that someone had access to Sam Phelps and intentionally placed him in that fire, but staged it to look like an accident.

"So if all that's true, then wouldn't everyone who was on his squad be implicated?" Zara asks. "Didn't they say Phelps was with them when they arrived at the fire?"

"I'm not sure, I haven't been interrogating them about it; I've been more focused on Spencer and Perry."

"Because they're the more glamorous deaths," she says. "But I think you're missing the underlying picture. If Farmer is right, then it means Phelps's entire unit conspired to kill him."

"And then start killing themselves?" I ask. "It doesn't make sense."

"No, I guess it doesn't," she replies. "But then how else do you explain Phelps getting in that house alone? On the second floor?"

I shake my head, flopping back on the bed again. "I can't. But something is definitely off here." I glance over at the clock. Eleven-fifteen. I need sleep.

"How are you feeling about everything else?" she asks, once the silence stretches between us too long.

I know she means finding the woman, but because we've been so busy, I haven't really given it much thought. "Same, I suppose. It just feels a little further away every day. Like I'm never going to find her."

"You'll find her. She's out there somewhere; it's just a matter of willpower. But if you want to quit, I'll support you either way."

"Ugh, why are you so damn nice," I say, grabbing my burrito. If I don't start eating it now, I'll fall asleep before I get the chance.

"Oh, I'm only nice with you. With everyone else I'm a complete asshole." She grins.

"Yeah, okay, go finish killing elves or whatever you're doing." I take a bite. It's not as warm as I'd like it, but the flavors are good. Better than I'd expected for the deep south.

"*Orcs*, how many times do I have to explain it? Elves are the pure form; orcs are the corrupted form."

"Goodnight Zara," I say, taking another bite.

"Sleep tight! Don't let the arsonists bite!" she ends the call and the room plummets into darkness again. I get up and switch on one of the lights, just so I can see to finish eating. Its only then I notice I've gotten some sauce on my blazer, which I quickly wipe off with a napkin. I only have the one with me, so I'll just have to live with it until I can get it clean. And most everything else in my suitcase is dirty too. Consequences of spending a week and a half trouncing around Savannah. I'll need to find a dry cleaner soon, until then, I'll just have to deal with it.

As I finish the burrito and toss the wrapper into the trash can, my phone lights up again. I absently think it's Zara again but when I see the name, I almost spit out what's left of my burrito.

"You've got to be freaking kidding me."

Chapter Eighteen

"FARMER!" I CALL OUT, HAVING PARKED HALF A BLOCK AWAY and having to run to the scene. The entire area has been taped off by the local cops and there are two more fire trucks here, both dousing the area with water. When Farmer texted me, I hadn't even had time to get out of my clothes, so it didn't take me long to get here. But from what I can tell, the blaze is already out. It probably helps that the subject of the fire was nothing more than a vehicle this time.

I duck under the tape and show my badge to keep the locals from stopping me. Farmer trots over. "I texted you as soon as we got the call." He points to the line of businesses further down on the main street. "Someone saw the vehicle burning, called it in."

"And you think it's related?" I ask, still huffing from my run over here.

"I had one of my guys run the plates on the car already. Guess who it belongs to?"

"One of Padilla's guys," I say.

He nods. "Ricky Black. The one who was conveniently off when we went by earlier today." He checks his watch. "Or yesterday now."

I glance at the two trucks that are here. "Either of these firehouse twelve?"

He shakes his head. "Out of the jurisdiction. But I'm sure Padilla knows by now. One of them would have recognized this vehicle. It was hard to miss."

I look at the remnants of the burnt-out husk. Most of what's left is metal, though there is some lime green paneling still visible under the soot. I also spot the shape of a figure in the driver's seat, the arms strung up perilously above what's left of his skull. "I assume that's Black?"

"Won't know for sure until the coroner gets a good look." He makes a motion to the ambulance parked over to the side of the scene, its lights flashing. "They keep coming, bless 'em. And every time there's no one left to save."

"Did anyone see what happened?" I ask.

"CPD patrolmen are going door to door right now," he replies.

"When can we inspect the vehicle?"

He looks over, monitoring their progress. Even though the fire is out, they'll have to make sure there can't be any flare ups. I can't help but imagining the whole car exploding just like in an action movie, but if flames did reach the gas tank it would just reignite the fire and burn longer. Hollywood likes to really exaggerate those explosions. "Maybe another ten, fifteen minutes?"

I nod. "Then I'm going to help them look for witnesses." The car is at the edge of what looks to be a residential area, set off from the main thoroughfare where all the businesses are. And every light around us is on, no doubt in response to everything that's been happening.

"Slate, you don't have to—"

"I'm tired and dirty," I say. "And if I don't keep moving, I'm going to fall asleep. So I'm going to help them canvass, see if we can't find someone who knows something."

He holds up his hands and takes a step back. "Whatever you say."

I head over to the CPD officer on scene and coordinate with him which houses they've already spoken to and which ones they haven't. I don't have high hopes for any of these places, but I begin the due diligence anyway. It's Friday night after all, someone might have seen something.

Three doors later I've come up with little more than nothing. One person heard some shouting, but figured it was neighborhood kids and decided not to look. Next thing they knew, there was a bright light outside their window. He did say he could hear the man inside, screaming for a few minutes until he went silent. That tells me what I'd already suspected: our killer is leaving his victims to burn alive.

Another person—a father—thought he saw another car but couldn't be sure. He'd been out smoking and had just gone inside when he heard what sounded like a bang. He looked out and could see the victim's vehicle, and what he thought was another car behind it, but he didn't get a good look. He just figured it was someone who'd gotten into a fender bender. The third door provides nothing of interest, other than a woman who seems overly eager to know if this is going to be on the news tomorrow. I leave her be.

By the time I get back to Farmer, he's begun his inspection of the car. I start near the rear, and notice where it looks like there could have been some back end damage from a collision. I can't say that happened tonight or not, but it might be a good starting point. "Farmer," I call out, pointing him to the back of the car.

"Rear-ended?" he asks.

"One of the witnesses thought they saw another car, thought it was just a minor accident. But what if it wasn't? What if the killer had targeted Black, and just waited until he could get him alone?"

"Seems plausible," he replies. "So we might be looking for a car that's damaged on the front."

"Yep. We should put out feelers to all the body shops in the morning, see if anyone brings one in. Though it would be helpful if we knew the make and model. Without a description it's pointless."

He shakes his head. "Accidents are always up on the weekends."

I make a motion at the car. "Find anything else yet?"

"No symbols if that's what you mean," he replies. "But it looks like the same accelerant was used. It's consistent with both Spencer and Perry's murders."

"But not Phelps," I say. He shakes his head. "We need to get in contact with Padilla, put his men in protective custody. Otherwise, he's not going to have anyone left," I say, running my hand through the strands of hair that have fallen down.

"But if the killer is someone on his team, then we'll never be able to uncover them. Not unless we begin searching through all their things. Hope we get lucky."

"I'm not too big on hope," I say. "But I don't see that we have much choice. Someone is obviously targeting Padilla's men, and the only way to keep them safe is to have them under guard."

Farmer shakes his head. "I don't know. That's also going to put an entire firehouse out of order. The city can't afford to do that."

"Then bring in personnel from other stations," I practically yell. "This is number four. I don't want the director of the FBI to ask me why we didn't put a stop to this when we're looking at four more bodies! There's no telling how far this killer will go. He could be looking to take out the entire squadron." I look back at the car. "In the most brutal way possible."

"He couldn't take out the entire squadron unless he was

willing to out himself," Farmer says. "Whoever is left is the culprit."

"Assuming your theory is right," I say, looking over the car again. I examine the ground around the vehicle. It's wet from all the water, but it doesn't look like its scorched. "Did this fire spread at all?"

He shakes his head. "No indications. It looks like it was confined to the car only."

I look up. No trees above us to catch the flames, no other vehicles close that could have been damaged. In fact, I don't see any collateral damage anywhere. "This was a surgical strike," I say.

"What?"

"Look at the surrounding area. He wasn't sloppy with it; he made sure the fire wouldn't go beyond this car. Just like you said at the paintball yard. He made sure the fire stayed within the one course. Whoever this is, they know fire management skills. They're proficient."

"Which backs up my theory," he says.

I have to admit, it does. Clearly, whoever is doing this knows what they're doing. They're taking things like environmental factors into consideration, even here, when they can't completely control all the variables. So they are careful. It also implies there's a conscience at work here; someone who doesn't want to inflict unnecessary pain. And yet they're willing to hurt these men, to make them suffer in the worst way.

I lean over to look at what I assume are the skeletal remains of Ricky Black. As with the others, the damage to him is concentrated around his face and neck, probably where the fire started and burned the longest. I can't imagine being lit on fire, then having it travel down my throat, burning me from the inside. I don't even like when I touch something too hot on the stove.

Farmer comes up beside me, examining the corpse as well.

"Call Padilla," I say. "We need to get all of his men to safety. Now."

"He won't like it," Farmer says.

"I don't care," I reply. "We have to put a stop to this. By any means necessary. This is the third death in as many days. If we don't do anything, I feel like we can expect another tomorrow. And another the day after that. If not sooner."

Farmer grumbles something then heads off with his cell phone in his hand. I move to the side as his forensics team heads into the area around the vehicle. It will take them some time to collect all the evidence left behind.

Curious that the killer decided to kill Ricky in his car. I can't help but wonder if the places where he's committing the murders have some significance. Obviously the bar where Greg Perry was killed was connected to the fire department in some way; it wasn't uncommon for them to get together there on occasion. I'll have to ask Padilla if the paintball yard was a regular haunt for his guys too. I could see it. But what about Ricky's car? What could have triggered him to burn the man in his own vehicle? I make a note to check the vehicular history of the car, see if anything stands out.

As I let the forensics team go to work, I walk the perimeter, looking for the same symbol. I don't expect to find it here, considering this is a mobile location. How could the killer have known this was where it was going to take place? Taking the time to leave the symbol after the fire would have been too risky; someone might have seen him. I'll also be interested to see if they recover Ricky Black's wallet from his pocket. If so, it indicates another change in how the killer is operating. It indicates he's taking more risks. Perhaps the car was just convenience; a way to eliminate Black without a lot of setup. Our trip to the firehouse yesterday may have spooked him. Which means he'll only get bolder and faster if he wants to finish what he's started.

The one good thing about having them all in protective

custody will mean that I can start questioning them one by one. I definitely want another run at McKenzie. He knows way more than he's letting on. And if I can get him away from Padilla long enough, I think I'll be able to crack him.

"Slate!" Farmer calling me breaks me out of my train of thought. I head over in his direction as he's speaking to the CPD officer in charge on the scene.

"Yeah?" I ask.

Farmer turns to me. "Good news. We found a witness."

Chapter Nineteen

"PLEASE STATE YOUR NAME FOR THE RECORD," I SAY.

"Layla Nicole Berr."

"Is that b-e-a-r?" I ask.

"No, b-e-r-r, it just sounds like the animal."

We're sitting in an interrogation room in the CPD's fourth precinct, the one closest to the location of the fire. The young woman across from us looks about as scared as she can be, using a thin blanket to cover her bare shoulders.

After canvasing all the houses close to the scene of the crime, some of the officers went out further, down to the businesses that run along the main thoroughfare there. Only two were still open, a club and a late-night fast food joint, but after a few questions, they managed to find Layla, who volunteered she'd seen Ricky earlier in the evening.

"I want to reiterate that you're not under arrest, Ms. Berr, nor are you a suspect in the crime. We just want to know what happened."

She seems like she's still in shock because she hasn't been very responsive since we brought her here. Farmer was the one who got the blanket for her, putting it around her shoulders. As soon as it was there, she grabbed onto it like it was a parachute.

"You told the officers you went out with Ricky in his car, is that correct?" I ask.

"I didn't know his name. But he had the lime green car," she says, in something of a daze. I can't tell if it's from the news itself, or if she took something earlier in the evening, though her pupils aren't dilated.

"That's right," I say. "Can you tell us what happened after you got in the car with him?"

She gives a little shake of her head, not really looking at anything other than the table between us. "Just…fooled around a little. He was driving us…I never should have gotten in that car."

"Why?" Farmer asks. "Did something happen?"

She glares at him like he has two heads. "Duh! He's dead. *You're* the one who told me that."

"I meant, did something else happen?" Farmer says, and I can hear that frustrated undercurrent in his voice.

I hold my hand up to him. "Layla, take your time. Just tell us what you can."

She takes a deep breath. "We got in the car and things were…good. He drove around the block from the club, but I could already tell by the look on his face we weren't going to make it very far. I tend to have that effect on guys." She seems to come back to herself for a brief second. "But then, before I can really get going, some jerk rear-ends us, before he can even get the car parked. It wasn't a hard hit, so I didn't see why he got so upset."

"You mean Ricky?" I ask.

"Yeah, whatever his name was. He got *pissed*. Jumped out of the car, started yelling, cursing. I'd had a few so I figured I'd just stay in the car, but then he gets freaked out, asking where the other guy is."

Farmer leans forward. "The other driver?"

"Yeah. I got out of the car and the other guy's door was open, but he wasn't there. There was no one in the car. I said something to Ricky—I guess—but I don't remember what. All I remember is him telling me to shut my mouth. I should have seen it earlier, with that stunt he pulled at the bar…nice guys don't do that. But he was cute, so I figured why not?"

"Wait, wait. Back up," I say. "You're saying when you got out of the vehicle, the other driver wasn't in the car, right?"

"Right," she says.

I skip over the other part as I'm not entirely sure what she's talking about. "Then what happened?"

"After he mouthed off at me, I left. I don't care how cute a guy is, it's not worth it. I just walked back to the club to meet up with my friends again, seeing as they're the only way I had back home." She pauses and stares at the table again. "But if I'd stayed…I could have died in that car, just like him, right?"

I exchange looks with Farmer. "Let's focus on what did happen, not what could have. You're here, you're safe. And we don't believe anyone is coming after you."

"But how do you *know* that?" she asks, the pitch of her voice going up a few octaves. "I mean, they could be waiting for me out there. As soon as I'm done with you, they'll finish the job."

"Layla," I say, in the most calming voice I have. "Trust me, this wasn't about you. If anything, I believe the killer may have spared you because you weren't his target."

"Spared me?" she asks.

I nod. "Based on the information we have; we don't believe you were in danger. We still don't."

"But…how can that be?" she asks.

I shake my head. "I'm sorry, but we can't reveal information about the case to the public."

"And you're sure he won't come after me?"

I nod. "I'm sure. Now, when you were walking away, did you happen to get a look at the car that hit you?"

She pulls the blanket tighter around her. "I think so. It was dark, but I think it was gray or black. Or, you know, that darker gray color, one of those."

"Any idea what kind of car it was?" I ask.

"I dunno. Not a very nice one, I know that."

"Sedan, SUV, truck?" Farmer asks.

"Sedan I think. It was smaller. Definitely not a truck or SUV. And not a Jeep. I have one of those, so I would have recognized it."

"If we showed you a few pictures, do you think you could pick out the vehicle for us?" I ask.

"I…I guess so," she says.

I look over what few notes I've taken. "Did you see anything else? Hear anyone else as you were walking back?"

She shakes her head. "Like I said I was still tipsy. And pissed. I just wanted to get back to my friends." I can see there's something else she's not saying, something deeper.

"Layla, I really need you to be straight here," I say. "If there's something you're not telling us…" I leave the words hanging in the air.

She sniffs once and shakes her head.

Farmer gives me a subtle shake of the head as well. Whatever she's holding back, she's not about to reveal to us yet. Maybe after some time she'll be able to. In the meantime, I want to get her pictures of some vehicles. We both stand. "We'll be back in a few minutes, Layla. Do you want anything? Something to eat?"

"It'll just bloat me," she says in a sad sort of way and lays her head on the table. Farmer rolls his eyes, and we make our way out of the interview room into the hallway. I motion to the patrolman standing near the door.

"Would you put together some images of standard model

dark sedans from the last five years for me? I want her looking over them."

"Yes ma'am," he says and heads off. I have to say, I'm finding the Charleston PD to be much more amenable to me being here than my previous postings.

"What do you think?" I ask Farmer.

"I think she was drunk and isn't reliable enough to give us any credible information," he replies.

"Except for the fact she was spared," I say. "The killer saw her in the car with Black and knew he couldn't attack him while they were together. That's why he jumped out of the car right after the accident."

"That's one hell of a supposition," Farmer says.

I shake my head. "It fits the pattern. This guy is careful. Meticulous. You were just commenting that he hadn't let the fire spread any further than necessary. He's not going to take an innocent life, not if he can help it."

"And what of Mrs. Orla?" Farmer asks. "What did she do to deserve his wrath?"

"I don't know. Maybe she was a mistake. All I can assume is Phelps was his first target and he didn't know what he was doing yet. But the evidence is clear, he could have killed them both and he waited until Layla was gone before attacking Black."

"Is that what the profile tells you?" he asks. I shoot him a glance and he actually smiles, though he shakes his head as he does it. "Hell, I don't have a better theory. But that's all it is, a theory. We still need to catch this guy."

"Where are we with Padilla?" I ask.

"I've got a call into him," Farmer says. "But it's the middle of the night. It will be morning before he can get his men rounded up. Not to mention all the paperwork this is going to take. Which, I believe, is your department."

He's right. Getting protective custody approval for twenty-four—make that twenty-three people is not going to be easy, cheap, or fast. "I need to call my boss."

He chuckles. "I bet you do. I'll go help get those pictures together." He wanders off after the officer.

I sigh, pulling out my phone. Despite the fact it's two-thirty in the morning, I don't have a choice but to call Janice. This is getting out of control, fast.

Chapter Twenty

THE MOMENT MY HEAD HITS THE PILLOW I HEAR A KNOCKING at my hotel room door. Why the hell would someone be knocking this early? It's barely three-thirty in the morning. Grumbling, I turn over, my exhausted and addled mind hoping it's just housekeeping, and they'll go away. However, the knocking only continues with increasing frequency.

"What, what, what?" I yell, getting out of bed and flinging open the door.

"You know, you really should be more careful around here, I could have been a stone-cold killer."

"Zara?" I ask.

She stands in front of me with one hand grasping the handle of a suitcase beside her and a warm cup of coffee in the other. Her platinum blonde hair is perfectly styled. "What are you doing here?"

"Nice to see you too," she says, smiling sweetly as she leans in for a quick hug. "Here, this is for you, I know you need it. I've already had two." She hands me the coffee and pulls her bag into the room, letting the door close behind her. "Oh, this is so much nicer than what I'd pictured." She looks around at the décor, which has been inspired by Charleston's rich history.

The coffee smells heavenly and I can't help but just stand there and inhale the aroma. But there's no way I'm drinking it this early; I'll never get back to sleep. "Zara, what's going on, how are you here? I just called Janice an hour ago."

She flings open the curtains and I can see daylight beginning to illuminate the streets below. "Better check your clock, sleeping beauty," she says. "It's almost seven."

"What?" I check my phone to find out she's right. "I can't believe it; I feel like I just fell asleep." After calling Janice to inform her about the developments in the case I was so tired I barely remember getting back to the hotel. I could have sworn I hadn't been down more than a minute. "Wait, how are you here?"

"Flying dragon," she says, opening her suitcase and flinging some of her clothes on the other bed.

"What?"

"I took the first flying dragon in from D.C. this morning. Big pink one. His name was Jean-Pierre. Super nice."

I grab one of her shirts and fling it at her. "Smartass." I take a sip of the coffee, relishing the aroma even more. I'm gonna need about a dozen of these things today. "Don't tell me you took another leave. Janice is going to have your head on a pike."

She shakes her head. "Nope. All official, baby. I'm your reinforcement. Despite getting like no sleep. When we spoke I didn't expect I'd have to get up in the middle of the night and fly down here, but those were my orders." She looks around. "Where's the rest of that burrito? I know you didn't finish it."

I have to admit I'm a little stunned. Though Janice didn't seem particularly fazed last night, I didn't expect any additional assistance from her. She told me she'd get the field office down here started on processing the protective custody orders.

I shake my head. "No way, I don't believe it. You skipped or something."

"It gets even better," she says, sitting on the edge of one of the beds. She's produced a bag of Fritos from somewhere and is crunching on them. "Janice sacked Nick this morning. Or last night. Margreeves sent me a text right after I landed. She made an announcement as soon as everyone was in the office."

"No way," I say. "Did Margreeves give you any details?"

"Just that his employment with the federal government was over and that no one was to engage with him on a professional level if he approached them."

"Damn," I say, sitting on the other bed. It'll be nice not having to worry about him when I get back to D.C. "I guess she just had him doing his exit work. But I still don't see why she sent you back down here after recalling you only a day ago."

Zara shrugs. "Who knows why she does what she does. Janice works in mysterious ways."

"Or she knows this case is huge and pulling you off was premature. This might be one of those rare times when she realized she made a mistake."

She tosses me a Frito, but it just bounces off my leg to the floor. "Don't tell her that. Plus, you have your hands full. And with Farmer being *el dicko*, you need all the help you can get."

"I think he's beginning to soften," I say, getting back up and heading into the bathroom to turn on the shower. Zara being here reminds me of everything we have to do today, which means I need to be ready and out of here in fifteen.

"You're saying I should turn around, go back home?"

"Of course not. Who else would bring me my coffee?" I say, holding it up in a mock salute to her before I disappear behind the doorframe.

A wayward shirt flies past the open door. Even though

nothing has changed in the case, I feel more hopeful than I have in days.

"Well, well, if it isn't Kid Rocket, back to join us," Farmer says as Zara and I make our way back into his office. When I called to make sure he was still here, I neglected to inform him Zara had returned. But he doesn't seem surprised.

"What the hell is Kid Rocket?" I ask.

"TV show from the 70's. You know that thing you used to watch before everyone stared at phones or computer screens all day long? Before your time, I guess," he says. "Anyway, energetic little thing. About half the size of everyone around him, though he was obsessed with catching the bad guy. Though to me he always seemed like he was on the edge of popping off."

"You want to talk about size?" Zara points to his gut. "I wouldn't be talking if I were you." She turns to me. "Seems to be about the same gigantic ass to me."

"Now children, play nice," I say. "We've got a shit ton of work to do. Did you talk to Padilla yet?"

Farmer tosses the file he was looking through on his desk. "You mean during the final fire inspection and the two hours of sleep I logged in the break room? Yeah, I did, but you're not going to like his response."

"Let me guess, he's not too enthused about being put into protective custody."

Farmer grimaces. "Outright refused. Said it was unnecessary and that it would put the public interest at risk."

"Oh, I can tell I'm gonna like this guy," Zara says, walking around to see the other side of Farmer's desk. She bends down, getting a good look at his screen. "What kind of security programs do you guys have? All we're using is the old

ATMOS system. Have they at least given the ATF something that was coded in this century?"

"What is she doing?" Farmer asks.

"*She's* assessing the operational capacity of your systems," Zara replies. "We recently dealt with something of a...not so much a breach, but a conflict of interest with a contractor who provided the FBI with one of its tools. They're still scrambling to find a replacement."

Farmer turns back to me, shaking his head. "Anyway, Padilla said neither him, nor any of his guys were going anywhere. Taking twenty-three men off the field would leave too large a hole in the system. It would be negligent."

I sigh. "Did you tell him about Black?"

Farmer nods.

"And?"

"He's mad as hell we haven't caught the guy yet. Called me a few choice names I won't repeat. But at the same time, he's not willing to lock himself in his home until this is over."

"Shit," I say. "What do we do, put a guy on each of them to watch their every move? I can probably pull some personnel from the satellite office here, but still, that's going to be a massive job. Assuming three shifts, that's at least seventy people. There's no way."

"I don't know what to tell—don't touch that!" Farmer says and Zara immediately backs away from his desk, a huge smile on her face. I give her *the look*, to which she only shrugs and smirks back.

"Did Padilla tell his unit what's going on?" I ask. "Did he give them a choice?"

Farmer shakes his head. "I doubt it. It wasn't a long conversation. He never had the time."

"Then we need to make the case to them ourselves," I say. "Otherwise, one of those men is going to be our next victim. And I'd really like to stop anyone else from getting killed if we can help it." I glance over at the clock. "Given his pattern, we've got until around eleven p.m. which gives us just over fourteen hours to find every person on that squad and convince them it's in their best interests to come in until we catch this guy."

"Even though one of the people we bring in might *be* our guy," Farmer says.

"Yeah, even then. I don't see we have much of a choice. The more people we can eliminate, the better chance we'll have of finding the killer and stopping him."

"Has anything come back from any repair shops?" Zara asks. "You said the car that hit the one you guys investigated this morning should have front-end damage, right?"

Farmer shakes his head. "And Layla wasn't much help either. She couldn't tell a Toyota from a Jaguar. Still, we've got an APB out on a vehicle matching what little she gave us."

"Really?" I ask. "Those are drastically different types of cars."

"Some people just don't have the eye for it," he replies. "I'm the same way with soda. Coke, Pepsi, Pepper, it all tastes the same to me. Can't tell one from the other."

"Now you've made a fatal mistake," I say, glaring at Zara. "She's going to test your hypothesis, see if that's really true or not."

Farmer immediately covers the foam cup on his desk. "That doesn't mean I can't taste anything." He turns to Zara. "I find out you're adding salt or some shit to my coffee…"

"You know what?" Zara says, appraising him. "I was wrong, he *has* softened some. And in only two days. Not bad."

Farmer takes a deep breath, glaring at her under hooded eyes. "When can you start coordinating with your satellite office down here? I can have my guys help with the canvassing, but it's going——"

My phone vibrates in my pocket and I hold up a finger while I answer. "Slate."

"Detective?" a shaky voice asks on the other end.

"It's Special Agent, actually. Who is this?"

"Dan McKenzie. We met yesterday, at the fire station?"

"I remember," I say, motioning for Zara to grab me something to write on. "What can I do for you, Mr. McKenzie?" Farmer's eyes go wide. I put the phone on speaker so they can both hear as well.

"You told me if I remembered anything else to give you a call." He sounds more than nervous. I would even say he's scared.

"That's right. Do you recall something about the other men?"

"No...well, maybe. But I just heard about Ricky. Agent Slate, we need to talk in person."

I don't want to lose him again and give Padilla the chance to intercept us. But I can understand someone not wanting to talk on the phone. When informants are nervous, they often prefer to meet in person. It gives them a greater sense of security. "I can do that. Can you meet now?" I check my watch. This will also give us a chance to get McKenzie under protection, though all the paperwork hasn't come through yet. But I'd still feel a lot better about him sitting in a waiting room here or at the FBI rather than out there where he's nothing but a moving target.

"Not now," he says. "I need to take my kids to soccer practice and my wife is still home. I don't want them to know anything about this."

So far, the killer hasn't shown any interest in any of the victim's families, but that could change. We might have to consider putting the families under protection as well, but we'll already be stretching our resources thin. I'm not sure we can manage it. But I'll deal with that problem when we come to it. Right now, I'm much more interested in what McKenzie has to say. "When's the soonest we could sit down?"

"Give me until about noon," he says. "There's a small

southern diner over off Old Towne Road, the Curly Pig, know it?"

Farmer nods. "Yes, we will meet you there."

"Okay. I'll see you then. Thank you, Agent." He hangs up.

"Well, that's one down," I say. "Only twenty-two more to go."

Chapter Twenty-One

"Heard from Chris?"

The question is so sudden it catches me off guard. Zara and I are sitting in the rental car outside the Curly Pig, waiting for McKenzie to arrive. The two of us, along with Farmer's entire team, spent most of the morning reaching out to the firefighters of station twelve, but only finding about half of them. Unfortunately, it seems like Padilla's word is law as only a few of them were even interested in talking with us, much less coming in for protection.

I don't know what it is about these "band of brothers" types, but I'm pretty sure if someone was hunting down the people in my squad, I'd want as much protection as someone was willing to offer me. But it seems to me like they all have some kind of understanding that they don't go against the wishes of their commanding officer. Almost like a code. I can understand that...to a point. But they are literally putting their lives in his hands, and I'm not convinced Padilla isn't wrapped up in this somehow. His constant refusal to cooperate is only making him look more and more suspicious by the minute. I'm hoping McKenzie will be able to shed some light on the subject for us.

I can't help but check my phone every few minutes. We have less than twelve hours until the next murder.

"Yo, you awake?" Zara asks.

"Yes, just avoiding the question," I say. "No, I haven't heard from Chris. Not since we came down to Savannah."

"Have you even *tried*?" she asks.

I let out a long breath. My relationship with my ex-brother-in-law is complicated. If he and his wife weren't taking care of my dog, we'd have no relationship at all. But at least they're not willing to hold a grudge against an animal for the actions of his momma. "I don't want to come off as nagging."

"It's not nagging if you just want to check up on your only child."

The thing is, Timber was Matt's dog too. And they're animal lovers, so I know they're taking good care of him. If I weren't absolutely sure about them, I would never have left him there. And it's not like it's a permanent arrangement, despite what my sister-in-law thinks. I just need to close this chapter of my life, get my head straight and get back to a normal routine.

"They've got that big yard," I say. "I'm sure he's having the time of his life with their other dogs. At least he's not alone all day long."

"I thought about getting a cat," she says.

I nod. "Makes sense. Nocturnal, always getting into things they shouldn't be…mischievous. Fits you like a glove."

"Same problem though," she says. "It would be alone most of the time. That's not as bad for a cat as it is a dog, since I'm convinced cats pretty much think we're all assholes anyway, but still…I'd feel bad."

A silence extends between us. "Thanks for coming back," I finally say. "I know this wasn't all Janice. You were in there somewhere."

She gives me a warm smile. "Maybe. But I couldn't just let you tackle this all on your own, could I?"

"No, you absolutely could have," I say. "I wouldn't have blamed you one bit."

"What's that supposed to mean?" she asks.

"Nothing. I've just felt—ever since losing Matt I've felt like I don't really fit in this world anymore. Like I'm an outsider."

She turns the air up a notch. As the heat of the day is settling in, its only getting warmer in the car. "I think everyone feels like that at some point. I've felt like that most of my life."

"Really?" I ask.

"Oh definitely. I mean, at the very least I was born in the wrong decade."

I bark out a laugh. "I can't imagine you being a sixties kid."

She shakes her head, her short hair doing a little swish. "Wrong direction. I should have been born in the 2040s or something. The technology of today is too limiting."

"You have the entire sum of human knowledge in your pocket!" I say. "What more could you want?"

"Totally immersive virtual reality simulations, brainwave connections to the grid, and most important, autonomous robotic bodies that look and feel human. You know, so we can live forever."

"Maybe you'll get lucky, and they'll have all that stuff by the time you're a grandma."

She starts chuckling, which turns into a full-on belly laugh. "A grandma? Me? I'm not even going to be a 'ma'."

"Really? You always talked about having someone to settle down with."

"Yeah, that doesn't mean kids though," she says. "At least not unless I can hire a nanny or something. If I don't have enough time for a cat, I definitely don't have time for kids."

"I know what you mean," I say. "Matt and I had the discussion early and decided to hold off for a while. Eventually I think we just accepted the idea that neither of us really wanted them. But it was gradual, not something we just sat down and decided one day."

"And now?" she asks. "Still feel the same?"

I have to admit, it would be nice to still have some part of him in the form of a child, maybe with his eyes or his chin, but it wouldn't change how I feel. And it would be unfair to the kid, to put that kind of pressure on them. I'm already doing that with Timber, I imagine it would only be worse with a human child. "No regrets in that department."

"Good," she says. "So where the hell is this guy?"

I check the clock on the dash. It's a quarter past twelve and I haven't seen any indication of him yet. "Maybe he slipped past us, let's check inside."

We both step out into the sticky air. "Past you? Ol' eagle eye? I don't think so," Zara says. We make our way into the Curly Pig and immediately my stomach flips at what would normally be the delicious smell of fresh bar-b-que, the bodies of Greg Perry and Ricky Black prominent in my mind. I swallow and force myself to keep from throwing up.

"What's wrong?" Zara asks.

"Could this have been a setup?" I ask. "McKenzie rubbing it in our faces?"

"I don't get it," she says, looking around. "I don't see the guy you described anywhere. How is this a setup?"

"Because it smells exactly like burnt human flesh," I say a little too loudly. A few of the patrons turn in our direction, their eyes wide.

"C'mon," Zara says, ushering me outside. "You think he's screwing with us? That he's been the killer this whole time and he sent us here for what? Just to mess with you?"

I shake my head, happy to get a fresh breath of air. "I don't know; but if Farmer's theory is right and the killer is one of the men on the squad, it makes sense. He fits the profile."

"But why out himself like this?" she asks. "Unless he's finished his 'job'." She uses air quotes to emphasize her point.

"We need to find Dan McKenzie, right now," I say. "Something isn't right. He feared something or someone yesterday. He might physically match the profile, but mentally? No way."

"Maybe he's just a really good actor."

And if that's the case, maybe I've been too confident in my own abilities lately. I could have overlooked McKenzie because he came across as meek. But then what was yesterday all about? I just don't buy it. Maybe the BBQ place was just an unfortunate coincidence.

"Here, I've got his address from the files we were going through earlier," Zara says, heading back to the car. "Let's just go to his house."

I nod. If his family is there, we'll have to be discreet. Part of me can't help but think about Gerald Wright, and how when we'd left him alone he'd kidnapped his own children and attempted to kill them. I hope McKenzie isn't nearly that sadistic…or stupid. But I can't get the feeling out of my gut that something about all of this feels off. I'll feel a lot better once we have McKenzie under guard where I can pepper him with questions regarding everyone in the squad.

Including Padilla.

The drive over to his home isn't far. Like most of the fire-fighters who work at station twelve, he lives relatively close to his home base, which makes sense. It's a modest neighbor-hood, like a lot of the neighborhoods I've seen in Charleston. Granted, I've been working outside of the city center most of the time, so the houses out here have a little more yard and land than those on the peninsula itself. It's also where I imagine most of the suburbanites live. Single-family homes, small plots of land, nice little neighborhoods where kids can ride their bikes without worrying about traffic.

We pull up to McKenzie's house which sits at the end of a

cul-de-sac. An open field sits behind the house which seems to empty into a marshy area, all of it covered with trees.

As soon as I step out of the car, an acrid smell hits my nose, like burnt newspaper. Zara and I exchange a look. I glance around for anyone who might be out grilling on a Saturday afternoon but see no indications it's coming from somewhere else. The cul-de-sac is quiet, empty. When I turn back to McKenzie's house, I can tell the smell is definitely coming from there. "Call Farmer," I yell at Zara as I sprint up the driveway. "And call 911!"

"Em, don't you do it!" she yells back and within a second she is hot on my heels. Just as I'm about to reach the front door she slams into me from behind, grabbing my waist and pulling me away from the house.

"What are you doing?"

"You have no id—" Her words are cut off by a massive explosion of heat, which knocks us both to the ground. The air is filled with sounds of crackling and burning, the deafening booms of more explosions. I feel like my skin is on fire. Debris and glass rain down on us and I cover my face to protect it the best I can, trying to crawl away from what used to be Dan McKenzie's house, which is now a raging inferno.

"Zara!" I yell out.

"Here," she calls somewhere beside me. "Get clear!"

"I'm trying!" The heat is searing. I can't tell if I'm actually on fire or not, but it sure feels like it. We crawl on our bellies until we're almost back to the street. Both of us turn to look back at the house which is engulfed in flames.

Somewhere inside, I hear a man screaming.

Chapter Twenty-Two

WE MANAGED TO MAKE IT BACK TO THE CAR AND BACK IT AWAY from the house, so it wouldn't inadvertently catch fire as well. But I feel like I've just run through a burning gauntlet. My blazer smells of smoke and ash, and I feel like my hair has been singed.

I look over at Zara, who seems more rattled than I'd expected. "Hey," I say. "We're okay." I take both her arms, looking them over for any burns, but find nothing. Her face shows no burns either, just a little dirty from crawling along the ground.

"Do you think the family was in there?" she asks. Her normal confidence has been wiped away, which, considering the circumstances, is understandable.

I turn back to the fire as sirens sound in the distance. "I don't think so," I reply. "That's not his style. But I bet McKenzie was."

"Did you hear the screaming too?" she asks. I nod. I'll be hearing that sound in my dreams.

Less than a minute later, the fire trucks arrive, one of them from station twelve. I recognize some of the guys from yesterday. As soon as they see the scene, their faces go pale. They already know whose house this was. And they probably already suspect who was inside. But it doesn't stop them from doing their job. They start coating the fire with water from one of the trucks while the other hooks up to the local hydrant.

A few moments later, Farmer pulls up, along with a few cars from the CPD. By now, the neighbors have come out to look at the blaze and the attempts to smother it.

"Slate, Foley, what happened?" Farmer asks, jogging up to us.

"McKenzie never showed at the restaurant," I say. "We think he's still in there."

"*Je-sus*," Farmer says, watching the men try to douse the fire. "Is that McKenzie's house?" I nod.

I can't help but go into analysis mode—it's the only thing that's keeping me from losing it right now. If I think too hard about what just happened, I'll shut down. "He's changing tactics again. The timing is off. It's not nighttime yet and he's never used anything with any kind of explosives in it before."

"Explosives?" Farmer asks.

"He blew the house up," Zara says. "Almost took us with it."

I reach over and grab her shoulder, giving it a gentle squeeze. She saved my life back there. If it weren't for her, I would have been right at the door when the whole place blew. I would have been killed instantly.

"This has gotten out of hand," Farmer says. "At this rate, he'll have killed them all by the middle of next week."

"We need to lock these guys down," I tell him. "I don't care if they want to do it or not. We lock them down or we find some reason to lock them up. Either way, they need to be off the streets."

"You're right," Farmer says. "We need to talk to Padilla, face to face."

"I'm sorry." Zara leans forward. "Can you say that again?

I thought you said Emily was right." She seems to be coming back into herself a little more, but I can tell she's still shaken. I know later I'll be a wreck. But not right now.

"I did," Farmer replies. "You need me to say any more?"

I appreciate her support; I really do. But right now, we need answers. "I want to canvas the scene," I say.

"Now?" he asks. "When the building is still on fire?"

I look over, and it seems like they have the blaze under control. A few more minutes and they'll have it down. Thankfully, it didn't have time to burn long. "Right now. While things are still fresh. We're getting closer. I can practically feel us closing in on him. And he's speeding up in an attempt to finish as much as he can before we catch him. It might be making him sloppy."

"Okay but stay back until they've cleared the house. Perimeter work only." He starts barking orders at some of his forensics teams who have just showed up in their own vehicles.

I motion for Zara to follow me to the far side of the property, on the left-most side of what used to be the house. "Are you okay?" I ask.

"Physically? I think so. Mentally I think I'll be scarred for life."

"You saved my ass. Literally."

She glares at me. "This is why I can't leave you alone anywhere." I drop my head. Running up to the house was stupid; I knew it at the time. But I thought if we could catch this guy in the act, it would all be over. I didn't expect him to blow the entire structure. "Hey," she says, causing me to look up. "I can't let my best friend just run into a burning building, can I?"

"Wasn't burning when we got here," I say.

She purses her lips. "It was burning. We smelled it."

"Yeah, well...thank you. I don't know how I can ever express my gratitude."

That wicked smile of hers returns. "Oh, I do."

My eyes go wide. "No way. Not doing it. I'll run back in that building before—"

"Oh yes. As soon as we're back in D.C. Karaoke night, you and me, up on stage, in front of the entire crowd. And we're doing Sir Mix-A-Lot." She presses a finger into my chest. "You're out of excuses now. I practically own you."

I let out a long sigh, turning back to the house which is still being doused with water. Due to how quickly the department responded, most of it is still up, but they'll have to check the structural integrity before we can go in. "Come on," I say. "Let's check the perimeter."

"Don't change the subject," she says, trotting after me. "*Baby Got Back* or *Monster Mack*. Your choice."

"I don't even know that second one," I say, trudging across the lawn.

"That's the beauty of karaoke, you don't have to. The words are right there for you to read. But you have to really try! You can't just monologue it."

I let out a frustrated grunt, knowing she's loving every second of this. I have never sung karaoke in my life, and I'm not about to start right now. I'll just have to get sick or something.

"C'mon, let's practice right now," she says, despite my best attempts to ignore her. "*My anaconda don't want none unless…*"

"No," I say, "Not doing it."

"You have to," she says. "It's in the contract."

I turn back to her. "What contract?"

"The friend contract," she replies, grinning. "Now do it."

"Zara—"

"Doooo itttt," she insists.

"*Ugh!* Fine. *Unless you got buns, hun.*"

"Yesss!" she says, doing a full body fist pump. "I cannot wait to get you up there. It's gonna be so good. We can make it a weekly thing, you know? Like a date. You're gonna be this great singer and get booked at all the dive bars looking for tribute bands. I can't—"

"Zara," I say, stopping a few feet from the backyard.

"Huh?" She looks around me. "Oh."

McKenzie's backyard is mostly hardscape. There's an elevated porch that's attached to the back of the house, but it's only a foot or so off the ground. Beyond it is a hardscaped patio that extends back into a sitting area and a fire pit, appropriately enough, surrounded by some chairs. The porch itself is singed from the fire, but it doesn't look like it was burning long enough to do a lot of damage. Instead, I'm more interested in the patio. In the center, painted around the fire pit, is the same symbol we saw at the bar where we found Greg Perry. A circle, with the fire pit in the middle, with two smaller circles on either side. There's no bisecting line this time. But my eye catches a small object near the middle of the fire pit.

"Gloves," I say.

"Already ahead of you," she replies. "You weren't kidding when you said ritual."

"Ever seen it before?" I ask.

"I don't think so. But it won't take me long to figure out what it represents. I'm great at image searches."

"The previous markings had the big circle with a line through the middle," I say. "But this one doesn't." I walk over, careful where I step, though it doesn't look like there is any debris this far away from the home. The stones are relatively untouched, other than a bit of green algae from not being cleaned in a while.

"Is that a wallet in the fire pit?" Zara asks.

I nod. "More than likely McKenzie's," I say, realizing now that we've lost the only person willing to tell us what was really going on. The killer must have gotten wind of McKenzie wanting to talk to us and decided to silence him before he had a chance. And the only person I can think of who could have known would be Padilla.

"You think his boss did this?" Zara asks.

"I think there's no way he's not involved," I reply. "He conveniently silenced McKenzie yesterday when we were at the station. Every one of the victims has been someone on his team. And he's refusing protection. I feel like that's enough to at least bring him in for questioning." I pull out my phone and take a picture of the scene. Then snap a closer one of the wallet. "Let's see if there's anything useful inside."

Zara picks up the wallet, opening it, and begins to remove the contents. From what I can tell it doesn't seem like anything is missing. She takes out McKenzie's driver's license and firefighter ID card, along with an insurance card, a couple of credit cards, a folded up fifty and a couple of twenties, and some old receipts. She also removes a torn piece of paper with numbers written on it. Something about the sequence seems familiar.

"What?" Zara asks. "You've got that look."

"I think it's a locker combination," I say.

Chapter Twenty-Three

AFTER CATALOGING ALL OF THE WALLET'S CONTENTS AND waiting for the forensics team to meet with us so they could maintain the proper chain of evidence, it takes a few more hours for us to fully walk the scene, given the dangerous nature of everything. Much like the bar where we found Greg Perry, the house is in ruins, and the hottest part burned right where we find the only body: in what seems to me like a rec room of sorts. The skeleton of a foosball table stands in the far side of the room and a large blackened television sits off to the side. The entire room smells of burnt plastic and metal, and of course, bar-b-que.

Zara covers her mouth and nose as we walk through, getting a good look at what remains of who I presume is Dan McKenzie. He's upright, affixed to a chair with nylon rope that's melted through what remain of his wrists, covering them in a gooey substance. As much as I hate it, I'm starting to get used to the smell of burnt flesh. It doesn't bother me nearly as much as the other times and I'm wondering if it's just because I've been exposed to so much of it over the past few days. McKenzie makes four bodies in six days. Leon Spencer on Monday, Greg Perry on Wednesday, Ricky Black yesterday, and now McKenzie. The killer is definitely moving quicker now. Sam Phelps was almost three weeks ago. Now he's killing one per day.

"Farmer?" I ask. The man walks over, inspecting the remains of McKenzie.

"Very similar to the others," he says after a cursory evaluation. "Same kind of accelerant, though I'm not sure why—" He cuts himself off as he walks over to inspect the stove. "Gas was left on. The crews cut it at the street as soon as they arrived, but it was on before the explosion." He looks over at the microwave, which is little more than a metal box. The door is completely missing, and the entire thing is black, charred, and warped. "Probably used the microwave as a timer. Could have placed a bit of aluminum foil inside. Or something he could have used to spark the explosion. He wouldn't have had much time to get out though."

We never saw anyone fleeing the house, but that doesn't mean the killer couldn't have gone out through the back, which actually makes sense, given where the spray paint and wallet were found. Though he would have needed to do that before the explosion, obviously. Perhaps while he had McKenzie tied up. "Have you heard anything from any of the engine crew?" I ask.

"Most of them are in a state of shock, but my bet is Padilla has made things clear," he says. "Either they listen to him, or they'll pay for it in some way or another. Whether that's less time on the clock, more cleanup duty, or something else, I don't know."

"We need to put an end to this," I say. "No more beating around the bush. I'm taking Padilla in for questioning, and I want the rest of the firehouse locked down. Talk to the city's fire chief, let them know we're dealing with an uncontrollable situation here until we have every member of this squad in protective custody."

Farmer nods. "I'll do what I can. But don't think that

things get any better the higher up you go on the chain of command."

"At some point, someone is going to have to admit it doesn't make sense to leave these men exposed like this. Hell, talk to the governor if you have to; get the national guard involved." The look on Farmer's face tells me he doesn't like where this is going. I had hoped we could contain this situation ourselves, but it's spiraling out of control, fast.

"What are you going to do?" he asks.

I glance at Zara. "We're going to have a talk with Padilla. Bring him in if we have to."

"There's nothing connecting him to any of the scenes," Farmer says. "We can't bring him in if we don't have any evidence."

"He doesn't know what we have and what we don't," I say, heading back out to the car.

"You're going to bluff," Farmer says.

"We like to call it creative lying," Zara replies, holding her fingers like she's pinching something. "It's good for my acting prospects."

"A word of advice," Farmer says as we get out to the driveway. He waits until two of the firefighters pass us. "I've played poker with the man. He'll call if he suspects a bluff."

"Then we'll just have to make sure we're really good at doing it," I say.

———

We head over to firehouse twelve before the engine returns, only to find Padilla isn't on duty at the moment. I find it strange that the firehouse captain isn't on duty when yet *another* one of his men has been killed in a fire.

"Correct me if I'm wrong, but isn't the fire captain usually on site when fighting a fire?" Zara asks as we make our way back to the car.

"That's how I've understood it," I say.

"Has he been at all the others?"

I think back. He was definitely at Greg Perry's. But I don't recall him being at the vehicle when we found Ricky Black. And he obviously wasn't at McKenzie's house just now, though I saw Lieutenant Olsen. I don't recall seeing him at the paint yard where we found Leon Spencer, though, I got there late. He could have been there when they were still battling the fire. As for Sam Phelps, I believe I read in the report he was on site for that fire. They all were.

"Now what?" Zara asks.

"We make another house call," I say. "And hope this one doesn't explode on us. Can you pull up Padilla's address?" I take off my blazer and toss it in the back seat of the car. It's nearly three-thirty and I'm roasting. The sun only seems to be making the air hotter and wetter.

"Got it," she replies. "Winchester Drive. About fifteen minutes away."

We drive over there in silence, yet the whole time I'm seeing if I can build a case against Padilla in my head. He's not my first choice for a suspect, but I'm trying to keep an open mind. And he's at the head of what links all these people together. But what would be his motive for killing his own men? Ever since that first night at Perry's scene, I've suspected there's been something off about him. Obviously killing McKenzie would have been to keep him quiet. But why the others? Were they all going to speak up as well? And about what? What could be so important he'd be willing to kill for? And how do the symbols and the wallets fit into the equation?

When we pull up to Padilla's address, I let out a low whistle. There are already ten other cars here, some in the driveway, others parked out on the street. The house is larger than most of the others I've seen, at least two floors and all brick. The second floor has a balcony in the middle which can be accessed by double doors, like a widow's walk of sorts.

"Looks like the captain is doing well for himself," Zara says.

"And in the middle of a party," I say. The smell of fresh hamburgers and hotdogs reaches my nose as I get out of the car and grab my blazer again, pulling it on. It's not as pungent as the BBQ, but I can still detect a familiarity in cooked meats to cooked human. I don't know how they do it.

"We may not be able to go at him as hard as you first wanted," Zara says. "If he's been here for more than a few hours—"

"That's what we need to find out," I say, walking up the entry walk that runs parallel to the driveway. I plan on knocking on the door, but the inner door is already open, there's just a screen door. Inside, the raucous noise seems to be coming from all parts of the house. "I don't think they'd hear us if we knocked anyway."

"Then by all means, after you," she says, giving me a low bow.

"Oh no, after *you*," I say, mocking her. She gives me a haughty nod, then enters the house with me right behind her. A staircase to the second level sits in the middle of the hallway, while rooms branch off to the left and right. People stand in each, holding plates or drinks or both, all chatting away. It's not much cooler in here than it is outside, but all the fans in the house are running, moving the air at least.

A few people glance over as we enter, but no one really seems to pay us much attention; they're all too engrossed in their own conversations. We casually make our way through the home, as a freight train of children come running down the stairs. I take a deep breath and flatten myself up against the wall as they run by, screaming and yelling at each other. It isn't until they've passed that I realize I was holding my breath.

Zara gives me a sympathetic look as we continue through the house. The kitchen is large and expansive, with a huge island in the middle and it opens up to a family room in the back. Instead of sliding glass or French doors, Padilla has something of an indoor/outdoor thing going on, where four or five massive panels have all been pushed to one wall, which opens up the entire family room and half the kitchen to the outside. There, a pool sits about ten feet beyond the house, surrounded by a lounge area, along with an outdoor kitchen, complete with grill, which is where the smells are coming from.

I stare at that grill and all I can think of is those men burning to death.

"Don't worry," Zara says. "I doubt they're serving human today."

"Hello," a woman says, approaching us as she wipes her hands on a rag. She's tall, thin, with a perfect bob of blonde hair and is wearing active gear, right down to the Asics on her feet. She can't be more than forty, though if I had to guess I'd say she's even younger than that. "I'm sorry, we haven't met. Are you friends of Joe's from another district?"

"No ma'am," I say. "We're—"

"FBI," Padilla says, coming in from the outdoor kitchen. "This is Agent Slate," he says, indicating me. "And…"

"Agent Foley," Zara says, giving them both a nod.

"Agents, my wife, Suzanne," Padilla says. The woman gives us a sweet smile.

"So glad you could join us," she says, oblivious to the tension between me and Padilla. "Help yourselves to anything, we also have plenty to drink. Water, soda, wine coolers and beer if you like. Joe here's been on grill duty almost all after-noon, churning out burgers and hot dogs. We also have vegan options, just in case."

I shake my head. "Thank you, but we're fine."

"I don't think the agents will be staying long," Padilla says, giving me the eye. "Is there something you needed?" Finally Suzanne seems to pick up on it.

"Oh, well, nice to meet you," she says, excusing herself.

"There are two of you now?" Padilla says as soon as she's out of earshot.

"We're like the Hydra, man. Keep chopping and more heads will keep popping up," Zara says.

"I haven't—" Padilla seems like he's ready to pop under the pressure himself, which is good. That's the reaction I wanted. The last thing he'll do is make a scene in front of all his friends and neighbors. He manages to reset himself. "What do you want?"

"Just a few questions," I say. "Do you have somewhere we can talk in private?"

He nods, pushing past us and leading us back down the hall through an adjacent door into a home office.

"I assume you heard about McKenzie?" I ask as soon as the door is closed and we're alone.

"Olsen called me an hour ago," he replies, then heads over to his desk and takes a seat. I can see that he's not as calm and confident as he was yesterday. He seems to be perspiring more, though that could just be the South Carolina heat. Of course, two more of his men have died since we last spoke.

"Still not willing to go into protective custody?"

"No, and do you know why?" he asks, but seems intent on telling me without giving me the chance to answer. "Because as soon as this party my wife's had on her calendar for two months is over, I'm getting a bunch of my guys together, along with the CPD and we're gonna go out there and hunt down this son of a bitch. I'm not losing any more men to some crazy bastard with a fire fetish."

"Or, you could allow us to take your men where we know they'll be safe and under guard and then you let us handle it."

"You've had more than enough chances to handle it, Agent Slate," he replies. "And the bodies just keep piling up."

"What did McKenzie know?" I ask.

He squints at me. "What are you talking about?"

"Yesterday. He approached Farmer and me. Said Sam Phelps had something on his mind before he died. I don't guess you'd have any idea what that would be."

Padilla shakes his head slowly. "No clue."

"Any animosity between any of your guys?" I ask. "Especially in the past few weeks? Anyone not getting along?"

"What is this, am I being interrogated now?" he asks, clearly offended by the tone he's using.

"Just trying to get to the bottom of this," I say. Zara has set herself up at the far end of the room, keeping a close eye on Padilla's body language. This is something I wouldn't be able to do with Farmer; especially with the two of them being so close. But Zara knows exactly what to look for.

"My team works as one unit. We can't have guys on the team if everyone doesn't trust each other. There are lives at stake here, and if someone screws up, someone dies."

"Is that what happened with Sam?" I ask. "Did someone screw up?"

"What are you implying?" he asks.

"Tell me about the night Sam died," I say. "I mean, I've read the report. But you were there, weren't you? You saw what happened?"

He shrugs, turning in his chair some so he's facing away from the window. "Just what I said in my official report."

"Go through it again for me, if you will," I say, giving him the death stare. He knows if he refuses, it only makes him look more guilty. But if anything in his report was inaccurate, he's afraid he might get caught in a lie.

"Look, there's nothing to go through. We get the call, it's late. I pull seven or eight guys, Sam among them. Whoever was on shift. We're over there in minutes, but the house is already going up like a roman candle. We get out, start prepping the engine, looking for the hookups. Next thing I know, Olsen is yelling at Sam as he rushes the house. He's in there before any of us can pull him back and it takes us a few more minutes until I'm comfortable sending my guys in after him."

"So you're saying he just ran into a burning building, without any kind of backup?" I ask.

He holds out his hands. "Yeah. It's crazy, I know."

"Right?" Zara says. "I mean, who would do that?" She shoots a glare at me which I avoid, turning my attention back to Padilla.

"How many years had you been working with Sam?" I ask.

"About five. He was a good firefighter. A good person." Padilla cuts his gaze away as he says it, which I find interesting.

"So why would a seasoned firefighter with all that experience charge into a building unaided?" I ask.

Padilla holds up both his hands. "Agent, I wish I could tell you. I don't know, some people snap sometimes. Maybe it just got to him."

"Did he say anything when you arrived? Or was he acting odd at all?"

I can tell Padilla is just about done with our questions. "If he had, it would have been in the report," he says, standing back up. "Now if you'll excuse me, I have guests to attend to."

"Kind of strange," I say as he moves to the door. "Having a cookout after so many of your men have died. Two in the last eighteen hours."

"My wife has spent weeks on this. I wasn't going to be the one to tell her we needed to cancel. She and I decided it would be better for morale if we didn't," he says. "What am I going to do, go out there and tell everyone that I lost *another* man and that they all have to go home? I can assure you of one thing, Agent, this bug isn't getting any more of my guys. We protect our own. We don't need the FBI *or* the ATF to come in and tell us how to take care of our own business." He moves past me and opens the door again, heading back to the kitchen and outside again.

"You didn't ask him about his alibi," Zara says.

"No need, we can just check with his guests here," I reply. "They're more likely to give us a straight answer than he is."

It only takes checking with two people to find out Padilla has been here all day, ever since this morning, prepping for the party. That effectively rules him out for McKenzie, the only victim I could see him having a motive for. His stubbornness not to cooperate seems like just that: stubbornness.

"What did you think?" I ask as we head back out.

"He's still hiding something," she says. "He seemed a little jumpy. What about you? You met him before I did."

"To be honest, Padilla has been all over the place. But he did seem upset we were there. I still don't know if I buy the story about Phelps, but I couldn't tell if he was lying or not. There's something there."

"Me either," she says. "So what do we do?"

I shake my head, opening the car door. A blast of heat hits me. "We can't *force* the members of firehouse twelve to accept protection, but at the same time I don't think we can just let them roam around seeking vengeance either."

"We can't keep tabs on all of them," Zara says. "There are too many."

My phone vibrates in my pocket before I slip into the car. "Slate."

"It's Farmer. I'm still out here on site. You'll never believe what just happened."

"Go ahead," I say.

"Lieutenant Olsen and half the guys on the truck here just agreed to protective custody. I've got my men bringing them to your office now."

"You're kidding," I say, glancing up at Zara. She mouths *"what?"*.

"Nope. I think this one finally put the fear of God into some of them. You better be there to meet them."

"We will, thanks, Farmer," I say, then hang up.

"Don't keep me in suspense, what is it?" Zara asks.

"Maybe a break," I say. "Let's go find out."

Chapter Twenty-Four

IT TURNS OUT SIX GUYS FROM STATION TWELVE AGREED TO THE voluntary protection, while two others took the engine back to the station. But what's most surprising is Lieutenant Olsen, Padilla's right-hand-man, leading the charge. I guess the captain's word isn't as iron-clad as I thought.

While six guys from the station isn't even a third, it cuts down on the amount of surveillance I'm going to have to assign for the remaining members. Since we can't count on the killer sticking to his normal time of killing anymore, I need eyes on every one of them right now. In the meantime, I want to take another run at Olsen, see if he knows more than he's letting on.

Farmer is already at the FBI satellite office when we get there, though he's standing outside smoking.

"Hell of a thing," he says as we approach, putting out the butt under his shoe. Seems like he's dropped any pretense of not doing it. "Never can seem to stop for very long."

"Did Olsen or the others say anything?" I ask as the three of us head into the building.

"No, they approached *me*," he replies. "Wanted to know if the offer was still on the table."

"Considering the chilly responses we got just this morning, I'd say McKenzie's death was a turning point."

"Maybe they decided they couldn't pretend like it wasn't really happening anymore," Zara says as we take off our weapons and any metal to get through security. Once we're past, I have the field office issue a temporary pass for Farmer, who accompanies us up to the second floor.

"Anything else from the fire?" I ask.

"Dental matched McKenzie, so it's definitely him. But nothing else of note. Just looks like he also had turpentine in his body when he began to burn. We'll know more from Dr. Lewis in a few hours."

"It's going to be the same," I say. "The only stand out is Phelps. Everyone else has had this ritualistic killing. I just need to figure out why."

"Maybe there isn't a why," Farmer suggests. "Maybe he's just weird."

"There's always a why," Zara says before I can. "Even if he doesn't exactly know it, there's a why."

Damn I'm proud of her. She has taken to field work like a mouse to cheese. And to think, she used to be intimidated by it. Look at her now. I like to think I played a small part in that.

"Oh, that reminds me," Farmer says. "Information came back on Ricky Black's car. Near the back right side of the vehicle, when they stripped away all the charring, they found remnants of fresh spray paint. It's possible the killer tagged the car before it burned."

I shake my head. "At least he's consistent."

"How did it go with Padilla?" Farmer asks.

"The man knows how to grill a mean burger," Zara says, though I'm not sure she ever actually tasted one.

"He was grilling?" Farmer asks.

"Having a cookout party, actually," I say.

He drops his head a second as we head to the holding

rooms. "Suzanne's party. Right. I got the invitation for that. Surprised he still had it, with everything going on."

"Multiple people confirmed him there all day," I say. "So this isn't his doing. At least not directly. But he's hiding something else. We're just not sure what."

"Want me to take a run at him?" Farmer asks.

All three of us stop, Zara and me with our mouths open. "You?"

"Maybe he'd be willing to confide in an old friend," Farmer says. "Rather than a new enemy."

I glance at Zara, she's as shocked as I am. I never would have thought Farmer would turn on Padilla, at least not directly. My shock must register in my facial expression.

"Don't look so surprised," he says. "I might have had on blinders before. But I'm beginning to see again."

"That's good," I say. "But let's hold off until tomorrow. You go after him right now and he'll suspect something. We need to give him time to cool down."

"You know, Stan, Emily made it sound like you were only getting to be more of a pain in the ass but you're turning out to be just a big pussy cat, aren't you?" Zara says in that condescending tone of hers that always puts me on edge when I'm on the receiving end. I can't imagine what Farmer thinks.

"Right," he says after a minute. "I've got to call my team. Then I can assist you with the interviews." He heads off down the hall.

"Why do you do that?" I ask.

"Do what?" Zara shrugs. "Not being a dickhead a good thing."

"Yeah, but guys like that, they build their personalities based on how rough and tough they are. You undercut that; you cull any progress we're making with him."

She scoffs. "Men and their pride. Farmer will be fine. I'm more interested in what these firefighters have to say."

Maybe she's right; I need to stop being so concerned with offending people. We check in with the Agent in Charge, SAC Bluell. He seems cut from a similar cloth as Farmer, though he's far less grumpy and is happy to let us take the lead on the firefighters while his team finishes processing all the paperwork related to keeping them safe. Each one will be taken to a different location with a small team of agents on them for the next forty-eight hours. Bluell also tells us they're in the process of evaluating if the families will need to be moved as well.

"What?" Zara says as we head down the hall to meet with Olsen, our first witness.

I'm sure she's seen the pained look on my face. "I just remembered, McKenzie said he had a wife and kids. Daughters. It's going to be hell for them."

Zara puts her hand on my shoulder. "Let's not think about that right now. Instead, let's go see what Olsen has to say."

I nod as we head into the holding room. Lieutenant Olsen sits on the small couch, which is barely big enough for one person, much less two. "Lieutenant," I say as we enter. "Good to see you with your shirt on this time." I see Zara shoot me a look and do her best to hold back what I'm sure is an epic quip.

He nods. "Agent…?"

"Slate," I remind him. "And this is Agent Foley." We grab a couple of folding chairs and take a seat across from him. "You won't be here very long, it's just until we get all the paperwork filed. Thank you for volunteering and for your willingness to keep you and your fellow firefighters safe."

"Kind of hard not to after seeing what happened to McKenzie," he says. "I was just at his house last weekend to catch some football."

"Football season ended in February, sport," Zara says.

"Sorry, soccer. They say *fútbol* all the time, you start to get used to it."

"So a lot has happened since we last talked," I say, leading off. "We're now looking at five deaths instead of three. I know I asked you this before, but is there anything you can tell me about all five men that they shared in common? Anything that might stand out?"

He shakes his head. "Other than being on the same truck sometimes, no, not really," he says.

"What about the night Sam Phelps died," I ask. "Were the other four there that night?"

For just a half second he glances off to the side before dropping his gaze. It's a telltale sign that someone is attempting to lie, but I'll check with Zara before noting it. It was so fast I could have imagined it. "Let me see. Perry and Black were both there, but Spencer and McKenzie weren't," he says. "At least I don't think so. I'd have to go back and double-check the logs."

I sit back like we're just having a casual conversation. I don't want him to feel like he's under an interrogation here. It might make him loosen up a little. "Anything strange about that night? About Sam in particular?"

"What can I say?" Olsen holds up his hands, almost in the exact same way Padilla did. "I don't know what happened."

"Were you there that night?" Zara asks, even though I know she already knows the answer to the question.

"I was. I drove the truck."

"We're just trying to figure out what might have been going through his mind," I say. "It seems strange that he'd just run in there like that."

"No, I get it, you're absolutely right. I wish I knew. I've never seen it before, but I've heard of other firefighters having something called adrenaline narcosis. A firefighter will be so focused on getting to the fire and putting it out that they'll just ignore everything else around them. I thought it was made up until I saw Sam that night."

I slide my gaze over to Zara, wondering if she's buying

this. I've never heard of adrenaline narcosis, and I doubt anyone else has either. If it does exist, it's never been officially diagnosed as a real disorder.

"So you think he just, what? Got too focused on the job?"

"Well, not exactly," Olsen says. "But Sam was one of those guys who would make sure everyone else was out before himself. He wasn't afraid to put his life in danger to save others. Maybe that combined with lack of sleep...I really don't know; I'm just spit balling here."

"No, I get it," I say, trying to stay casual. "Sometimes people do strange things. You just hold tight, and we'll have you out of here and somewhere more comfortable soon."

"Hopefully somewhere with a minibar," he says as we get up and head for the door.

"I'll see what I can do." Zara and I head back out to the hallway.

"Did you catch that?" I ask as soon as the door is closed behind us. Zara gives me a knowing nod. Both Olsen and Padilla are holding something back, but I don't know what. I check the time. It's going to take another hour at least to get through these interviews.

"So...shirtless, huh?" she asks, leaning up against the wall.

I shake my head. "I was getting nowhere. I went into the locker room."

"Emily Rachel Slate," Zara says in mock outrage. "How could you?"

"Door was open," I say. "I walked right in."

"I was wrong about you," she says as we make our way back down the hall. "Under all that seriousness is a tigress somewhere, just yearning to be free."

"Yeah, well this tigress is more than happy with just catching our killer and calling it a day. I'd much rather spend an evening with a book."

"C'mon, you get a peek at anything?" she asks, nudging me.

"Don't worry, everyone was covered. More or less."

"Wow," she whispers. "Legend."

I just roll my eyes. We've still got five more to go before we can release them.

It's going to be a long night.

Chapter Twenty-Five

SLEEP COMES IN BOUTS, AND I KEEP WAKING UP IN THE MIDDLE of the night thinking my phone is ringing. Somehow, I make it all the way through until morning without a call from Farmer. We managed to finish up all the interviews and fill out all the paperwork last night, placing all six of station twelve's "volunteers" in different hotel rooms across the city. Fortunately for us, I was able to convince Bluell that I didn't think taking their families into protective custody was necessary, given the killer's history.

But at the same time, as Zara and I trade off bathroom time to get ready, I can't help but think the only reason I didn't get a call in the middle of the night is because we already have the killer, in one of the hotel rooms.

Then again, it could just be a coincidence. He might have moved up his timetable on McKenzie because McKenzie was about to talk, and now he's back on his regular schedule. It's impossible to know for sure.

As I'm buttoning my blouse both my and Zara's phones buzz at the same time. "Message from Farmer," I say. "The paint from all four locations is an exact match."

"That's about as useful as a camouflage golf ball," she

calls from the bathroom. "We already knew it was the same guy."

"We figured it was, but this will make it solid when we nail him," I reply. "If we can take him alive, there'll be no way he won't go for life."

"Do they have the death penalty in South Carolina?" she asks, poking her head around the corner.

I cock my head. "I dunno. Maybe?"

I pull up Bluell's contact info. He picks up on the second ring. "Bluell."

"It's Emily Slate. Any development on Padilla's roving gangs last night?"

He gives me a long sigh. "We worked with CPD to keep an eye on them, but a lot of those guys work together, so I know we lost sight of some of them for a while. The good news is most gave up before midnight. As far as we know, we're not missing anyone else this morning."

"Good to hear, thank you," I say.

"Let us know if you have any luck convincing the others," he says. "Otherwise we'll hold down the fort."

I hang up and finish getting ready. We dropped our suits off by a twenty-four-hour dry cleaner last night on rush. They were hanging on our door when we woke up this morning. It feels good to be back in fresh clothes.

"What's the plan?" Zara asks. "Keep going after Padilla's people?"

I'm not willing to risk that we don't have the killer in custody—he might have just taken the night off last night. And if we do already have him, he's not going anywhere. I want to know what McKenzie wanted to tell us, and I'm hoping his work locker will give us a clue. His house is a complete loss, there's nothing salvageable there. But the locker at his work on the other hand...

"We're going back to fire station twelve," I say.

"Yeah, let's crack those skulls!" She says that with too much enthusiasm, but it still makes me laugh.

"Even better. This time we're going to crack a lock."

"So how do we play this? Go in all rough and hard, flashing badges and guns?" Zara asks as we park and head over to the station. Looks like there is a full complement in the station today, which is surprising given how many were out late last night. I clock Padilla's car is here as well.

"No, I don't want to make a fuss. We don't have a warrant and I don't want Padilla to stonewall us any more than he already has. I need you to distract him and the others while I search McKenzie's locker."

"You better hope that slip we pulled from his wallet was the combination," she says.

"It was. No way it wasn't. Why else keep it in there?" I ask.

She quirks her mouth at me. "So just cause a distraction, huh?"

"Think you can handle it?" I ask.

"Look who you're talking to," she says. "I've got this."

We split off, with Zara heading for the main entrance where the fire engine is. She stands right outside the entrance and waits for me to get on the far side of the building, so I'm just around the corner from the door that leads into the other side of the building. I give her a nod.

"Attention Fire Station Twelve," she calls out. For such a small person, she can really have a booming voice when she wants to. "I am here to place every one of you under arrest."

I drop my head and rub my temple. Maybe we should have switched roles.

"What the hell?"

"Whaddaya mean under arrest?"

"Who are you?"

Firefighters start coming outside from all parts of the building to confront her. She has her badge on full display as she's fielding what I'm sure are to be the first of thousands of questions. This goes on for a good two minutes before Padilla finally storms out of the door I'm right on the other side of, making a bee-line for Zara. "What in God's name do you think you're doing here?" he yells.

I take the opportunity to slip in the door he's just vacated, and head quickly through the station. A few other men are still in the building, but upon hearing the commotion outside, they head to join everyone else.

I head back to the locker room, which seems deserted. I double-check the shower area anyway, just to make sure. I then find McKenzie's locker, with his name still on the tag. I've got the combination memorized, but I check my phone anyway and turn the dial. Once to the right, back to the left and back to the right again. It clicks and opens on the first try.

Never that easy, I remind myself.

Inside are a bunch of McKenzie's things, including his uniform coat and helmet. I push them to the side, looking for anything personal, anything that might indicate what he was so anxious about. There's a pile of old clothes, and a few books which look like training manuals. I open the small cubby at the bottom expecting to find his boots inside, but instead there are more personal items. Mostly photos that have little bits of tape on them, like they were recently hanging somewhere. I go through them, finding a few that were taken at the paintball yard. And a few more taken at Billy's Backwash. All of them have different members in the unit in them, none feature the same people. But at the same time, this is significant. I don't see Dan himself in any of the pictures, until I come to one of the last ones.

"Whoa," I whisper, looking closely at the image. It was taken here, in the locker room. It features Sam Phelps, Leon Spencer, Greg Perry, Ricky Black, Dan, Jay Olsen, and a *woman*, all of them in their firefighter gear. All of them with their arms around each other and big smiles on their faces. "Who are *you*?" I ask the woman, even though there is no one else around. I check the back of the photo, but there's no marking anywhere to let me know who this could be. Though, looking at the photo closer, I see where it was taken from, just on the other side of the island. Keeping the picture in my hand, I walk around the island, lining up where it was taken. I compare the names on the lockers in the picture to the names on the lockers now. One is different. The one in front of me reads Browning, K. But in the picture, it reads Davis, A.

Davis, A. Why hasn't anyone mentioned you to us? I head back over to McKenzie's locker, knowing I'm pushing how much time I have left, but I keep going through his stuff anyway. There's an old day planner at the bottom of the cubby. I don't have time to go through it, so I slip it in my pocket along with the pictures and put everything else back as I found it.

Was this what McKenzie wanted to tell me? About A. Davis? I'm going to see if I can't get Zara to run through the firehouse records when we're done here, see if we can't figure out who she is and more importantly, *where*. Everyone else in that picture, other than Lieutenant Olsen, is dead. We might have another body out there we didn't even know about; I'll need to check with Lewis at the morgue to make sure.

As I'm headed out, I'm so lost in thought I nearly bump into Padilla.

"Slate!" he yells. "What are you doing in here?"

"Making sure none of your men were in here, hiding," I say. "I assume you heard Agent Foley's announcement."

He practically laughs. "Yeah, you go ahead and arrest all of us. See how well that works out for you. I'm sorry to tell you, but your partner doesn't have the authority she thinks she does." He shakes his head. "I can't believe you come into my station on a Sunday morning and try to pull this shit. My guys were out half the night looking for the man you can't seem to catch."

All I want to do is slam his face down on a table and force him to tell me about A. Davis, but I have to give him a sweet smile instead. "Yeah, I heard you lost a few before you even got started. I think if you'd had a few more at that fire yesterday you wouldn't be so gung-ho about enacting vigilante justice. And just because you're buddies with the CPD, doesn't mean you have any more rights to apprehend criminals than a civilian does. And if I find out you're going out there any more with your little mob, I will bring federal obstruction charges against you."

He gives me the look I'm most used to from people in power. The look that tells me I'm just a little fish in this man's big ocean and I have no real pull. "I have a lot of friends," he says. "Even in your office. You better be careful who you order around, *Agent*."

"Have a nice day, Captain," I say, feeling the calendar and photos in my pocket. I turn and leave him there and head to rejoin Zara outside. Most of the crowd has dissipated, though one of the firemen has stayed behind. He's leering over her, engaged in what I'm sure is stimulating conversation. He's the same man who attempted to hit on me when he was wearing nothing but a towel. Walker.

"Time to go," I say.

"But Brett and I were just getting acquainted," she pretend whines.

"Doesn't matter," I say. "Better luck next time, Brett."

He shoots me a wink before heading back to the station. I feign disgust and return to the car with Zara. "So?" she asks. "Success?"

I nod, starting the engine. "Big time."

Chapter Twenty-Six

"Angelica Davis, 1945 Margrove Street, Riverland Terrace," Zara says after spending less than a minute going through the FBI's system. We returned to the satellite office to try and make sense of these photos and see if they help provide any clues to the killer's identity.

"Who prints out photos anymore," she says, glancing over at them again. "And who uses a day planner?"

"Not everyone is as technically savvy as you," I say. "Some people like to use pen and paper."

"So inefficient," she says. She's been studying the photos for anything we might have missed while I've been going through McKenzie's calendar, looking for anything else that might stand out. So far, it's sparse. It doesn't look to me like Dan had much of a social life outside work. Everything on the calendar is either a meetup with one person from work or a bunch of them.

"I'm assuming Angelica Davis was a member of fire station twelve?" I ask.

"Yep," Zara says, returning her attention to her screen. "Hired in 2016, terminated earlier this year."

"Terminated," I say. "Why?"

"Reasons listed here are poor work ethic, and inability to cooperate well with others. Signed Captain Padilla."

I take a look at the picture of all of them together again. She doesn't look like she's having any trouble getting along with anyone from this image. "And she's still alive?" I ask.

"Seems to be, as far as I can tell. No Jane Does in the morgue matching her description."

"Then she's a potential target," I say, getting up. "C'mon, we need to find her. Do you have a current job listed?"

Zara searches again for a moment. "Nothing that I can find. Maybe she hasn't found anything else since she was let go."

"Then let's hope she's at home," I say.

"Do you want to call CPD for backup? They can get there quicker than we can to keep an eye on the place."

"No, I don't want anyone knowing we know about her. Not even Farmer. Not until we figure out what's going on here. I don't want to find out we inadvertently put her life in danger because we got sloppy."

"Fair enough," Zara says. "Lead the way."

The drive takes us about twenty minutes. Thankfully, today isn't nearly as muggy as the past few days have been. Still, I drive with the windows up to prevent any of that wet air from seeping into the car. When we pull up to the address, I can see that Ms. Davis has come on some hard times. The house is small, but practical. Green siding, with a cute white, picket fence surrounding the property and even a small arch at the gate. But it's all in disrepair. The house needs a new coat of paint and some of the boards on the fence are falling off. The grass is long like it hasn't been mowed yet this season, none of which makes me feel very good about this situation.

Davis could have been the killer's first target, even before Sam Phelps. Maybe before he decided to use fire as his main weapon. And the house is far enough from its neighbors that no one would report any smells, even in this heat. I don't look forward to knocking on that door.

"Car is in the driveway," Zara says.

She's right. And it isn't covered in pollen or dust, which means it has probably been used recently. I feel slightly better.

We make our way up the walkway and I give the door a couple of knocks before stepping back. About a minute passes with no response, so I go up and knock again. "Ms. Davis? Are you home? This is the FBI."

"So much for subtlety," Zara says.

"Warranted," I reply. "Might make her realize we're not here to harass her for money or something else." I glance around again. I can't imagine she doesn't have at least a few creditors coming after her, given the state of things.

Finally we hear a deadbolt unlatch and a moment later the door opens, revealing a brunette woman in a tank top and pajama bottoms. She has a mug in one hand, and a skeptical look on her face. It's the same woman from the picture, no doubt, but this version of her looks hollowed out, like she hasn't been eating or sleeping enough.

"Ms. Davis?" I ask. She doesn't reply. "I'm Special Agent Slate, this is Special Agent Foley. As I said we're with the FBI. May we have a moment of your time?"

"What does the FBI want with me?" she asks.

"It has to do with the recent string of deaths in the area. The ones involving some of your fellow firefighters."

"Those assholes aren't my *fellows*," she says with palpable disdain. In the picture I saw she looked to be in her early thirties. This woman looks like she's closer to forty. Even if the picture was taken a few years ago, it's one hell of a difference.

"Please," I say. "We have reason to believe you might be in danger."

"If you must," she says and steps back from the door. "Excuse the mess."

I nod and walk past, as does Zara. The house definitely

has an odor to it, but I've smelled worse. However, there are tissues or other bits of trash along the floor, like she didn't even care to throw them away. Empty cups or cans sit on most of the available surfaces, and the small table in front of the TV is covered with empty to-go boxes and plastic trays. It looks like Angelica hasn't been out much lately.

"Is there anyone else at home?" I ask.

"Just me," she says, heading back to the kitchen. We follow her back and the situation doesn't improve at all. Back here even more food containers are strewn all over the place and the smell worsens. An overflowing bag of trash sits on the other side of the dirty counter, trash littering the floor around it. "Oh," she says, noticing where my eyes have landed. "Just ignore that. Trash day is on Wednesday." Part of her sounds embarrassed and another part sounds indignant, like she can't make up her mind which one she is. It is clear she's having a difficult time, though.

"I...uh, assume you've heard about the recent string of deaths," I say.

"Just what's been on the news," she replies.

"No one has contacted you? From your former place of employment?"

She gives me a mirthless laugh. "No."

I shoot a glance at Zara, who gives the two of us some space as she performs a visual inspection of the house. "Some of the information has been kept out of the news, to prevent a public panic," I say. "But so far, every victim was at one time a squad member of firehouse twelve, where you used to work."

She raises her eyebrows as if this information surprises her. "Who? I know about Sam...but who else?"

That's not surprising. Because he was the first, Sam's face has been all over the local news, calling him a hero who died in the line of duty. But the others we've been keeping quiet, at least until we've captured the killer. As far as the public knows, these are just random citizens, not connected.

"Leon Spencer, Greg Perry, Ricky Black and Dan McKenzie," I say.

Her expression doesn't change, though I'm looking closely. I can't tell if this is news to her or not. If it is, she's doing a fantastic job of hiding it. But I can't discount that she might be the connective tissue I'm looking for, not Padilla. "Huh," she finally says. She turns and walks over to the cabinet and pulls out a small Altoids case. "You mind if I smoke?"

What is it with people involved in this profession and smoking? I'd have thought witnessing what fires do to people firsthand would be the best kind of deterrent. She opens the case to reveal a handful of rolled marijuana cigarettes. Ah, that makes more sense. She pulls one out, lights it, and takes in a deep breath before exhaling.

She holds out the cigarette to me. "No thank you," I say, and she takes it back, holding it gently. I notice her fingers begin to shake. "Were you aware of these men's deaths?" I ask.

She shakes her head. "I had no idea. I just knew about Sam."

"Ms. Davis, can you tell us what happened with your job? Why were you let go?" Zara comes back around, standing on the far side of the room so we're both not in her immediate eyeline. Angelica has to split her attention to watch us both, which often has the effect of occupying the part of the brain that's trying to come up with lies. It makes things harder for them, and easier for me to spot someone doing it.

She tries to play it cool though. "Difference of opinion, I guess," she says.

"The official record says you were let go due to poor work ethic and an inability to work with others," Zara says.

She takes another drag. "Why am I not surprised?"

"Was that not the reason?" I ask.

She stares at me a long time before answering, as if she's attempting to judge my character; to see if I'm worthy of the knowledge. "I had a grievance," she finally says. "They didn't want to hear it."

"What was the grievance?" I ask.

"You know what? I'm not doing this," she says, putting out the cigarette. "I think we're done here."

"Ms. Davis," I say, pulling out the photograph and handing it to her. "Every person in this picture except you and Lieutenant Olsen is dead. You can't tell me that's a coincidence."

She looks at it a brief second before turning away, her eyes growing watery. Her emotions are right on the surface and she's not doing a thing to keep them in check. "Please leave," she says, her voice smaller now. I put the photograph away and she seems to relax a hair. I'm afraid if I push her any further, she might crack. We don't have any choice but to back off for now; to give her some space. It doesn't seem to me like she's afraid for her life, but something is definitely going on. Though, by the time Sam Phelps died, she had been off the force for almost two months. She wouldn't have had access to his equipment to sabotage it.

I nod, though I hold out my card. "I can see this is very difficult, and I'm sorry to be the one to tell you all this," I say. "But we're trying to stop a killer. If you can think of anything that might help us, or if you can tell us anything that might connect these men to each other, please, give me a call. Anytime."

She doesn't take the card, only holds herself with both arms. I move a couple of cups to the side on the hallway table and lay it there before Zara and I let ourselves out. Ms. Davis doesn't come after us, so I just gently close the door and we make our way back to the car.

Zara glances at me and I can already recognize the emotion in her eyes. I feel it too. Ms. Davis is hiding some trauma. From what or whom I don't know, but I can guess. "You felt it too?"

Zara nods. "How could anyone not?"

"She's the key," I say, motioning back to the house. "The key to all of this. Somehow."

"Do you really think she could have murdered five people?" she asks.

I open the driver's side door. "I don't know. Grief and pain can make people lash out in unexpected ways. The killer seems more coordinated, more methodical. I'm not saying I'm ruling her out, but I don't think she's in the mindset to do it as cleanly as our unsub has been."

We both get into the car and sit there a moment, watching Angelica Davis's house. There's no movement in any of the windows. If I had to guess, I'd bet she's still in the hallway where we left her.

"Now what?" Zara asks.

"Now we inform Farmer," I say.

Chapter Twenty-Seven

I'VE SPENT TOO MUCH TIME MOVING BETWEEN OFFICES lately…and after meeting Angelica, I don't really feel like going back. Zara and I decide on a brunch place instead, and call Farmer to meet us there so we can figure out how to move this thing forward.

I know Angelica sits at the middle of this case, somehow, but all the parts haven't lined up for me yet. But the very fact that her existence was obfuscated from the beginning makes me suspicious. Why didn't Padilla, or Olsen for that matter, ever say anything? And was this what McKenzie was going to tell us? Did he know what happened?

Zara doesn't say much on the way to the brunch place, a small hole-in-the-wall joint off the beaten path and away from the tourists. I imagine she's probably thinking the same thing I am, someone has abused Angelica, mentally and possibly physically. You don't go from having the iron will of a firefighter to someone who barely leaves their own home because you got fired. Even if no one in the city would have hired her, she could have moved to a different district or even gone to one of the areas outside of the City of Charleston's reach. A lot of the small towns that surround the city aren't under their jurisdiction. She wouldn't have even needed to move; they aren't that far.

We take a booth in the back. As soon as we sit, Zara pulls out her phone and begins working on it furiously. "You looking her up?" I ask.

She nods. "I want to see what we can gather from her online profiles. If I need to, I'll go deeper using the database."

I leave her to her work as I run through more scenarios in my head. Angelica is fired from the fire department, then two months later the murders begin, starting with Sam Phelps. So what happened to trigger the first one? Did it just take the killer that long to respond, to set it up to make it look like he died by accident? Could she have coerced someone still working at the firehouse to help her get revenge for whatever happened to her? An accomplice that had access to Phelps, and who was an expert on fire management. They could have been in it together.

"This is cozy." I look up to see Farmer standing there, sweat on his brow. "Took me forever to find you in here, this place is like a maze."

Zara slides out of the booth and scoots next to me as Farmer gets in the other side. "You said you had an update?"

I let Zara keep working as I fill in Farmer on all the details we know so far about Angelica Davis, though I leave out how I came upon this information in the firehouse.

"So you're saying you think she killed them out of some kind of retribution?" he asks after I've finished.

Both Zara and I glare at him. "That's not what she said."

"That's what you implied," he says. "I mean, we don't have a better suspect. She's pissed off, slighted by the department, looking for revenge. And she's going to get it, one person at a time."

I shake my head. "It wasn't like that. This woman was *broken*. She's not out there doing anything. At best, she's working with someone who is, but even that's a stretch."

Farmer scoffs. "You're being too sentimental. We should just bring her in for questioning. She'll give us a straight answer."

"You haul her into a station and put her in a bright room with no way out and she'll just shut down," I say. "We could barely get anything out of her where she felt somewhat secure."

"Then you need to eliminate her as a suspect because right now she's looking like our best option. Padilla is pissed; I've been fielding questions from him since ten a.m. about you two and that stunt at his station this morning. I'm assuming that's where you conveniently found this information."

I lean forward. "Last time I checked, we don't work for you. I don't care if you have to field questions from God, I'm conducting this investigation in a manner which I deem appropriate."

Farmer lets out a loud huff, but before he can continue, Zara speaks up. "You don't get it because you're a man. But all women above a certain age have an understanding about something like this. We recognize it because we've seen it countless times before. It's in the way someone's eyes will avert when you bring up a name, or the tightening of a body when someone walks through the door. And do you know who that person always is?"

Farmer looks like he's on the verge of answering, but wisely keeps his mouth shut.

"It's always someone they trusted, that they felt secure around," she replies. "It's so common it's almost comical. But women instinctually know what abuse looks like, even if there aren't any physical scars. We can just tell. Because in one way or another, we've all been on the receiving end of it at some point during our lives." She takes a breath. "Why do you think Emily and I work so hard?"

I have to say, I'm prouder of her in this moment than in almost any other. This is classic Zara, standing up for those who can't stand up for themselves. The fact that she even has to explain this to him is ludicrous, but it's something we accept as women. And it won't be the last time.

"You're saying someone assaulted her?" Farmer asks. I swear, I don't see how guys can be so dense sometimes. But when the world has always catered to you, it makes you blind to the struggles of others.

"In one form or another," I say. "Physically, mentally, emotionally. Maybe all three. It's hard to tell. But someone is keeping a secret; Padilla didn't want us to know about her. He's had plenty of opportunities to mention her."

"If that's true," Farmer says, "He'll just say it slipped his mind. Or he didn't think it was relevant. Either way, he's got an easy out."

"Right," I say. "I think maybe we take another run at Olsen, armed with this photograph." I pass it across the table to him. Farmer stares at it a moment.

"You think Olsen might be the killer?" he asks.

"He's the only other one out of this group left alive," I say. "I don't like to gamble, and I certainly don't have the money to do it. But I'd be willing to set my pension on Olsen being involved in this somewhere. Maybe he's the killer, maybe not. But he's involved. And if by some miracle he isn't, then he's a target."

"Do you still have eyes on Davis?" Farmer asks.

"I tasked one of Bluell's agents to keep an eye on the house while we were away," I say. "She's familiar with our car, but she won't recognize one of Agent Bluell's. I don't trust the CPD, considering half of them were out with Padilla's little brigade last night. Davis could still be a target too; I didn't want to take any chances."

Farmer stares at the picture a little longer, then reaches into his coat to pull out his packet of Marlboro's before cursing and putting them back. "Damn smoking bans. Soon enough I won't even be able to smoke in my own home."

"Maybe that's a good thing," I say.

"Uh-huh," he replies. "Tell me that when they keep pushing and outlaw red meat as well. Or alcohol."

I turn to Zara. "Find anything?"

"Still going through her socials, but there's not much over the past few months. An errant post here or there. Before that though…" She turns her phone so I can see. Lots of pictures of Davis with her squad. Lots of pictures of all of them out together, some at Billy's Backwash and a few at the paintball yard. Even some at McKenzie's house. In a few I spot Ricky Black's green Camry. "Social butterfly," I say. In all the pictures she looks happy, relaxed, living life to the fullest. "Wait," I say. "What's that?"

"What is it?" Farmer asks.

I take Zara's phone and select one of the pictures. About half of them are in it, but Greg Perry has his arm around Angelica's waist. "Look at this," I say, showing them both.

"Were they dating?" Zara asks.

"Maybe," I say, handing the phone back to her. "Or maybe it's just friends on a squad. But it looks like it's more than that."

"She had to have known Perry was married," Farmer says. "It wasn't a secret."

"But maybe they were," Zara suggests. "And Perry's wife found out."

I think back to the woman we met when we went to Perry's house to inform her of his death. She already knew about his one affair with Kyla. Did she know about this one too? And if so, and it drove her to murder, why kill all the others too?

"I don't think that's it," I say. "She would have killed Angelica first. Maybe before Perry. The fact she's still alive means whoever is going after these men could be doing it for her benefit."

The waitress finally appears and brings us some waters. I

can see why this place is out of the way of the tourists. We've been here probably twenty minutes already and still haven't seen a menu. But that might work to our benefit. After going over some of this, I really want to talk to Jay Olsen again. He clearly knew about Angelica and never said anything either, so what else is he hiding? The only problem is he's an expert liar. He hasn't slipped this entire time.

"Let's go see Olsen again," I tell Zara. "I want to squeeze him." As I make a motion for her to get out of the booth, my phone rings. "Slate."

"This is Fields, I've got eyes on Davis. She's leaving her house, medium-sized suitcase in hand."

"What?" All three of us are out of the booth in a heartbeat. "Stay on her, we're on our way."

"Do you want me to try and stop her?" she asks.

"No, keep a tail, but don't let her know you're following. I want to see where she goes."

"Understood," Agent Fields says. "I'll keep you updated."

"C'mon," I tell Zara. "It looks like we might have a runner."

Chapter Twenty-Eight

ZARA AND I HEAD OFF IN FIELDS' DIRECTION AS FARMER offers to take another shot at Olsen. He's probably thinking Olsen might respond better to a weathered career man like Farmer than he does to Zara or me. We're probably ten years Olsen's juniors already, not to mention we look even younger.

I keep Zara on the phone with Fields as we try our best to catch up with her tailing Davis. Our arrival must have finally spooked her into action, though I'm not sure where she's headed. If she's decided to flee the city, I'll have to radio CPD to assist in stopping her before she gets much past North Charleston. But she could be going to see a friend or a contact, in the event we come knocking again.

Honestly, at this point, anything is possible.

Fields keeps us updated and soon we're on 526 heading north out of the city. I'm about to radio in for backup when Fields turns off, following Davis to Charleston International Airport. So she is running, after all.

"Call the airport," I tell Zara as I focus on driving. "Find which flight she's taking and where."

"On it," Zara says, holding her own phone to her ear.

"Fields," I say on my own phone. "Stay on her until she enters that terminal. I don't want to lose sight of her."

"10-4," Agent Fields says. While I don't think she'll disappear from the airport, I don't like the idea of losing track of Angelica Davis, for even an instant. We're coming up on noon, which means the killer might be ready to strike again, if his pattern from yesterday holds. And this woman might be our only way to find out who is behind all of this.

We're only about eight minutes behind Fields by the time we get to the airport. I pull through to the secure gate, showing my badge. The officer there directs us through and I park just as Zara is getting off the phone.

"Flight 1933 to New Orleans," she says. "Boards in twenty-two minutes."

"What's in New Orleans?" We slam our doors and run for the main terminal.

"I don't know," she replies. "It could be out of desperation. The first flight available."

She's right. Davis might not care where she's going, as long as it's away from here. But is she running because she's scared, or because she doesn't want to be connected to the murders? I would think if she were trying to get out of the country, she would have taken a flight straight to Mexico.

We enter the large terminal, which is at least twenty feet tall with a large dome in the middle. The baggage and check-in gates flank us on either side, while the center leads down through some shops to security. I glance over and see a tall woman in a dark suit, scanning the crowd. Zara and I jog over to her. "Fields?"

She glances at us. "Yes, good to meet you. She's right over there, in line to go through security. Her bag is small enough to be a carry-on."

"She's not wasting any time," I say. "Did she spot you?"

Fields shakes her head. "Been too focused on getting here as fast as possible."

"Thanks," I say. "We'll take it from here."

"Good luck," she says.

"What do you think?" Zara asks as we make our way for the line.

"Slow and quiet," I say. "We don't want to spook her." We slip into line behind the last person. Davis is closer to the front, about to go through the detector. As soon as she presents her documentation and puts her bag on the scanner, she steps through. "Let's go," I say.

We duck the rope over to the precheck line and I show the TSA agent there my badge and my credentials for carrying a firearm into an airport. He waves me through after examining the documentation. I keep an eye on Davis while he does the same for Zara. We bypass the body scanner, considering we have our weapons on our hips, and slowly make our way into the main atrium. Davis is looking at the gates like she's never been here before, trying to decide where she needs to go.

Just as we begin walking toward her, she turns and her eyes go wide. I can see in that instant she's gonna run, no matter what I do. But she must know there is nowhere to go. Not in here. "Davis, don't do it!" I yell out. At that she takes off.

"Dammit," I hear Zara say as both of us break into a sprint after her.

"FBI, stop!" I call. People start screaming, there is a panic of chaos all around us. This is exactly what I was trying to prevent. People get jumpy at the airport, for good reason. I don't draw my weapon because I don't want to make a bad situation even worse, but at the same time Davis is fast.

She takes off down one of the gate corridors, though I don't know where she thinks she's going to go. These all just lead to airplanes or empty gates. We're catching up to her, but we're not close enough to stop her. Ahead of her, Fields steps out from behind a column and tackles her as she's running past. Her momentum takes her off her feet and she falls back, smacking the floor.

Zara holds up her badge as we reach her. "FBI, everyone remain calm. The situation is under control." Fields already has cuffs on her by the time we get there.

"Nice job," I say, huffing. "How'd you get in here?"

"Other security gate, down there," she nods. "Figured she might give you a little trouble."

"Please," Angelica says. "Just let me leave. I don't want to be here anymore."

"Angelica Davis, you're under arrest for public endangerment," I say as Fields helps me hoist her up. Zara keeps talking to the people around us, trying to calm them.

"I just want to go," she says. "I didn't do anything wrong."

I feel for her, I really do. But she's a suspect in a homicide case and I can't let my personal feelings get in the way of my job, as much as I would like them too. I had hoped we could avoid pressuring her like this; that we could have gone back to her house and questioned her again, but her actions have forced our hands.

A couple of airport security officers come running up and we inform them of the situation. I'm not willing to waste time trying to take Davis to the FBI's satellite office, that will take another hour. "Do you have an interview room we can use?" I ask the officers. "We need to ask her some questions."

Fields prepares to head off, but I stop her. "I'd like another pair of eyes on this. Since we won't have the interrogation tape."

She nods. "Of course."

Zara and I guide Davis as we follow the security officers into the guts of the airport, until they bring us to a security office. It's about as spacious as one of our interrogation rooms, complete with a table and a few chairs inside. "This will work, thank you. Can we get some water?"

They leave the three of us inside with the door cracked while one of them leaves and the other stays outside. Fields stays by the door while Zara and I take Angelica to one of the chairs and help her sit down. I take the cuffs off her, though it seems like she's gone completely limp. Getting anything out of her now is going to be a challenge.

"Angelica," I say, sitting on the other side of her. "I need to know what's going on here. For your benefit as much as anyone's."

She glances up at me, then back at the table again. I wait until the officer has returned with a water for her. He leaves it on the table then excuses himself. Fields closes the door all the way and Angelica jumps as it clicks.

She's wound way too tight. Like the last rubber band on a watermelon. If I squeeze too hard the whole thing goes.

"Angelica," I say softly. "What's in New Orleans?"

"Algiers Point."

"And what's in Algiers Point?" I ask.

"An old friend." Her responses are emotionless, like she's been drained of all her energy.

"Someone you trust?" She nods. "Someone who's been watching out for you?"

This time she shakes her head. "We haven't spoken in years. But he always promised to help me if I needed it."

"What do you need help from?"

She looks at me, then at Zara, and finally at Agent Fields. "Are you FBI too?" Fields pulls out her ID and shows it to her.

"Has someone been threatening you, Angelica? Is that why you're running?" I ask. She shakes her head and reaches for the water. Her hand is trembling, but she manages to grab it and take a few sips. "Then why?"

"Because I don't want any part of what's going on here," she whispers. "Someone is coming after us. I don't want to be next."

I sit back. It's not hard to tell she's frightened. She seems too rattled to lie so easily like that, which makes me believe she really doesn't have anything to do with the murders. No accomplice out there, exacting vengeance for her. But at the same time, it doesn't mean there isn't someone working on their own. "Can you tell us what really happened at work? The real reason why you were fired?"

"I quit," she says, setting the cup down.

I shoot a glance to Zara. "That's not what the record says."

"Padilla makes the rules, he can write down whatever he wants." When she mentions Padilla's name, her words become sharper for a moment. There's extra vitriol there.

"Why did you quit?" I ask. She doesn't reply. "Something happened, didn't it?" Finally, she nods. I grit my teeth. The last thing I want to do is retraumatize a survivor. But we need to know what really happened if we're going to find out who is doing this. "Can you tell us?"

She takes a deep breath. "We weren't doing anything we hadn't done a hundred times before."

"Who's we?" I ask.

"The FireDogs." A quizzical look from me causes her to elaborate. "It's what the others called us, because we were first tier, and we always hung out all the time. Like a second family. Leon, Ricky, Greg, Dan, Jay, Sam, and me," she says.

"You were a team within a team," I say. She nods. "Okay, go on."

"All of us were out like any other night a few months ago. Except for Sam. He had some family thing he had to do. I keep thinking if he'd been there, maybe…" she trails off.

"What night was this?" I ask.

"March seventeenth. Things between me and Greg had started to turn more…serious over the previous few weeks. I thought Greg was okay. He could be a jerk but at the same time he had this energy about him; he could entertain an entire room. He said his marriage was basically dead and I probably shouldn't have done it, but you've seen how I live. I don't have a lot of other people in my life."

"Where were you?" Zara asks.

"Started out at Billy's" she says. "Closed 'em down. Then we headed over to McKenzie's place because it was closest."

"I assume you were drinking?" I ask.

She gives me a pointed look. "We were always out drinking. Not much else to do between shifts." I make a motion for her to continue. "We went over to McKenzie's a lot. He's got that big house. And his wife was always really nice to all of us. Treated us all like family. But she and the girls were away that night. At her mother's or something, I don't know. Greg and I ended up in McKenzie's bed, you know how it is after a long night. Everyone was being rowdy like a bunch of teenagers whose parents were away." She pauses and puts her hand to her head, her entire body visibly shaking. "At some point I realized Greg wasn't the only one in there. Ricky had shown up too. I don't remember how."

"Angelica," I say, putting my hand on her remaining one on the table. She jerks it back like I've stabbed her. "You don't have to continue if it's too hard, I think we can guess what happened." I glance up to Zara and even over to Fields. They both have that look in their eye, that recognition. Angelica takes a breath like she's going to hyperventilate if she doesn't.

"Just tell me this. Was it all of them?"

She shakes her head. "Just Greg and Ricky. The others knew though. They were there."

"Okay," I say. "It's okay. You're here with us now. You're safe." She takes another shaky sip of water. "I need you to take five deep breaths. In...and out." I take the time to breathe with her. She does it, though when she finally looks up there are tears in her eyes.

"I assume you reported what happened?" I ask.

She shakes her head. "I couldn't, not at first. I thought maybe Jay would say something, since he was there. And he was my Lieutenant. But he never mentioned it and never said he'd be taking it to Padilla. Everyone else pretended like it never happened. Eventually, though, I couldn't take it. I couldn't take working with them anymore. I went to Padilla and filled out a report."

"What happened to the report?" Zara asks.

She shrugs. "He probably destroyed it. I waited a week. Then another and nothing changed. Finally, I asked him about it, and he pretended not to know what I was talking about."

"He didn't want the scandal," I say. "All this is because of a coverup."

"I don't know what's happening," she says. "All I know is if they are all dead, I might be next."

"They're not all dead," I say. "Olsen is still alive. He's in protective custody."

Her face darkens. "You're *protecting* him?" It comes out as a snarl, as if some caged beast has been let loose.

"We didn't know what was going on. We still don't know who is doing this. We're trying to get as many of the members of firehouse twelve into protection as we can until we stop this killer."

"It has to be Olsen," she says. "He's the only one left."

"Him and Padilla," Zara says. This has just become a lot more complicated. But at least it narrows the suspect pool. Olsen might have gotten worried that one of the other guys would crack and decided not to take the chance on letting them open their mouths. But a quadruple homicide is no small feat. And how does the messaging fit in? Not to mention he was on site for two of the murders. I'm not sure he could have burned Black's car and McKenzie's house, then made it back to the station in time to go out on the calls.

But if Padilla knows as well, maybe they're working on it together. Which could explain why Padilla responded to two and Olsen responded to two. They were both covering for the other one. The more I think about it, the more I can see it making sense. But then I remember Sam Phelps. How does he fit into all of this? Why kill him if he wasn't even there?

"What about Sam?" I ask Angelica. "Why would Olsen have killed him?"

"Because," Angelica says, "I told Sam everything. He was going to expose all of them."

Chapter Twenty-Nine

"Hang on," I say. "Back up. You told Sam about what happened at Dan McKenzie's house?"

Angelica takes a deep breath and another sip of water. She seems calmer now, more even. I'm hoping to keep her distracted enough so she can stay out of that dark space in her mind. "A few days after I quit, Sam came to see me at my house. Sam was the consummate Boy Scout, always trying to do the right thing for everyone. But he was a little naïve. He wanted to know why I suddenly quit and why all the guys were acting like I never existed. He said he couldn't get a word out of them. To him it was like they turned their back on me, which is just something you don't do. Not when you're supposed to be part of a team like that. Then again, you're not supposed to *fuck* each other either.

"I didn't tell him everything that happened, but like you, he figured most of it out himself. He said that he wasn't going to let them get away with it; that I deserved justice for what happened to me and by the time he was done, I would be able to sue the city for physical and emotional trauma. To be honest I wasn't sure if I wanted to go through all that, not publicly, but I wanted Greg and the guys to know they couldn't just get away with what they'd done. They had to pay, even if it was just their reputations that suffered."

"So Sam was going to expose all of them," I say. "When?"

"As soon as he could. He said it was better not to wait, in case they could still find forensic evidence at the scene. Though, given it was Dan's bedroom, I doubt that would have been possible."

I'm trying to imagine how that would have gone, given Sam didn't witness the event. Maybe he thought he could coerce one of the actual witnesses into talking. "Did he manage to make a report of his own?" I ask. "What did Padilla say?"

She shakes her head. "I have no idea. The next thing I know, the captain is on TV talking about a hero firefighter who died trying to save an old woman from burning to death." She looks completely exhausted and spent, but at least her hand isn't shaking anymore.

Sam died before he could expose them for what they did. "How long after you told him did the fire happen?" I ask.

"Same day," she replies.

I sit up straighter. "Wait, you're saying that the same day Sam Phelps told you he'd get justice for you, he ends up dead in a house fire?"

She nods. "Wasn't more than six hours later."

"Jesus," Zara whispers.

"That's what I said," Angelica replies. "I couldn't believe it at first; I thought it was a mistake. I even went down to the firehouse after it was all over to confirm for myself. And you know who was there waiting for me?" I don't take my eyes off her. "Olsen. He confirmed Sam had died in an accident. I had a screaming match out there in the parking lot with him. I couldn't believe that it was just an 'accident'. Sam wasn't stupid and he wasn't careless. He was good at his job."

I crack my knuckles absently. "What did Olsen say?"

"He wouldn't tell me anything else. Except when I threatened to go to the police. Padilla obviously wasn't going to do anything, and I couldn't let them get away with it. I'd get the police to investigate Sam *and* my assault charges all at once."

"You never made that report, did you?" I ask, seeing where this is going.

She shakes her head, taking another sip of water. "Olsen implied that if I wasn't careful, I could end up in an accident of my own."

"Holy shit," I say. "That's it. Olsen killed Sam Phelps."

"I didn't want to believe it at first. They were best friends, as close as brothers. I never thought Jay could ever do anything to Sam, not like that. But the more I thought about it, the more it was the only thing that made sense."

"Angelica, I'm so sorry you've had to endure all of this," I say. "I can't even imagine what you're feeling."

"Switches between rage, numbness, and pure grief," she says, off the cuff. "Sometimes all three." She downs the rest of the water, looking like she's just finished a gauntlet.

"I have to hand it to you," Fields says. "You two have uncovered a right mess."

"Think we can tell Farmer?" Zara asks.

"I don't know. He and Padilla are...or at least were— close. He's been willing to go this far to investigate him, but if he finds out Padilla participated in a coverup that includes the death of one of his own men as well as what happened to you," I nod to Angelica, "he might buddy up."

"I got the impression that making a formal police report was pointless," Angelica says. "They're all in league with each other."

I look up at Fields. "That true?"

She shrugs. "As much as any place. A lot of them run the same calls, so they're going to get close. It's a camaraderie thing. Nothing has stood out to us enough to flag it."

"Still," I say. "I don't think we can count on the CPD to be completely honest with us. We'll have to keep this in-house for the moment. Only when I'm satisfied we can trust Farmer do we bring the ATF back in."

"What do you want to do?" Zara asks.

"My bag!" Angelica calls out, looking around the room as if she's just now realized she doesn't have her suitcase with her. "Where is it?"

"It's right outside," Fields says. "I grabbed it from the terminal."

"Please," Angelica says. "Just let me get on a flight out of here. I don't even care where anymore. I just don't want to be here."

"You shouldn't have to be afraid to live in your own city," I say. "It seems someone is out there enacting vigilante justice for you, and possibly Sam too. Who else knew about what happened?"

"No one," she says. "I didn't tell anyone other than Sam."

"Who else at the station knew?" Zara asks.

"It's not like it was something they wanted getting out. Fire departments are notorious for dealing with sexual assault cases with their female fighters. I've heard about enough of them. Never thought it would happen to me, though," she says. "I can't see any of them talking about it to anyone."

"Someone talked," I reply. "Someone who was there that night, or Sam. Either way, we need to find out who that is. Because whoever knows is rampaging through this city."

"I never wanted to see any of them dead," Angelica says. "I wanted them to hurt, but not die. Especially Ricky and Greg. But the others too because they didn't have to just stand around and do nothing." Tears start falling from her eyes again.

I put my hand on her small arm. She doesn't pull it away this time. "Just hang tight here for a minute, okay? Agent Fields will stay with you." I look to Fields who nods. I motion for Zara to follow me out into the hallway.

The other officer acknowledges us then goes back to what

he's doing. "We need to get alibis on Angelica for all five murders," I whisper to Zara once we're back out there.

"I know you don't think she did it, why go to the trouble?" Zara asks.

"Because I don't want to leave any room for doubt. They are waging a war against her. We're going to make sure none of it ever blows back in her face. Once we have the alibi, I want to keep her in protective custody, just in case I've called this thing wrong."

"You know her Jeep isn't even close to the car Layla described hitting Ricky Black. And it doesn't have any damage anywhere."

I nod. "I know. Doesn't mean she couldn't have used someone else's car. I just want to make sure if this ever sees a trial, a prosecutor will have a paper-thin case against her. If Olsen and Padilla are arrogant enough to do this, I have no doubt they'd try to crush her in a court."

"Okay," she replies. "I'll get right on it. In the meantime, we're still no closer to finding our killer." Zara glances at her watch. "And no idea when he'll strike next."

"Right," I say, looking back at the door one more time. "I have an idea about that. Let's get moving."

Chapter Thirty

AGENT FIELDS TAKES ANGELICA BACK TO THE FBI SATELLITE office while Zara and I follow so we can use the office's resources to work on our individual projects. Regardless of what happens, I'm not letting Olsen and Padilla get away with this. But I don't want Olsen dead either; I need him alive to pay for his crimes against her. Which means we need to beat our killer to the punch. He can't get to Olsen, not right now, which gives us some breathing room. And considering he only seems to be going after people who were there that night, it means we shouldn't have to worry about putting any of the rest of station twelve into custody anymore.

But I don't inform Farmer yet. I want him to stay busy working on that side of the case while Zara and I do the real work. The only problem is he already knows about Angelica, so if he and Padilla are still buddy-buddy, he could very well blow what little advantage we have.

Once we're back at the office and I'm sure Angelica is in good hands, Zara and I set up at some of the empty desks they have there. I call Janice to keep her up to date on the most recent developments while Zara does more background research on Sam Phelps.

"What'd she say?" Zara asks as soon as I get off the phone.

"She laughed," I reply. Zara arches an eyebrow. "I know. It seemed genuine too."

"About what?"

"The fact that I keep stumbling into these cases," I reply. "She sent me here to investigate a simple fire, that's it."

Zara smirks. "She probably thinks you're the mastermind behind all of them. Setting yourself up for a promotion."

I exhale, running my hand through my hair. "God, I hope not."

"Em, I'm just kidding," she says. "You need to relax. I mean, as much as you can."

"I'll relax when we've got him in custody and don't have to deal with any additional fires," I say. "Did you find anything yet?"

"Okay. Angelica has a good alibi for two of the murders, but not the other two, assuming we're not looking at her for Sam Phelps."

"We're not," I say. "Go on."

"She was in Jupiter, Florida when both Greg Perry and Ricky Black were killed, as evidenced by credit card receipts and video footage," Zara says. "She got back home on Saturday morning."

"What's in Jupiter, Florida?" I ask.

"Sister," she replies. "Lives down there with her husband and kid. Records shows she goes down there about once a quarter or so to visit. This lines up with her most recent trip."

"But she was here for Spencer and McKenzie," I say. Zara nods. "It'll have to be good enough. Let's just hope we can find out who is really doing this."

"Got something for you there, too." She taps away on her computer for a minute, the clacking of the keys falling into a rhythmic pattern. "Since we now know Sam Phelps isn't part of this most recent string of killings, I decided to investigate him a little further."

"Makes sense," I say. "I should have realized his death wasn't directly connected because the M.O. didn't line up. No turpentine, no fluids in the body, no restraints."

"Right. He's a victim just like Angelica. Here's what I've got so far: Samuel Phelps, born 1989 to Marie and William Phelps, both still living. One younger brother, Andrew. His family is Charleston born and bred, been living here their entire lives. He has no record of any kind, went to Clemson, graduated, worked in the private sector for about three months, then applied to be in the fire department. Has been with them ever since."

"Sounds like sitting in an office didn't do much for him. Friends, romantic interests?"

Zara shakes her head. "The only close friends I can find are the FireDogs. Don't see anything about a steady girlfriend or boyfriend." She sits back. "It's like with us. Hard on families. That's why they lean so hard on each other—only they know what it's like. Perry was on the verge of divorce already. Spencer and Black didn't have anyone. McKenzie seems like the family man—though given what we know about Angelica now, not very family-like. Even if he didn't participate himself. He still had a hand in the coverup. They all did."

"It's horrific," I say. "Even more so when you think about the lengths Olsen and Padilla have gone to in order to keep it quiet. I'm sure Padilla knows the scandal could cost the city millions and ruin any chances he has of keep climbing the ladder."

"Are you thinking about hanging Olsen out for bait? See if we can't draw the killer in?"

"Maybe," I say. Olsen would probably never agree to it, not until we threatened him with the information regarding Angelica. But at the same time, even if he did agree, I don't think I want to take that chance. Our killer is smart and ruthless. We hang him out like a piece of meat, we're likely to lose him before we can close ranks. Especially if he's the last one. The killer may decide he has nothing left to lose, and that's the last situation we need. "But I want to talk to Phelps' family first. See if they knew anything. Maybe Sam was so upset he didn't keep Angelica's secret to himself."

She looks around the edge of the computer at me. "The brother?"

I nod. "The parents are probably too old to get in and out of those locations without risking life and limb. Fire is fast. But a young man in his prime?"

"Bent on avenging his dead brother," Zara says, and I feel a familiar pang in my stomach. I know what it's like to try and get justice for someone you love. Someone who was killed.

"Do you have an address on Andrew Phelps?"

"Sure. 3044 Sycamore. Apartment 2458."

"Let's go," I say, already out of my chair.

When we reach Sycamore Apartments, I search all the vehicles in the parking spaces for any that might have front-end damage, though I don't find any. Given it's a Sunday, the lot is almost full. A couple of people are grilling on their balconies and again I'm struck by the stench of burning meat. I have to pinch my nose closed, otherwise all I'll be able to think about is the charred and still-cooking bodies of our victims.

"Oh, you're right," Zara says, sniffing the air. "It's very close, isn't it?"

"Too close for me," I say, my voice nasally. "Let's find him."

It takes only a few moments to locate 2458, on the second level. I give the door a good knock, but no one answers.

"Farmer actually tried to shoot that girl the last time you

did this, huh?" Zara asks. She's also pinching her nose. I realize how stupid we'll look if Phelps looks through his peephole. But then again, maybe that will help disarm him.

"I really thought he was going to take the shot," I say. "She was just scared."

"He's kind of like those guys who can only prove their toughness in one way, physical force," she says.

"He's old guard," I reply. "That's how it always used to be done. That stops with us."

"Damn straight," Zara says and holds out her fist. I give it a bump then pound on the door some more. I put my ear up to the door itself.

"Ya'll lookin' for Drew?"

I turn to see a young man, maybe about seventeen or eighteen. He's wearing swimming trunks that contrast with his dark skin and coming from the next apartment over. "Do you know Mr. Phelps?"

"Sure. But he ain't here today. I tried to get over to use his PlayStation this mornin'."

"When was the last time you saw…Drew?" I ask.

The kid shrugs his lanky arms. "I dunno. Maybe two or three days ago. He's been out a lot lately."

"What's your name?" I ask, approaching him.

"Damien," he replies. "Why?" As I get closer his attitude seems to change. He goes from friendly to skeptical. I wonder how often he's had run-ins with cops.

"Damien, I'm Agent Slate with the FBI." I show him my badge. "Do you know where Drew would be?"

"Oh shit, the feds?" Damien says, his eyes going wide. "What'd he do? He kill somebody?"

"We just want to ask him some questions," Zara says.

Damien changes again; now he's practically bouncing up and down on the balls of his feet. "He did, he killed somebody didn't he? They deserve it?"

"Why do you ask that?"

"Drew don't like to see nobody get hurt that didn't deserve it," he says. "These guys were messin' with me, they live over on the other side of the complex, and Drew saw 'em, and they don't mess with me no more. I don't know what he told 'em, and I don't care, neither."

One glance to Zara tells me we're thinking the same thing. Andrew—or Drew—might be out there trying to avenge his brother's death. Which means we've had it wrong this entire time. It wasn't about justice for Angelica, or maybe it was on some level, but it's really more about justice for Sam.

"Does Drew have a place he goes on Sundays usually?" I ask Damien. "Anywhere you know where he might be?"

"Nah, I know he goes over to his folks' place sometimes."

"Okay, thank you for all your help," I say.

"Hey," Damien yells as we begin to head back to the car. "You find 'em, don't hurt 'em. He's done more for me than the cops ever did." He turns and runs down the other set of steps on the far side of the hallway, which leads to the apartment common area and the pool.

"Vigilante justice," Zara says as we make our way back down the other staircase that leads out to the parking lot.

"Yep," I say. "And probably a good dose of rage. Explains why the victims are all in such sorry shape. He's punishing them for what they did to his brother and Angelica."

"We gotta find him and get him off the street," Zara says.

We get back to the car and I'm backing out of the space before Zara can finish closing her door. "We can't issue a warrant, not without some evidence connecting him to the crime. Maybe we'll get lucky and he's at his parents' house for a visit in between killings."

"You really think it's going to be that easy?" Zara asks.

"Hell no. But it's worth a shot."

Chapter Thirty-One

As we head to the Phelps house, I go over everything in my head. It's easy to see now how I had it all wrong from the beginning—that Sam was never part of the pattern and the killer started with Leon. Still, with Angelica's testimony, we should be able to put Olsen and maybe even Padilla on the hook for Sam's murder. We just need to find some evidence implicating them. But now that we know what to look for, it should be a lot easier.

Still, my first priority has to be finding Andrew Phelps and seeing if we can tie him to any of the crimes. I think there's enough of an established pattern that if we can link him to one, he'll go down for all of them. He fits the profile, and now I finally understand where all that anger he's showing toward the other FireDogs is coming from. I really want to believe Farmer is with us on this, but given his full breadth of behavior, I'm not willing to blow the entire case on what little I know about the man. He could have known about Padilla this whole time and been directing me away from him. Then again, he might have no idea at all.

We pull up to the Phelps house, which looks to be even smaller than Angelica's. Probably built in the sixties. It might be small, but it's well kept. The lawn is mowed, and garden beds line the front of the house and along the small walkway from the street. It looks like a nice place to grow up. I can just imagine a couple of kids pulling up on their bikes, laying them down and running into the house for a snack before heading back out again.

Something else pangs in my heart. I'm not usually so sentimental, but there's something about this house that just screams typical suburban family. And now we have to go in there and tell them in addition to their already dead son, we suspect their only remaining child of being a murderer.

I shake my head. We don't need to reveal any details about Andrew. It will be harder for them later, but it might make them more cooperative now if they think we just want to talk to him. Plus, it isn't like we have any hard evidence yet, just a theory and a set of circumstances that happens to fit. No need to cause them additional grief.

Just as I'm getting out of the car, my phone buzzes. "It's Farmer," I tell Zara.

"You going to tell him?" she asks.

I honestly don't know. I pick up. "Slate."

"We've got a problem here," Farmer says. It sounds like he's been running. "I just got a call from the 911 switchboard, routed to me through CPD. They've received multiple calls about a hostage situation down at station twelve."

"What?" I say, getting back into the car. Zara does the same. I switch the phone to speaker. "Who's the hostage?"

"We think it's Captain Padilla," he replies. "I haven't been able to get him on his cell or the radio. No one over there is picking up. CPD is already on the way and I'm going to meet them there."

"You think it's our firebug?" I ask.

"The 911 calls report a strong odor of turpentine, so yeah, I think it's him," he replies. "A witness saw a man inside the station shouting, but he didn't look like one of the other firefighters. She said he had longer hair, down to his shoulders and wore a baseball cap. She also said he looked like he worked out." I glance at Zara and she nods. The description matches what little we have on Andrew Phelps.

"We'll be there as soon as we can," I say and hang up. I peel away from the Phelps house so fast the tires on the car squeal. "Shit."

Zara checks the time. "He's right on time, twenty-four hours from McKenzie's death."

"But why take Padilla hostage?" I ask. "He wasn't there that night. And he's never taken a hostage before."

Zara shakes her head. "I don't know, he's the only one who can answer that question. You think he's willing to go up with Padilla? Burn the whole place to the ground?"

"Must be," I say. "Unless he's left himself some kind of back door we don't know about. But in about two minutes that place is going to be surrounded by cops. I just hope we get there before they decide to breach. Because this guy will kill Padilla, no question."

"What's he thinking?" Zara asks. I know she's testing me to see if I can get inside the killer's mind.

Looking at it from Andrew's perspective, he must already feel cornered. He knows we're on his trail, that it won't be long until we catch up with him. So he might be thinking he just goes and takes down Padilla in a blaze of glory, ending it on his own terms. Andrew doesn't seem to me like someone who is willing to quit before he's finished a job. But that still leaves Olsen...and that might be our only bargaining chip.

"He's angry, and desperate," I say. "But he's not completely off the rails yet, otherwise the whole place would already be on fire. He wants something. Maybe a microphone, to announce what Padilla and the others did."

"You want to give it to him," Zara says.

"I would love nothing more," I say, "If there weren't lives

in imminent danger. Andrew might actually be the link we need to take Olsen down. But we can't do that if he's dead."

As we drive, I can't help but think about what Andrew must be feeling. He's obviously hurting because of the death of his brother, but what would cause him to snap and go off to kill these men? Why not make the case against Olsen and the others? But then I have to remember that he'd have to trust the CPD to go after all of Angelica's assailants. And unless he has direct evidence connecting Olsen or any of the others to Sam's death, then he couldn't make a credible accusation. So maybe he's doing the only thing he can to make things right in his own mind. I have to admit, part of me agrees with him.

This entire time I've been looking for the woman who killed Matt, I've never really thought about what I would do when I caught her. Somewhere in the back of my mind I assumed I would bring her in and charge her, but there was no evidence of foul play anywhere on Matt or Gerald Wright. Which means I'd have no recourse once I actually found her. She could be walking down the street and stop right in front of me, and it would make no difference. All I have is a hunch, and the knowledge that my husband was in perfect health before his death. The fact that he and Gerald Wright died in the exact same way is the only thing connecting this woman to my husband's death. And I can't even prove it.

I have to wonder, if I actually found the woman responsible…would I be content with letting the system play out as it's been designed? Which means she could walk away with zero consequences? Or would I decide I needed to enact my own brand of justice while I had the opportunity?

It's a question I can't answer. Who knows, if I were in Andrew's shoes, maybe I'd be doing the same thing. There are some crimes that are so heinous that there isn't a punishment harsh enough to balance the scales. Not even the death penalty.

We see the lights before we reach the station. The

normally quiet street is a buzz of activity, as the CPD has blocked traffic in both directions. I manage to maneuver our car into the oncoming lane to avoid all the stopped traffic. Some of the other drivers beep their horns as we have nothing on the car signifying it anything other than a private vehicle, but all of my attention is on the station itself.

"FBI," I yell out the window at the patrol officer trying to stop us. I show him my badge, giving him just enough time to jump out of the way before I run into him. Still, there are enough police cars here that we can only get so close.

I pull over on the side street and hop out. "We need to find Farmer," I say.

Zara and I make our way around the vehicles before coming around to the parking lot of the station. A barricade of vehicles has been set up in front of the entrance, which is a far cry from what it looked like this morning. I spot Farmer over speaking with a CPD officer.

"Farmer," I call out. He turns to us. "What's the situation?"

"Single hostage, we've confirmed it's Padilla," he says. "Sniper got a look at him about four minutes ago, but it wasn't a clean shot. Neither of them are in the windows now."

I notice the fire truck is still in its spot in the garage, and the garage door is open as well. The rest of the fire crew stands off to the far side of the parking lot, speaking to a group of three officers. "What happened?"

Farmer shakes his head. "Best I can tell, gunman with a large backpack and suitcase came in, firing off two shots to get the people to scatter. When Padilla came out, he took him hostage. Been in there about twenty-five minutes so far."

"Any word from him?" Zara asks.

"Nothing so far. We don't even have an ID."

"We do," I say. "We think it's Andrew Phelps." Farmer knits his brow. "Sam Phelps' little brother. We believe he's taking revenge for the firefighters responsible for Sam's death."

"Wait a second, what?"

I shake my head. "I don't have time to explain right now. Did you talk to Olsen?"

"I did, but he's as stoic as ever. Nothing but cryptic remarks. Whatever he knows, he's keeping it to himself."

"Oh, he knows stuff all right," Zara says.

"I'm going to need you to get him down here, right now," I say.

"I'm not pulling him from protective custody in the middle of a crisis, are you crazy?" Farmer says. "Plus, that's your jurisdiction."

Maybe now isn't the best time, but I need to know. "Did you know? About the charges?"

"Charges, what charges?" he says.

"The ones Angelica Davis filed against five of her fellow firefighters," Zara says. "Two of whom sexually assaulted her while the others witnessed the event."

"What?" Farmer yells, causing more than a few people to look over. "When was this?"

"About two months ago," I reply. "She tried reporting it, but Padilla covered it up."

Farmer turns toward the building, gritting his teeth. "That son of a bitch. He's been playing me the whole time."

I grin. Farmer's reaction seems genuine, good. We need him on our side right now. "Olsen is the key to what Andrew wants. He's looking to exact revenge. Apparently, he and the others killed Sam Phelps because he was going to expose them for what they did. Somehow Andrew found out and now he's taking revenge for his brother's murder."

"How would bringing Olsen here help?" Farmer asks.

"I have a feeling Andrew would much rather kill Olsen than Padilla," I say. "He's the last one who was there that night. And he used to be Sam Phelps' best friend. He's been

Andrew's ultimate goal this entire time. No wonder he let us take him into custody. He knew without us he was next."

"I'll call Fields," Zara says. "See if she can't get him down here. But it's going to take some time."

"That's fine," I say. "Because I want to talk to Andrew myself."

"Hold up," Farmer says, putting his hand on my shoulder. He takes it right back off again. "The CPD has dedicated negotiation teams for this kind of thing. They're trained."

"And I know how his mind works," I say. "I have a better chance of getting him to stand down than anyone else does." I see the look of disapproval on his face, but it doesn't matter. "Look, I'm not asking permission. I'm telling you. Now find me a megaphone."

Chapter Thirty-Two

"FIELDS SAYS SHE'S WORKING ON GETTING HIM HERE, BUT IT'S going to take time." Zara tells me after she gets off the phone. "Apparently Olsen is very comfortable in his new digs and doesn't plan on leaving."

"I don't care if she has to drag him down here in handcuffs, I just want him here. In case nothing else works."

"Here," Farmer says, walking up to me with a megaphone in his hand. "I told the commander you were taking control of the scene; he wasn't too happy about it."

"Thank you," I say, taking the megaphone. "The local cops never are, but he'll get over it. If he's doused that place in turpentine, how long do we have?"

Farmer shakes his head. "Minutes maybe. It depends on how much he had with him and if he's really soaked the building. It's masonry construction, so it won't burn as fast as a frame building, but it's going to get very hot in there very fast, like an oven."

"I wonder why he hasn't tried communicating yet," Zara asks, looking at the building. There is no way Phelps doesn't know about all the activity outside. Maybe he's waiting on us to make the first move. I'm about to oblige him.

"Do you have a picture of Phelps?" I ask Zara. She nods and pulls it up on her phone, showing me. He's handsome, in a casual sort of way. Not the killer I was picturing. For a brief moment I pause; there's still a chance our firebug is someone completely different. But in my gut I feel like Phelps is our man. Maybe I want him to be, just because I know what wanting revenge can do to a person. And given our constraints, it's worth the risk.

I turn to the building, megaphone in hand. "Andrew Phelps, this is Agent Emily Slate, with the FBI. We know you have a hostage inside the building. State your demands so we can come to a peaceful resolution."

I see some of the officers behind the vehicles in the lot ready themselves. Some have their weapons already pointed at the building, and I know there is already at least one sniper up on the nest, keeping watch. My goal is to take Phelps alive. Part of me needs to hear his side—to know what has pushed him so far that he's taken all these lives and caused all this carnage. My first priority has to be preventing any more death. But a deep part of me needs to know what motivates him, if for no other reason than to prevent the same thing from happening to me one day.

"Nothing," Farmer says, watching the building. "He doesn't want to talk."

"He wants to talk. Otherwise he would have torched the place already," I say. "He just doesn't know how to start. He never imagined himself in this position. By capturing Olsen before he could get to him, we put a wrinkle in his plans. Notice how much sloppier this job is than all his others."

"Then what do we do?" Zara asks.

I level the megaphone at the building again. "Andrew Phelps. I know you're scared, and I know you're angry. I want to understand why you're doing this. Will you talk to me?"

I hear at least one officer snicker behind me. I spin,

locking my eyes on him. He's a little older than me, glaring at me with an obvious disdain. "Something on your mind?"

"Yeah, just shoot the bastard when he shows his face," the officer says. "None of this back-and-forth bullshit."

"You better hope this back-and-forth bullshit works," I tell him. "Otherwise, you're going to have at least two more deaths on your watch. Not everything can be solved with a bullet."

He scoffs and turns away. I look at the other officers who have their weapons trained on the building. Some of them are looking at me with skepticism. They don't believe this will work. But I don't need them to believe, I just need them calm and collected. Anyone gets an itchy trigger finger, and the entire operation is over.

"Look," I say, calling out again. "We know you want Olsen. We can get him for you." Do I care I'm basically offering up Olsen on a platter for this killer? No, because it will never happen. But I need him to believe it will. I need him to believe we're serious. I turn to Zara. "How far out is Fields?"

She shakes her head. "No update. I bet he's not cooperating."

"FBI!" A voice calls from the building. I can't see the owner of the voice, but I have to assume it's Andrew Phelps.

"I'm here," I call back.

"I'll talk. But only to you."

"State your terms," I say.

"Leave your weapons, come into the building slowly. Don't try anything," he yells back.

"Absolutely not," Zara says before I can even consider it.

"It might be our only chance to speak with him," I say. "I can talk him down."

Farmer takes a step closer to us. "And what if you can't? You're putting your life in his hands by going in there. Is it really worth it?"

Maybe it isn't to them, but to understand this man—to get inside his head—I have to try. I take my blazer and my holster with my service weapon off, handing them to Zara. "Em," she says, leaning in. "Don't. Not for Padilla."

"I know what Andrew is going through," I tell her. "I need to at least try. Wouldn't you rather see Padilla in a cell for the rest of his life rather than burned to a crisp?"

"Right now, I'm not so sure," she replies. I give her a stern glare. "Fine. No, he doesn't deserve to die. But neither do you. This guy is unhinged. He pours turpentine down people's throats for God's sake."

"He's not going to get that chance with me," I tell her.

"Great, now we're going to have to pull another body out of the wreckage," the same cop from earlier says.

"Take care of that for me, will you?" I ask Zara as I pull my hair into a bun on the back of my head. I don't want any loose strands anywhere.

"Hey, jackass!" Zara yells at the guy. "You're off the scene. Report to your watch commander and tell him you're not fit to be here."

"What?" the guy yells. "You can't do that."

I leave them to argue, maneuvering around two of the vehicles and making my way slowly toward the building. "Andrew, I'm coming in. I'm unarmed." I keep both of my hands up as I close in on the building. From what I can tell, everything seems normal and in place. Except as I get closer, I can smell the turpentine the witnesses reported. It's strong and pungent, almost to the point where it burns my nostrils. Those bags he was reported coming in here with must have been full of the stuff.

"Andrew?" I ask as I reach the large open door in front of the engine. "Where do I go?"

"In here." I follow his voice through the familiar rooms until I reach the locker room. Padilla is in the middle of the room strapped to the end of the island of lockers with a series of nylon ropes, just like the kind we saw around Greg Parry's arms and legs at Billy's Backwash. His face is covered in bruises, but he's still breathing. The entire room is soaked in turpentine. The floor is covered in it, like a shower that has overflowed and spilled everywhere. Padilla himself is covered in it too, his clothes slick. He barely glances up when I enter, coughing once before dropping his head again.

Next to him stands a young man, no older than twenty-five, blonde hair down to his shoulders with a baseball cap on. He's dressed in normal-enough clothes, jeans, shirt, sneakers. His face might be young, but his eyes are alert, scanning. On the bench beside him is a tin of turpentine, along with a metal funnel.

"Andrew Phelps," I say.

"You already knew who I was," he says. He's got a zippo brand lighter in one hand, and he's opening and closing the metal cap with the telltale *click, click*. He could light this entire place up at any second.

"I spoke with Angelica Davis," I say. "She told me the whole story."

"About what they did to Sam?" he asks, tears in his eyes. His whole body is practically trembling. He could light that lighter at any second. I nod, slowly. "About the coverup?" He shoots an angry glance at Padilla.

"About all of it," I say. "But you haven't been doing this for Angelica, have you? I'm sure you feel for her, but you're really doing this to avenge your brother."

"He was just trying to do the right thing!" Phelps screams, mostly at Padilla who tries to collapse into himself and fails.

"Listen, I understand why you're upset," I say. "I recently lost someone I love too. They were murdered, just like Sam."

"Who?" he asks.

"My husband. He was…killed a few months ago."

"Why?"

I shake my head. "I'm trying to find that out." I'm

surprised he's showing so much interest in *my* life, given he's the one with the grievance here. But it also tells me he's not so far gone. I just need to figure out a way to talk him down.

"If you know what they did then you know I have to finish this," he says, looking over at Padilla. "It was supposed to be him and Olsen together. Sam's best friend and his commander. But then you got involved. You made me hurry."

"I know this all feels like it has to happen right now," I say. "But let's just take a minute to breathe. Padilla isn't going anywhere, and I have my people bringing Olsen down here at this very moment."

He chortles. "You're not going to trade one life for another. The FBI doesn't do that."

I lean forward, just slightly. "What if I told you I believe in what you're doing?" I see Padilla's eyes go wide and he coughs again.

"You're lying," Phelps says.

I shake my head. "I've dealt with my fair share of pigs over the years. Men who think they can just come and take what they want. I may not want justice for your brother like you do, but I do want it for Angelica. She and your brother suffered at the hands of these men, and you were actually brave enough to go out there and do something about it. To make sure they couldn't hurt anyone ever again. I applaud you for it."

He eyes me suspiciously, like he's trying to decide if I'm deceiving him or not. I can tell he's not stupid, which means I have to be as convincing as possible. "I did what the police won't do. And I saved a lot of people the trouble."

I nod. "You absolutely did."

"So then…what? You're going to deliver Olsen in here to me and just let me burn the place down with both of them in here?"

It's a direct call to my bluff. If I say yes, he'll know I'm lying. No law enforcement officer in the world would make that deal. And if I say no, he could just decide to cut his losses and light the place up. "Andrew——"

"It's *Drew*," he says, his words clipped.

"*Drew*," I correct. "I checked your background. You've never been in trouble with the law before. You've never even gotten so much as a parking ticket. I want to understand. Can you help me do that?"

"What's to understand? They took a life without cause," he says, almost like he's a scholar on the subject. "All I'm doing is fixing the balance."

"What about the symbols?" I ask. "The wallets."

"I had to make sure everyone knew who they were, so that their crime couldn't be covered up," he replies. "Burning a body makes identification difficult. I wanted to make sure there was no doubt as to the identities of these men. The symbol was a way to mark them. It's the international sign for karma. One bad deed balanced out by a good deed to rectify it."

Karma. Zara is going to lose it when she realizes she didn't figure that out. I should have seen it too. "People lose loved ones every day," I say. "What makes this so different?"

He hesitates. "I assume Sam was the one who told you about what happened to Angelica."

He nods. "He told me about it right before he headed off to work. Said he was going to file a formal complaint while he was on his shift, and if they didn't listen, he was going direct to the Assistant Chief for the city. I asked him if he thought that was smart, to threaten them like that, but he wasn't worried. He and Olsen had grown up together, he trusted the man, even if he'd made a bad call that night with Angelica. He was sure Olsen would back him up.

"But as soon as I saw the news that night, I knew exactly what had happened. They'd betrayed him." He actually laughs. "It's so stupid when you think about it. These organizations. They claim to be bound by something stronger than blood. They claim that they are all one big family, that everyone is a brother or a sister. Tell me, would you have sex with your sister and then kill your brother if he was going to tattle on you? I'm the only *real* brother he ever had, and I supported him one-hundred percent. These other bastards were nothing but a bunch of liars and killers." He turns, his rage infecting him, and starts slamming his fist into Padilla's face, over and over.

I glance at the lighter in his other hand, weighing whether I can get to it in time or not. But before I make my move, he stops, breathing hard. Padilla looks to be unconscious as his entire body sags against the restraints. "They don't know what family really means," Drew whispers, his anger clearly still in control.

"I know what it means," I say. "And I know why you're so angry."

"Do you?" he yells, turning at me. "How many people have you killed to get justice for your husband? Huh?"

I decide now is not the time to lie to him, but his question pierces me in a way I didn't expect. *Would* I kill to find out what happened to Matt? "None," I say.

"Exactly. You don't have the same conviction, you're not dedicated, like I am. I'm not willing to let any of them hurt anyone else ever again. What are you doing to stop the people who killed your husband from hurting someone else?"

"This isn't about me," I say, my hands still up. "We're talking about you."

He clicks the lighter again, this time igniting the flame. For a second I think it's going to light the fumes in the room and send the whole place up, but it just flickers and burns. "No. Now we're talking about *you*. What have you done? Tell me."

I don't see that I have much choice. But if it keeps him talking, that's all I need. "Alright. I'm looking for the woman who killed him. Trying to track her down."

"Track her down, what is she, some kind of contract killer?"

"I don't know," I say. "She has multiple names, multiple addresses. I haven't had any luck so far."

He narrows his gaze at me. "You'll do it. You'll find her. After all, you found me and I covered my tracks well. But the question is, what will you do with her once you catch her?"

It's the same question I've asked myself over and over again. I honestly don't know. He must see it in my eyes. "I'll tell you what you do," he says. "You make her feel the same pain she makes you feel, every day you're not with him." He nudges the funnel with his leg. "You make sure she feels the pain inside and out, and you make sure she dies in agony, because you have mercy that she didn't show you. You're willing to let her agony be brief, while she has sentenced you to a lifetime of it. And in that way, you beat her. You do your husband proud."

I can't help but feel the twinge in my stomach and the prickle of tears in my eyes. It might be the turpentine, but really I know that part of me recognizes what he's saying as truth. I want her to feel the pain she's caused me, and I want her to know she can't just get away with what she did.

But the other, more rational side of me knows that it's a path I can't follow. If I start down that dark corridor, I'd never be able to come back. I have to shut that door in my mind, and make sure I never open it again.

Drew takes a deep breath, like he's finally calming himself and I start to relax a little. He seems more in control now, less likely to do something rash. "I know you're only here to make sure I don't kill anyone else," he finally says. "And I know you'll never give me Olsen. I just have to accept that five out of six will have to be good enough. Maybe the knowledge that Olsen's actions not only killed his best friend, but his entire team and his commander too will be enough to weigh him down for the rest of his life. This can't go on." He waves the lighter back and forth precariously close to Padilla's clothes. It's a miracle the flame doesn't jump the distance. But then again, Drew knows about how to control fire. He has since the beginning. Because he learned about it from his brother.

"I appreciate the chat, but it changes nothing," he says. "Go. Find the woman who did this to you. I'll give you time to escape. It's time to end this."

"Drew——" I begin. But he shakes his head.

"No more talk, this is your last chance. I'd hate to have to kill you too."

"You won't," I say. "You haven't killed any innocent bystanders yet. Only those involved. As long as I'm here, you can't light the fire."

He looks at me with a sad sort of expression. "I'm really sorry, but I tried." He takes one last look at the lighter, then tosses it.

Everything erupts into flame.

Chapter Thirty-Three

BEFORE I CAN EVEN MOVE, PADILLA'S ENTIRE BODY IS COVERED in fire. Drew turns away from the blaze, holding his hands up but the flame is moving fast. Within seconds it has spread to the accelerant all over the floor and I have to jump back just so I don't get burned. Padilla screams, the fire having awoken him and that telltale smell of burned flesh returns as the man literally cooks right in front of me.

The sprinkler system goes off, but the pitiful amount of water spraying out isn't enough to combat the fire that's already raging. Drew retreats back to the showers, where I know there is no way out. But at the same time, I can't just leave him in here. I vault over the growing flames as they spread and I sprint past Padilla, not even bothering to slow down. There's nothing I can do for the man; I can't cut him down in time to save his life. But I might still be able to save one life today.

In the shower room Drew has turned on all the shower-heads, and the cold air combining with the heat from the fire in the locker room combines to form a thick steam that makes it impossible to see anything. I'm already drenched from the locker room, but more cold water douses me as I make my way through the open showers, trying to see through the steam as the heat from the other room begins to spread. The walls are warming up, creating even more steam, mixed with smoke. Soon enough we won't be able to breathe. I get down low, trying to spot him. I think the only reason I can breathe is because the water is keeping the air relatively clean down here, but there's no sign of Drew anywhere.

"What are you doing?" he yells from behind me, and pain erupts in my side as a boot connects, knocking me over. "You were supposed to leave! I gave you the chance to get out of here."

I scramble away from him, trying to put some distance between us. "I can't just let you kill yourself. I have an oath to uphold," I manage to say.

"Yeah?" He comes barreling at me through the steam and I barely have enough time to put up my hands before I'm knocked backward on my ass again. "It's my destiny to die in here, just like it's yours to go out and find your husband's killer. I'm not dying in jail; I know what I've done."

I use his distraction to sweep his legs out from under him, causing him to splash down on the tile. I grapple with him, doing my best to try and get him under control, but he delivers a sucker punch to my kidney, which shoots a new wave of pain through me. I cough and fall back, holding my side as he gets back up. "But it's too late now. We're both trapped in here. You've accomplished nothing."

"No," I say, starting to feel the first tendrils of the smoke enter my lungs. He's right, it won't be long now. "I did my job. I at least tried."

He coughs once. "Your job got you killed."

"Better than my obsession." I deliver another kick to his unprotected midsection. He staggers back, the air knocked out of him. I use the chance to deliver a few well-timed punches, then aim for the carotid artery. He's disoriented, and one good hit interrupts the blood flow, causing him to collapse in on the ground, unconscious.

Even with the water on full blast, the smoke is still making its way into the room, even if the flames aren't. I crawl over to the entrance to see sprinklers are still trying to contain the fire, but with all the turpentine, it burns anyway. What I can see of Padilla isn't moving any longer, he's more than likely already asphyxiated. A black cloud of smoke hangs on the ceiling, and it only seems to be growing. Retreating back into the showers, I search for a way out. Above me are windows that provide some ventilation, but it isn't enough. Black smoke is escaping through all of them. I get back on all fours and crawl back to Phelps. I can try to carry him through the locker room, but there's no doubt in my mind I'll end up with third degree burns on most of my body. Plus, I'm not even sure I can lift him; he's not a big guy, but he's got some muscle, and muscle is heavy. But that has to be preferable to dying in a fire, right? I just need to make it out to the hallway and hope the fire hasn't spread too far yet.

Then I remember, I'm in a *firehouse* dammit. I crawl back to the locker room. The last few lockers up against the entrance to the shower area are within reach. I wrench the closest one open, and grab the two pairs of turnout gear inside: pants, jacket and helmet. I don't have time to go with the full breathing apparatus. I carry them back into the shower area, and pull on the oversize pants and jacket, securing it around me. I then slip the helmet over my head and return to Phelps. It takes me precious minutes to get him into the protective gear of his own, but he won't make it if I don't.

I take a moment to gather myself, then grab Phelps by his dirty turnout jacket, and begin dragging him out of the shower and into the inferno. The place is engulfed, but thankfully a lot of the turpentine on the floor seems to have burned off. I drag him as fast as I can, feeling the heat all around me.

Farmer was right about this place being an oven. The heat is enough to make me woozy, but I keep yanking and pulling as hard as I can. The fire practically wraps itself around us as I'm trying to get him out of here, and for a few short seconds, I feel like we'll both be overwhelmed.

Finally, I make it out into the hallway, which is also on fire, but extra ventilation ensures the heat level is much lower out here. It only takes a few more minutes to reach the exit, where I realize three teams of other firefighters are already dousing the entire building with water.

"Em!" Zara yells, her, Farmer and some of the others running up to me. Farmer and the others take care of Phelps. He's whimpering, and his makeshift turnout gear is black from the flames. There's no way he got through that unscathed.

"Are you okay?" Zara asks. I begin to reply, but I can only cough as a fit takes over me and I go to my knees, all the strength seeping out of me. A pair of paramedics come up to me and help me back up, leading me over to a nearby ambulance. I hear Farmer shouting orders to keep the fire contained, that they've almost got it under control while the cops do their best to keep bystanders back. The paramedics get me to the ambulance and start pulling the turnout gear off. Underneath, I'm shivering, which strikes me as insanely funny, given how warm it is outside.

"She might be going into shock," I hear one of them say as an oxygen mask is slipped over my face. I try taking a deep breath but have difficulty catching it. I take a few shallow breaths instead as I'm wrapped in a warming blanket. Zara is right there beside me the whole time.

"Is she okay?" she asks.

"We need to get her checked out," one of the paramedics says, indicating I should lie down on the cot.

"I'm coming with you," Zara says, climbing up into the ambulance and sitting right beside the paramedic as she monitors my vitals. The last thing I see before they close the doors is fire station twelve, still on fire as teams work to extinguish the flames. For the first time since I came on this case, I can rest easy. We caught the guy. The killing spree is over.

I glance up at Zara and give her a brief smile, which she returns, but it's pinched. I wish I could reassure her, but I feel like if I say anything right now, my throat might tear itself apart. Instead, I hold out a hand, which she takes.

I focus on breathing as the ambulance rumbles through the streets. Slow breaths.

In…and out.

Chapter Thirty-Four

"ALL RIGHT, LIEUTENANT OLSEN...OR SHOULD I SAY MR., since your title has been revoked by the city?" I say, sitting down across from Olsen. He's been moved from his comfortable hotel room to this interrogation room in the FBI satellite office where he's been detained for three days while I regained my voice and was cleared by the hospital.

It turned out I'd inhaled more smoke than I'd realized, and I was on the verge of carbon dioxide poisoning. But a day in the hospital and fresh oxygen for thirty-six hours and there was no lasting damage to my lungs or internal organs. My blood toxicity is down as well. I was told by the doctors had all that cold water not been running, I probably would have died in that room.

Phelps suffered second-degree burns on multiple parts of his body and one third degree, but he's going to make a full recovery. Which is good, because I'll need his testimony to put Olsen away. Of course, none of it absolves him of his crimes; but he plans on pleading guilty to all counts in order to avoid needing to drag any of the families through court. The footprint we found matches his shoes and his vehicle shows damage that matches the back of Ricky Black's car. I feel like

Drew realizes now that even if he didn't kill anyone other than those involved, he's affected a lot of lives…family members, friends, etc. You can't just kill who you want and think it's going to make everything better.

Which brings me back to Olsen.

"Cat got your tongue, Mr. Olsen?" I ask. Zara is right beside me, her eyes boring into his, not flinching a bit.

"I'll never go down for anything," he finally says. "I never did anything wrong."

"Sure about that?" I ask. "Because Angelica Davis says you threatened her life after Sam died, telling her that she might have her own brand of accident. Not to mention both she and Drew Phelps knew about the incident on the seventeenth, two months back. The incident you never reported and Padilla conveniently covered up."

"You don't have any proof," he says. "It's all hearsay."

"I'm sure once we exhume both Sam Phelps and Mrs. Orla and investigate their deaths as murders instead of accidents, something will come up. Our friends at the ATF are going back over that house inch by inch as we speak."

It's not hard to see this rattles him. "Just answer me one question. Was Sam Phelps already unconscious when you placed him in the home, or was he still awake? My guess is unconscious, as he would have been easier to move. One of your co-horts sabotaged his breathing device so that it delivered CO_2 to him, knocking him out. Then you carried him into the home where you'd already taken care of Mrs. Orla, and you lit the fire. Then Padilla and the rest of the team arrived on the engine, didn't they? You waited for the fire to burn for a while, making sure it would be long enough so that both of them would look like they died in there, and then you went in and "found" him. In time for the eleven o'clock news. Convenient."

Olsen just looks away, shaking his head.

"I really have to wonder what kind of person could do

that to their best friend?" I say, continuing to push him. "Drew was right, you were like a brother to Sam, and you betrayed him. But I guess if you have aspirations for moving up in the world, you always have to step on someone else to get up there, don't you?"

He remains stoic, determined not to say a word. That's okay, I didn't really expect him to. If we can link any of the deceased to the crime scene, then it will all come back on Olsen, because he's the only one left. Padilla perished in the fire, but at least he didn't have turpentine poured down his throat.

"I think you'll find after Ms. Davis makes her accusations; the Fire Chief is going to be looking hard for a scapegoat. And since you're the only one who survived, I'd expect the hammer any day now."

He squints and I can see he's doing everything he can to hold back a biting retort. But Olsen isn't stupid enough to talk to us without a lawyer, I just wanted to come in here and rattle him a little bit. Just seeing the look of hatred and rage on his face is reward enough for me.

"Alright Mr. Olsen, we'll leave you to your thoughts. But remember, you cut a deal before any of this comes down and it will be a lot better for you in the long run." I wait a beat then stand, Zara doing the same. "Best of luck to you."

As soon as my hand touches the handle of the door, I hear him shift in his seat. "Wait," he says. "What kind of deal?" I give Zara a knowing grin. She sends it right back. *Bingo*.

"We found another set of tire tracks, out on the other side of the house," Farmer says. "Fortunately, the mud out there was deep, so they weren't worn away. Now that we know what we're looking for, we're seeing a lot that we missed the first time." He takes a breath. "That *I* missed."

"Hey now, don't be so hard on yourself, you also missed the fact that your buddy was covering up an assault charge," Zara says, grinning.

Farmer glares at her, then takes a long swig of his beer before turning his attention back to me. "How do you stand her? Does she point out all your flaws all the time too?"

"Nothing to point out," I say. "I'm flawless." Zara just about spits her drink out, but manages to retain it and high-fives me instead.

"Anyway," Farmer says. "We're thinking Mrs. Orla was murdered with one of her own kitchen knives. I don't expect to get any prints, but it's keeping with the overall theory of the crime. We'll find something out there. No matter how much people think fire gets rid of everything, it always leaves something behind."

"I guess I can't blame you for not knowing that it was in fact a double-homicide brought on by a bunch of rogue fire-fighters attempting to cover up an assault that could ended the career prospects of at least half a dozen people," Zara says. "Y'know, not really intuitive."

"Thanks," Farmer says, tipping the neck of his beer to her. "Next time I'll make sure to be on the lookout for that, though." He takes another swig. "Did you talk to Phelps again?"

I nod. "I went to see him this morning. He goes before the judge in less than a week. He's sticking to the guilty plea. Seems like he's a lot like his brother. He just wants to do the right thing now. In exchange, the state won't pursue the death penalty. But he's still facing five murders and millions of dollars of property damage. I don't think he'll get the option for parole."

Farmer shakes his head. "I understand he's hurting. But to go off and kill five people, and in the brutal and inhumane way he did it…I just don't get it."

I want to agree with him, but part of me *does* understand. I can't seem to get Drew's words out of my head. *How far would you go to find out who killed your husband? Would you take a life to know?* These are questions I thought had easy answers, but seeing as we are no closer to tracking down the woman who killed Matt, I really have to question the reality of the situation. And if we do find her, what then? "He's disturbed, that's for sure," I say. "Even if his heart was in the right place, his actions most definitely weren't."

"I guess you two will be heading back up to D.C.," Farmer says.

"Tomorrow," I say. "I for one will be glad to be out of this heat."

"Oh, come on, admit it. You like it," Zara says, giving me a little shove.

"Trust me, I've had all the warmth I can take for a while. I wonder if Janice would be willing to transfer me to Montana for the summer."

"Not likely," Zara says. "Both you and I probably have a pile of cases a mile high on our desks."

"Well, we'll won't miss you," Farmer says, though he smirks when he says it. "I've had just about enough of the goddamn FBI."

"Right back atcha, you grumpy old bastard," I say, clinking my glass with his. "Feel free to look us up if you ever decide to visit the nation's capital."

Zara leans forward. "She's speaking for herself only. Don't look me up. I'm a hermit."

Farmer grins and drains the rest of his glass. "Least I can do then, is at least buy you one more round before you go." He motions to the bartender we'll need another round. "For a job well done."

"I'll drink to that," I say. "Light me up."

Zara gives me a big shove for that one and Farmer boos.

I admit. I absolutely deserved it.

Epilogue

THE LINE RINGS TWICE. HE PICKS UP JUST AFTER THE SECOND ring, like always. "Report."

"Tailing subject now. Current location is 3045 Augusta."

"The brother-in-law's house."

"Yes, sir. Looks like she's picking up her dog."

"Do you have eyes on her right now?" His voice is gruff, but emotionless. Just what I've come to expect.

"Always."

"Any indication you were spotted?"

That gets under my skin. But these are the people that pay me. It isn't like I can mouth off to them. "I'm good at my job."

"Apparently not good enough, otherwise she never would have found your aliases, not to mention your previous accommodations."

"They were nothing more than dummy houses I only used once each, on assignment for another clients," I say. "They weren't designed to be invisible. Though I still don't know how she found out about them."

"Any indication she found anything at any of the locations?" Sometimes I hate this faceless voice I have to speak to.

But at the moment, he's the one paying the bills. So I have to put up with it.

"There was nothing to find. Each location was wiped clean before I left. I don't know if she'll continue the search. The events down in Charleston seem to have taken some of the wind out of her sails."

"I'm very glad to hear that. Because if Ms. Slate keeps digging, we're going to have a problem. One that you will be required to rectify."

"Wait a minute," I say, lowering the binoculars and settling into my perch. "You never said anything about removing Slate from the equation. This was the question I asked you in the beginning and you said she wouldn't be a problem."

"It seems Ms. Slate is more tenacious than we gave her credit for. But you should really blame Wright. It was his big mouth that got us all in this mess to begin with. Had she never been in Stillwater, she wouldn't know about your intervention."

"Listen," I say, dropping the volume of my voice, despite the fact there is no one else around and my equipment shows no one is hijacking our signal. "You want me to take care of an FBI agent that comes with additional costs. That's a lot more heat than I signed up for."

"We'll have to hope it doesn't come to that, then, won't we?" he asks in that patronizing tone of his. I want to curse him out right over the line, but I hold my tongue. "Stay on her. I want to know her every movement for the next few weeks as she settles back into her life in D.C. Let us know immediately if anything about her routine changes. Anything that might indicate she's on to either you or us."

"There's only so much I can do without getting into her apartment," I say.

"Then get in her apartment. Watch her twenty-four seven. Trust me when I tell you, you do not want her digging into this any further. If we get burned, you go down with us."

I roll my eyes. "So you've told me."

"Then do what you're paid to do. And for God's sake, don't show your face to her anymore."

"I already explained that," I say. "She was supposed to be at a doctor's appointment. What was I supposed to do? Run away, causing even more suspicion?"

"Just don't let it happen again, otherwise we'll have to take alternate measures." I grit my teeth. He means they'll bring in someone else to take care of me. This job, sometimes. Fuck.

"I understand," I say. "Slate won't be a problem anymore."

"Good." The line goes dead.

I turn my attention back to my subject, still on the porch of her brother and sister-in-law's house, though now she has her dog back at her side. That dog is going to be a major impediment if I'm going to get into her apartment. It's going to require some special precautions so that he never knows I was there.

I watch as Emily Slate seems to speak cordially with her sister-in-law, only for her brother-in-law to finally appear and close the door on her. She stands there a moment, then finally turns and heads back to her car, with her dog in tow.

I've had eyes on this woman ever since she found my place in Savannah. And it seems like I'm going to have eyes on her for a long time to come.

Looks like I better get comfortable. Emily Slate and I are going to be spending a lot of time together...even if she doesn't know it.

The End?

To be Continued...

Want to read more about Emily?

Special Agent Emily Slate has seen her fair share of death ever since joining the FBI. But never anything like this...

Emily's most recent case brings her to a sleepy New York town to investigate the gruesome death of a fellow FBI agent. Except when she arrives, Emily discovers this was no home invasion gone wrong. This was a calculated kill, undertaken by a disturbed and brutal individual.

As Emily begins her investigation, the trail leads to a local author, who the killer is using as inspiration for his kills; copying details from the author's books as templates on how to kill his victims. As the bodies pile up and the danger grows ever closer, Emily begins to suspect the author herself may be the killer's ultimate target.

But just as Emily thinks she has a handle on things, her own husband's killer surfaces with a warning for Emily. One that will turn everything she knows upside down...

Find out what happens in *Her Final Words*, available now from Amazon. Get your copy now!

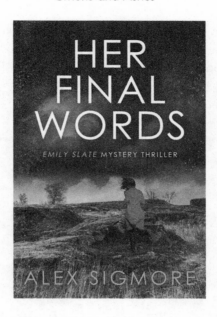

Scan the QR code below to get your copy of HER FINAL WORDS!

FREE book offer!
Where did it all go wrong for Emily?

I hope you enjoyed *Smoke and Ashes*. If you'd like to learn more about Emily's backstory and what happened in the days following her husband's unfortunate death, including what almost got her kicked out of the FBI, then you're in luck! *Her Last Shot* introduced Emily and tells the story of the case that almost ended her career. Interested? Scan the code below to get your free copy now!

Not Available Anywhere Else!

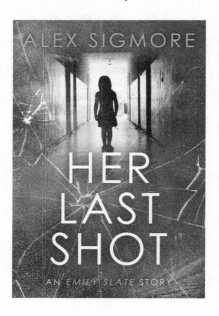

You'll also be the first to know when each book in the Emily Slate series is available!

Scan the QR code below to get your FREE copy today!

The Emily Slate FBI Mystery Series